Praise

"I value the prism of Julia's personal experiences, which highlight the incrementally vanishing societal norms. The book is both a tribute to one woman's resilience and a call to America for serious and honest reflection."

—Simkha Y. Weintraub, LCSW, former Rabbinic Director, The Jewish Board, New York, New York

"Susie Stein beautifully captures the worlds of family and community in the fifties and sixties in small town New England where we grew up."

—Dr. Kym S. Rice, Interim Director, The Corcoran School of the Arts and Design

"When Julia discusses her medical case with a doctor who finally listens, it is a culmination to this very personal novel that also provides a social commentary on the years 2007–2019."

—Zachary Sklar, screenwriter, Olivebridge, New York

"The story will draw you in; the writing will keep you there."

—Roman A. Draba, retired business executive, Milwaukee, Wisconsin

"The poetry of the author is beautifully written; the telling of the heroine's story is very truthful and real."

—Patricia Jones, retired personal aide, Waterbury, Connecticut

"I love the story line, and it has captured my interest in following Julia to the end of the tale."

—Diana Simons, insurance agent, Brookfield, Wisconsin

Other Works
(Published as Susan G. Stein)

<hr />

2005, Wood Place Imprints, *These Are* Not *Your Husband's Portions,* nonfiction, with Dr. Patricia H. Dolhun. Cited as #6 for year-end gift giving by Booklist Wisconsin.

1995 *October Roses*, "The Never Ending Stream," Juried competition.

1979–1983 *World Press Review,* dozens of translations from French.

Translation of "The Enigma," by Patrick Rousseau, *Substance,* University of Wisconsin-Madison, 1981.

Additionally, Stein has published letters and articles in the *International Herald Tribune, The New York Times, Milwaukee Journal Sentinel, Wisconsin Bankers Association newsletter,* and *The Business Journal Milwaukee.*

A VALENTINE TO AMERICA:

What Happened to Our Country?

—a social commentary—

SUSIE GIGI STEIN

A Valentine to America

© Wood Place Imprints LLC 2021
Milwaukee, Wisconsin

www.529bookdesign.com
Interior design: Lauren Michelle
Cover design: Claire Moore

Author shot and interior photography by Erol Reyal
Portrait of Marilyn Monroe and cover art by Rachel J. Schneider

Ten percent of royalties from *Valentine* will go to Feeding America Eastern Wisconsin.

https://www.feedingamericawi.org

Dedication

I dedicate this book to those who have gone before, namely to my incomparable parents, Betty Lois and Harold Stein. I offer a loving nod to my unusually prescient children, Rachel and Daniel, now young adults. And a reverent thanks to my brother, Jeff, the best internist ever, and those true friends of decades, or new friends along the way, who stayed the course, of course—you know who you are.

I dedicate this novel to my Milwaukee family of choice and to those doctors and their teams who provided comfort and effective protocols in my arduous, thirteen-year-long search for answers to the simple question: How do you take a perfectly healthy fifty-five-year-old woman and wreck her life?

I wish to thank the superb skills of eminent screenwriter and journalist Zachary Sklar, who provided inspiration during innumerable healing times and great direction as a reader (more than once) of the manuscript. My editor, Lisa Cerasoli of 529 Books, has provided dynamic critique, patience, and great insights as a new sharer of my writing. Without her expertise, this book would never have been.

Thank you to my daughter, Rachel J. Schneider, for the beautiful cover art and illustration of Marilyn Monroe, and to Erol Reyal for my author shot. Thank you to Lauren Michelle at 529 Books for your interior design skills.

Lastly, I wish to thank the many sponsors of this artistic endeavor, without whom my novel would not have come to life.

A VALENTINE
TO AMERICA

What would happen if one woman told the truth?
The world would split open.

I am working out the vocabulary of my solitude.

—MURIEL RUKEYSER,
Beloved Sarah Lawrence College professor and writing mentor

Introduction

This is a tale of Boomer wealth gone mad, of community and family disintegration, of a nation reeling from the Second Great Depression, and of a patient desperate to get answers to her doctors' most intransigent case, at least for those who actually paid attention to Julia's midnight (or three in the afternoon) cries of pain, inescapable and unpredictable.

This story was told to me, Dear Reader, by Julia Fields. Every word in it is true, carved out of years of incomparable disarray, molded by twentieth- and twenty-first-century illnesses, her disparate community of national healers, and her loyal community of family, friends, and colleagues.

But Julia survived; she beat all the odds and surprised everyone.

I recorded our sessions. Some chapters appear in the first person—in Julia's voice—from the blizzard of journal entries, letters, and emails she shared. Together, we created a framework for telling this story of an unusual time in the heroine's life and in the world she observed. I took my notes and recordings back to my studio and delved deeper into this woman's experiences.

Why did it happen? Lady Jane and Prince Hal, high school sweethearts, they started it all, this tale of memory across time, a story unraveled by their only child, Julia, telling it as she saw, lived, and breathed it. These connections involve many people and places. They are real, they are etched in her brain, and they are here as she lived it, in Millennium America, a country of blazing glory and one desperately seeking a center during the eight years of the first black president of the United States. There followed the frightening rise of the first reality show president, in a spectacular upset at the 2016 election. Julia struggled in a "Health Uncare System," with staggering societal woes spread across a continent of majestic mountains, Great Lakes, and goodwill in common folk.

This tale is one of hope and surprises, finding answers for many puzzles. Julia told it in her irrepressible way, sharing paintings and photographs, jewels and teacups, news clippings and tennis trophies, yearbooks and her father's U.S. Navy Seabees' photos, now archived at Stanford University's Hoover Institute library. Her landscape is broad terrain, the feelings translated into words, the memories of her origins and those going back to two mesmerizing and complicated parents.

How did she survive?

Was it humor, the passage of time, finding her voice in her verbose middle-of-the-night emails? Was it our remembering/recovery sessions together, or—even at the outer reaches—some of the medical protocols that perhaps, despite their frightful costs and meandering successes, made Julia well?

This tale may surprise or shock you, but that is only because you sat out the economic and moral collapse of

America, while minding your own challenges during the quaintly named "Jobless Recovery," and while keeping daily news at bay: harsh news reports that created the story of so many in Julia's world and turned hers inside out, over and over. She landed on her feet but relapsed frequently.

Please keep this story in your hearts. Read it when you need a passion for healing or when you need harmony in your life and your work.

Julia would want it that way.

PART I
JULIA REMEMBERS

CHAPTER 1

Julia Meets the World's Most Celebrated Actress

Marilyn Monroe was Julia's father's customer. It was the fifties. There were no security guards for the World's Most Famous Actress; there were few unlisted numbers, and there was no Caller ID—that scourge of human communication, which banned so much understanding in Millennium World, eclipsing community and caring. "Marilyn," as she was known to Hal, was to be served well and speedily during the down-to-the-studs renovation of an eighteenth-century farmhouse in Roxbury, Connecticut, amid rolling hills and long, winding roads. There was a new one-room writing cabin built for her beloved Arthur Miller, and, short as it was, it was a marriage of kindred souls, the top American playwright of his day, a college dropout with no literary criticism classes to maul the great writer within, about to marry The Face That Launched a Global Following. She was a twenty-something woman and easy to talk to, as Julia did in 1957.

"I am sorry," Marilyn said. "No pictures, I'm a mess. I was just picking blackberries in the woods with my stepchildren." And so it was that Julia Fields came to discuss hair, rather than use her infallible Brownie camera on that bright and never-to-be forgotten summer day.

When Julia was young, she was a black-haired beauty. But in the 1950s, blondes were featured in Breck shampoo commercials and all the rage, and she sometimes wondered whether it wouldn't have been better to have been born a blonde. She fought like crazy when someone said her hair was brown: "No, black," Julia would respond. "It's black like my eyebrows, see?"

"I wish I had blonde hair like you," she ventured once the photo shoot was clearly not happening.

The Most Famous Actress of Her Day looked down at Julia's pitch-black pigtails and said, "Julia, I would do anything to have black hair like yours."

That did it! Marilyn Monroe told her she had black hair, so Julia had the ultimate authority on her side.

A girl does not forget a brief exchange like that, not for one day, when she had shaken both Marilyn's hand and the playwright's, though she did not know even what a play was, being five years old. The Brownie camera lay unused during the thirty-minute ride home, on the backseat of the car, where seat belts would be tangled today, three across in a big boat of a DeSoto.

As the daughter of Hal, prince to Lady Jane, there were many Marilyn stories, told and re-told throughout Julia's life—stories of finding the rabbi for Marilyn's conversion to Judaism, for their wedding, for finding the perfect colors of appliances that would please the World's Most Famous Actress in her weekend home, away from the city and Sutton Place.

These and many other conversations are private no longer. Marilyn's conversion was heartfelt; she studied hard for many months, as Julia would read at the Jewish Museum in New York in 2015 in an exhibit about famous Jewish actresses.

Marilyn found her new bathtub's surface too coarse for her derriere and called Hal to see whether there might be a remedy.

Marilyn was no cook, so when she wandered through the 1950s showroom, she deferred to Arthur as to which stove and refrigerator they would install. The Great Playwright marveled at how Hal could remember the names of hundreds of bins of industrial and plumbing supplies, as the bins were coded by numbers.

On the second visit to the white farmhouse with black shutters, in typical Litchfield County fashion, the aura of Marilyn's glowing beauty told Julia that this was happiness—a career in film, a world-famous husband, and a home in the country, aside from the mansion-like apartment on Sutton Place.

In the end, none of it mattered. Marilyn was haunted by childhood demons throughout her short life, and worldwide fame did not alleviate it. The actress was stalked by lover upon lover, in and out of marriage, and she was remembered frequently as the interloper in the Young President's marriage. None of this mattered to Julia, as few of the people critiquing Marilyn had ever met her in person. It was all speculation and projection, as may well be 90 percent of what people say and how they interpret things, as Julia later learned in her Sarah Lawrence College creative writing classes.

Julia had seen Marilyn without makeup and in "dungarees," as they were called then—country weekend outdoor pants, not $250 designer pants. And she was   G O R G E O U S beyond anything Julia had seen in real life. No one, no theory, and no biographer could dim those days in 1957, forever a treasure for Julia. It was the Real Thing, simple Stop-by Visits, a wish to please a customer, no appointments needed, just as her father had done for hundreds of customers—as Lady Jane reminded her— since starting his career at Brass City Plumbing Supply Company, Inc. during summer jobs in high school.

On their second visit, Marilyn just appeared at the door, answering it herself. Introductions were made once again. Julia knew not to bring her camera this time, no point to it. She smiled when the actress pulled on one of her pigtails, complimenting again the black color.

Julia would think of Marilyn Monroe for the rest of her life, a poster-sized photograph in her home, so as to remember the visits to the striking beauty and the dungareed movie star.

It was a different country. There was customer service everywhere. It was not just her father's habits—everyone was only as good as their name and their behavior.

There weren't seven pages of paperwork before each new doctor's visit. There were house calls! Julia had many, after her tonsillectomy, painful and depleting, causing the pediatrician to make six house calls. During rheumatic fever, a portable X-ray machine accompanied the doctor because every blasted doctor thought she had pneumonia and kept irradiating her lungs. One of Julia's prepubescent legs grew to the right size; the other was too small, very gimpy. As if that weren't enough, all manner of antibiotics was shot into Julia by a doctor in a world and time and place that knew not the hazards of the surfeit of antibiotics.

Nope. No way that Marilyn would have committed suicide, not in the eyes of Prince Hal, Lady Jane, and Julia. There was something else at play, even if they could not

5

identify it in 1962. Just five years after meeting Marilyn, Julia was sitting around the campfire at summer camp when the news of the week was read. The counselor said that Marilyn Monroe had died, presumably from a drug overdose. Julia was horrified—it could not be. This lovely, charming, stunning-without-makeup woman had killed herself? It wasn't possible. Something else must have happened; some crazy pharmaceutical cocktail from a negligent "psychiatryst" (as Julia spelled it in her journals) might have done it. Maybe someone poisoned her at dinner. All these thoughts ran through Julia's mind, because she did not want anything to tarnish the lifetime memory of those two magical days in the yard of the engaged couple, wherein The Most Famous Actress in the World leaned over to Julia, looked her straight in the eye, and disparaged her own dyed blonde hair, wishing for black hair like Julia's.

Of course, The Most Famous Actress in the World did have very dark hair until Hollywood made her into the Blonde Bombshell, arming her with a new name and fame unparalleled in president's offices or barbershops.

But now she was gone.

Hal referenced them as Arthur and Marilyn to his dying day. There was no need for last names. He shared funny stories about the calls Marilyn had made, asking for a replacement for *this* or *that*. "Calling herself. Think of that. The Most Famous Actress in the World called my dad," Julia so often remarked during our discussions.

And so, Dear Reader, it was a different world, with people doing their own life's work, even famous people, even The Most Famous Actress in the World, calling Julia's dad for a fridge or bathtub upgrade. No intermediaries. No gatekeepers.

CHAPTER 2

Packing, Unpacking, and Repacking

There was no end to it.

Her mother's perfect towels in quadruple colors, the soft pinks, apple greens, pale blues, and whites of home furnishings. Two homes, interchangeable in her lifetime, now reduced to boxes coming to Julia in Milwaukee, where she is newly alone and in need of every conceivable home furnishing for the rooms and terraces overlooking the ever-expanding city skyline of Milwaukee.

You got it: Jane's gone, Julia is still here.

Unpacking. Repacking. Throwing out expired prescriptions, expired foodstuffs in Longboat Key the previous week, as part of the Simple Estate settlement—getting the condo ready for sale. It was no vacation, her first trip to the luxurious and immaculately landscaped Longboat Key condominium in eleven months. The prior time had been a fitful thirty-six-hour stay to pack up her mother's clothes and ship them back to her other home in the lush Connecticut hills.

Julia was haunted by memories when visiting Longboat. There was a deadly silence everywhere, except for the familiar bounce of tennis balls from the lanai, where she retreated to get off her aching feet. The sounds of her parents' words sliced through Julia's mind, their platitudes, their worries, their plans for the day—the simple, ordinary words of a sixty-five-year romance, now truly buried in the Connecticut terrain they had enjoyed since they were high school sweethearts.

For Julia, Longboat Key would always have special meaning. It was her favorite American resort town. Longboat Key meant scrumptious parties and birthdays at Harry's, tuna fish salad equal to a New York deli at the Blue Banana and many other small restaurants, in a place where even the fancy people wore "casual attire," serving up simple, pricey food. Julia would miss its solace for the rest of her life—the immaculate, twice-daily watered Har-Tru blue tennis courts and the ever-so-small swimming pool alongside, with its perfect redwood deck, where Lady Jane would watch all of Hal's and Julia's tennis matches. Jane required constant solace from the sun in her broad-brimmed sunhats. Her feet were also suspiciously given over to arthritis and bone spurs, as were Julia's from the time of Jane's death.

The Bayport Condos in Longboat proffered 200 quaintly labeled bronze plaques for all its precious trees and shrubs, with darting pelicans by the hour. There were

Julia's treasured moments at Dreamweavers, a boutique with handmade and ready-to-wear attire, where Jane would insist on buying Julia something to remember the trip by. Here, they regularly bought one-of-a-kind, hand-painted dresses or something from the off-beat jewelry collection. It was intended to thank the dutiful daughter for her many years of sixteen-hour days of organizing the apartment in advance of widowed Jane's arrival, for unloading the seven suitcases from the car that was shipped in advance, crammed to the brim with luggage and boxes, paraphernalia of all kinds, lest Jane forgot one useful outfit or a single CVS item.

"You don't have to thank me. It's what daughters are supposed to do."

Jane was no one's fool. She was cagy, witty, and charming, and every inch Julia's mom: beloved by many, misunderstood by most, and an insomniac of epic proportions. Only she could devour an entire box of Social Tea Biscuits at bedtime or during middle-of-the-night insomnia for decades and never have it show. She was a perfect size 6, like Julia, until she stopped exercising and blew up to a size sixteen. She stopped exercising because everything hurt, and she was exhausted all of the time.

These symptoms were exactly like those that evolved precipitously in Julia, just prior to Jane's ever-so-quick death one week to the minute in intensive care, where was precious little "care," intensive or otherwise. Through her deathwatch week, Julia was there for Jane during the many hours of few medical or nursing staff helping her mother or even checking in. It was a sloppy hospital room, but Julia was there from nine in the morning to three in the afternoon and straightened it up all day long. Together, they kept track of Jane's needs, processed the prior day's mail, emptied the trash, massaged her bed-ridden feet, or laughed like teenagers together over their final shopping expedition—purchases from the lush Christmas catalogue just arrived from Neiman Marcus. It was a holiday season Jane would never know, and black velour sneakers she never wore. But Julia did, for more than a decade until she passed them on to a friend, when her own feet blew up to a size ten.

Julia wondered whether there was a relationship—feet to feet, insomniac to insomniac, and within a month of Jane's death, everything hurt Julia as well. She attributed it to exhaustion, having heard Jane's prediction: "If you keep going like this, you are going to collapse." Naturally, the relentless demands of Lady Jane made Julia's days and weeks both long and troubled. As the fall of 2007 progressed and the world's greatest insomniac began to sleep ten to twelve hours a day and never once mentioned pain, Julia took heed and was ever more vigilant with the inimitable caregiver Wanderful, so named because of an inscribed watch at her tenth anniversary of working modest half-days here and there for the Fields. The house was so spotless, there was really nothing much for her to clean, but her precise 8:30 a.m. appearance made Jane feel good, especially in her widowhood.

The year these events started during the winter of 2007 and 2008, when everyone wore heavy sweaters in Milwaukee until well into June. Summer followed a winter of hellish proportions, with the goodly neighbor Gregg shoveling out Julia's car at 6:15 a.m., and then shoveling over and over again throughout the day. Julia hated the ice and the snow. She telecommuted to her clients more often, as she was afraid of falling with her numb and painful two left feet. She preferred having the fake fireplace's warmth on her back and was forever mesmerized by the city spread out in front of her, serving both as inspiration and as memory of earlier years in Brew City—or, as Julia coined it, Mil-ride-ee. No one walked. Everyone drove, and they all gained weight eating prizewinning cheeses, drinking craft beers, and huddling inside during Milwaukee's eight months of winter, prior to the inversion of weather patterns, with Julia's New York pals receiving far more snowstorms and blizzards.

Julia said this as a mantra: "*I am a survivor. I have survived the deaths of Lady Jane and Prince Hal. I will survive this American healthcare confusion and its mind-numbing costs—no system at all. It's all chaos, delays, and sub-specialists, unless you have a sore throat or the flu, a knee replacement, a routine cardiac procedure, or a typical cancer caught early in the game. It is a labyrinth for patients to follow, as my doctors rarely talk to each other.*"

Julia had no idea, in the beginning, what other institutions she would have to survive—the impact of years of depleted retirement savings to support the new America of a bare bones health insurance system. Costly, third-class insurance, but Obamacare at least gave her some bennies. Even the doctors, physicians' assistants, nurse practitioners, and hospital clerks often complained to her, wasting the short appointment time by reiterating their own insurance stories.

Jane had come to know firsthand the slippery slopes of the Milwaukee banks, quickly slipping her home mortgage to unknown financiers half a country or half a world away, with no notice aforethought. The Bank of Ill Repute made loans as if it were giving candy to a three-year-old: "Here, have some more money, it will make you feel good, there is no need to worry about your recent charges. We will finance them, and you will just pay us back in a few months. We understand," the banker declared. "You have a short-term cash flow crisis. We are here to support you."

Not exactly. The Bank of Ill Repute went down the tubes during the period of Julia's mortgage. Half the staff was out on the street. She had trusted the bank; the bankers had been told to lend to flimsy, risky people. Julia had no steady source of income, only her infrequent writing gigs and a steady translation gig that paid something on the order of six cents per word. This same bank continued to send Julia overdue notices for her safety deposit box for four years after she moved her money elsewhere. In any case, the safety deposit box was nearly empty—just a few sheaves of paper. Julia seldom wore her heirloom jewelry of four generations when she was too ill even to walk around her apartment, but she liked knowing that these memories were always nearby, in a pillbox or some weird hiding place that a potential thief would not think to look, so well-hidden that Julia lost track of them at times.

That is, until she had to pawn a few one year. She pawned a few the next year, too, receiving mere pennies on the dollar, but it was *cash*, that useful commodity so scarce in Millennium World. It justified an occasional pedicure or play at the Milwaukee Rep, the Milwaukee Chamber Theater, or new winter boots at Picardy Shoe Parlour, purchased during the 70-percent-off clearance weeks.

Years later, Julia only patronized Target. She discontinued manicures and massages, so helpful for the pains of, as she named it, FibroFuckingMyAlgia. It was correctly diagnosed in an excruciating EMG exam in the hospital in May 2008—*bingo*, her last test after she'd flunked lupus and many others. The ensuing diagnoses were often wrong, but some of them correct, if not correctable. Julia ate for $50 a week, no restaurants, cut her hair herself, and gave up on overlaying her gray hair with chemicals galore. Her aide, Megan, helped Julia walk to the shower and stood by her side, drove her to the store, and walked with her to the closet to help her get dressed. With peripheral neuropathy, there was no closing buttons or snaps in fewer than five minutes of ultimate frustration. All of this, no one ever knew. It was off their radar. They could not take hearing about Julia's pain, and many complained they did not know how to help.

Uh, how about a dried-up dandelion? Shall I send you a postage stamp so you can send me a card, a real card, not a virtual one, which I find virtually tasteless? Julia wondered.

Megan was more than a helper and a television news producer, she was like an adoptive daughter, bringing Julia surprise bouquets of flowers at just the right time, bringing epicurean foods she had cooked from scratch. And she was just an email away. Very traditional, that lady Megan—no cell phone and no texting.

Julia had been called resilient and a Renaissance woman all her life.

Right or wrong, these were her sobriquets throughout her life, healthy or sick, married or single. And the accomplishment of so many things, even games of tennis on occasion, made it impossible for most to understand how she could be in so much pain with so many incurable diagnoses.

They did not have U.S. Navy Seabee Hal as a father or Lady Jane, resolute genius, as a mother. Very simply, Julia kept this lineage going. She prayed a lot, and she wrote her head off. She knew there were many who had neither a dime of savings left nor any healthcare coverage. Some days, Julia thought it was perhaps better, a life without doctors and nurses bungling her case from meds to tests, getting paid whether right or wrong.

• • •

Welcome, Dear Reader, to Millennium World, Milwaukee, Wisconsin, where the electoral wall would fall in November 2016.

A Letter from a Friend in Phoenix

Julia,

It's now 5771, I looked it up, the Jewish calendar year.

You are one of a kind. Inexplicably not of this world. Light years beyond "Old School." Eloquent. Passionate. Righteous. All of the desirable character attributes listed in the table of contents in The Book of Virtues, *personified. What's more amazing is...there you are...over your ears in all the shit that gets piled on you, and you STILL believe people are good and will change their evil ways and see the world as you do. I know your father taught you never to give up, but...as much as I'd like to jump on your bandwagon, I have NO FAITH in people. None. I remain Teflon-coated. Won't allow anyone from the outside world get to me. There's too much evil/ignorance. I can't change it. So, I will swallow my one-a-day Fukitol pill and wear my shirt with "I hate people" on it. I will tread lightly on the world...reusing, reducing and recycling and being the best person I can be...but I will never expect these things from anyone else. They can't do it. They won't do it. They don't care about things right under their nose. They don't even read books any longer.*

Keep trying to feel better,

Hugs,
Millie

CHAPTER 3

Julia Tries to Rock Her Career Back

Dear Reader, it was not the best of times in Milwaukee, where no one walks, but rides in cars or buses, and in convertibles from the first spring day through fall days in the fifty-degree range. The economic crash may seem to be last year's news, but manufacturing, printing, and a host of other industries hadn't recovered yet. This array of unemployment trickled down, not the Reagan cash theory, but in the vast number of job seekers who could not find work, were fired for all sorts of specious or illegal reasons of sexual orientation, age, and religion, or whose positions were eliminated. This was the backdrop for Julia. It stank. Many people said it was her age, others said to just "suck it up," others had insane ideas about how she should make a living.

Why don't you find a job with benefits? She submitted some five hundred applications through the decade and was a finalist three times.

What about using your network? She could not attend easily her usual networking events; Julia, as Jane, found standing for more than a minute to be excruciating: Standing was the worst.

Why don't you do a national search?

That last one really inflamed Julia, as she loved Milwaukee more than any city in America. It had been home since 1987, and she was not moving. She had just moved into and fixed up the loft apartment, a perfect home, her favorite of all time—a glorious space with high ceilings, and her first home with central air. It had "concierge service," which meant your packages were left at your door and your plants watered when you were out of town. Julia wasn't buying anything on the internet, or at Bayshore, the poor cousin to Milwaukee's Mayfair Mall, so she had no packages to be carried up to her apartment. But still, she could dream of a different time when she might be able to afford ordering some socks or a needed pair of slippers. She hadn't taken a vacation in two years, ohmygod. It was like living in a hotel—no handymen to pay for changing light bulbs, and no light bulbs to try to locate among the 1,000 varieties at the Holt Avenue Home Depot. Her beloved *Milwaukee Journal Sentinel* and *The New York Times* arrived by 5:00 a.m., that delivery woman having to get out in the black of night at 3:30 and finish her route by 5:30, before starting her day job at 6:00, all in service of her husband's Almighty Health Care Costs of Staggering Proportions. Julia shed a tear when she read the note to please not call up the office if the paper was late. *No, please don't do that. They will deduct five bucks from my small salary. Here is my cell phone number: Just call me, Miss Fields, and I will pick up a fresh copy of the papers that may have been stolen by vagrants in your foyer or by your neighbors.* Julia never called the office again to report a missing newspaper. In fact, she walked up the street herself to Pick 'N Save and bought copies when they did not arrive. She left the carrier a note not to work even longer than her fourteen-hour workday.

Julia loved the warm, immaculate garage downstairs for the car. She also loved the three terraces with fake redwood floors and plenty of space for her stationary bicycle, treadmill, flowering plants, herbs, and vegetables—when they were not inside, relocated to Julia's winter garden in the extra bathroom. Julia ventured out on the terraces when she couldn't sleep through the night, which was usually, and the trees and her metal lawn menagerie of a giraffe, turtle, and bird sculptures comforted her. She wished upon the first star she saw. Then, often, she went right back to sleep in the Vermont-styled sleigh bed, the night air soothing her spear-like pains everywhere and the numbness in her hands and feet.

As for finding work, people had all sorts of polite but useless things to say: It was her age, her stage of career, "the market," blatant sexism, she was overqualified, and then the one no one likes to discuss in Milwaukee—anti-Semitism. It was plain as day. One jerk even said to her

21

face: "You are too old, and you are Jewish," as the reasons she wasn't suitable for a job for which she met all the requirements. Julia left the charming Plaza Hotel Café that July morning and thought about the interview for a few weeks. And then she found a lawyer, but he flaked out at the last minute—something about a conflict with another contingency case. He was probably going to make more money on that one. She found another one, ironically named Autumn, as 2008 had an early autumn that year. The man who uttered the words did not retain counsel for some time, but when he did, bang, he went for Julia's jugular, seeking a trial, for which Autumn would be charging Julia fifteen thousand dollars. "Fifteen thousand dollars?!" Julia shrieked. "You must be kidding. I haven't earned $15,000 yet this year. It is a 'Jobless Recovery,' surely you must know and understand that?"

Clearly, Autumn did not.

But Julia was invincible. She worked six hours a day or more on her client search. She cut out every single expense she could from top to bottom, from buying books and magazines to scheduling the weekly massages so necessary to relieve her FibroFuckingMyAlgia pain. Knowing her circumstances, what people said was incredible: "We're leaving for China." "We just came back from Paris." "We are retiring next month." Their experiences were a relentless barrage of what she could now only dream about. Julia worked every weekend on her writing and client search. And no, please, you idiot from hell, a forty-eight-hour weekend in Madison visiting her son, Joshua, in law school was definitely not a vacation, just a breather, sleeping on his street-procured leather couch.

Michael was a brief fling, an inverse image of Julia. He was disorganized, flirted with waitresses one-third his age, never read a newspaper or magazine, scrolled endlessly for answers through the 1,615 office messages in his inbox, and ate precisely the food that could kill him, given his advancing type 1 diabetes.

Oh, but he was charming on their first few dates. He complimented her every outfit, he held her hands at the movies, he let her drive his car to the beach in Sheboygan—Jackie Mason land, as Julia had learned in her childhood. Yes, a rabbi turned comedian, whose jokes she copied down in the Catskills hotels after skiing all day. Julia's father told a national conference of plumbing supply wholesalers that it was helpful if salesmen brought a joke with them, as his young daughter kept a log of jokes and told them to her friends.

Michael was the sort of boyfriend that once made them scrumptious smoked turkey on his immense grill, preposterously sized for a person living alone for twenty years, twice divorced and without children. He was immaculately dressed, with every silver hair in place. He told her she was gorgeous and brilliant, said all kinds of stuff, and then, *poof.* He disappeared into his jobs, had two of them, and his misery, and no way, they couldn't be friends.

How can you be friends with someone who doesn't respond to postage stamp letters pertaining to his place of work, a former client agency of Julia's? These were business questions! How can you be friends with someone who wants to sit twenty feet away from you during the televised presidential political debates? *And frankly, how can I be friends with an ex-boyfriend whose mind is blown to smithereens, who says that they only had a couple of dates?* Julia questioned. Uh, twice a week for four months is not a couple of dates. And really, how can you be friends with someone who is glued to the idiot box, who has no reading material by his bedside or next to his favorite, oversized, leather living room recliner with a cup holder?

Eloise, Julia's therapist, predicted Michael would be suicidal by February. "That's just what I've been thinking," Julia said. "And I have no training in this stuff, but I know male depression when I see it. And he fits the model to a T."

Okay, so the two-to-twenty dates were a brief diversion from ye olde client and job search, except that Michael kept encouraging her to look nationally. He never listened, he never remembered. And, no, she was not going to leave the Midwest, where the quality of life was superior, just like the name of the longest residential street in Bay View. And, Milwaukee was more superior every day, compared to the rest of America. It was something about the Midwest, the open spaces, the early morning appreciation of the day, of earnest efforts, of no one having to go to just a few select colleges or else feel they were unsuccessful from day one after high school. Julia treasured the Wisconsin Idea, a formerly free ride to the thirteen branches of the University of Wisconsin, but no longer available for all high school graduates to any branch. More recently, just the smarties, the top 20 percent of the high school senior class in the state wishing to attend Madison were accepted, and it was no longer free, but still cost just one-quarter of a private East or West Coast university. The whole state focused on education as requisite, with property taxes beyond astronomical. But Julia's Dear Milwaukee, while sporting ignominious honors in 2009, such as multi-generational severe housing segregation, a huge uptick in opiate deaths, and many unwed teenage mothers, also had Class with a capital C. It had the Lake of Turquoise Beauty, a huge and clean beach just north of downtown. And it had Boomers and Millennials linked in new downtown apartments, places unlike anything that Brew City had ever known until its Urban Renaissance, heralded many years later by the *New York Times*.

But Michael could not know or absorb all of this; he was new in town, did not explore Milwaukee, and he had never raised children, as she had taken both Jenny and Joshua to the emergency room a total of four times, or watched their fevers spike to 104° in a New York minute. He had never sent anyone to college for $55,000 per year before socks, per child. He had siblings he never spoke to; Michael was the Alone Ranger.

Not Julia. She loved her friends, and she kept in touch with many for decades, internet schminternet, Julia just called them up, preferred telling jokes and hearing human voices. For a while, the new apartment was her favorite home of all time, it was also solitude to the max. Music only went so far to accompany her writing. And, of course, she could not afford cable. She had sold her television and found out she never missed it for a minute, could watch most everything from her telephone—that Whole World in One's Hand. "You betcha," she said to herself, admiring her ingenuity.

And then, boom, one morning at six o'clock, a friend sent Julia an email about a consultant position. By 6:00 p.m., the interview was set for the following day. Three days later, it was a deal—a half-time consultancy at Milwaukee's largest housing agency. Whoa! Julia was reeling from the shock. And then, she made the leap. She re-launched her writing business with an artistic and appealing new website. With artist fees, internet fees, and a welter of contract worker insurances demanded by Ye Olde Client Redux, there went Julia's first paycheck.

But what was she to do? Suffer another year of gig searches? She started to color her hair again at home, acting against anti-chemical Healing Rules from the Women Hippie Healers at the alternative health clinic she frequented. Everything needed replacing with a disease like fibromyalgia—from Teflon pots and pans to her Estée Lauder™ makeup, and what?! *No nail polish?! Yikes!* Half-time work was most certainly not enough to live on, but it was plenty of nothin', and Julia reviewed the contract with her decades-long advisory circle of mentors.

And so, with one solid client, Julia was back to work. It was not easy. It was a whole new project, it had legal, banking, insurance, and accounting tasks and fees of endless proportions. The paperwork took more time the first week than the actual work, in a country of way-too-many regulations. But it was real work, it was learning a new client, it was served up in a huge building with an enormous, if ominous at nightfall parking lot in Milwaukee's center city, with guards at every entrance. And the employees were kind, they worked hard, and they appreciated Julia. One blurted out, "I love Julia!" at the very first board of directors meeting. It was a new start and a new way to frame the week, leaving Julia enough time to write opinion articles and letters to the editor on all seven days. She was never once in her fifty-seven years at a loss for words, written or spoken, as her friends regularly reminded her—they really had to go cook dinner, or grab a shower, they could not talk on the phone any longer. Much to Julia's shock, in her time of excruciating pain and living alone, the Whole World Was Unavailable to Take Your Call and about a zillion of them did not have the courtesy to call or write back.

As ever, Julia was just trying to make a good impression, denying her excruciating pains every second of the day. She was not a slave to work, never had been, but merely enjoyed providing her clients with the instant responses that mattered, whether penned on her phone from the dentist's chair or during face-to-face sessions. She provided service in the Economy Sans Service. Julia was resolute, and every call or email or text was answered before dinner every single day, always and with no exceptions.

A Letter from Julia to Michael

Good Morning, Michael:

I have reached the same place as you did several weeks ago—"no love connection." But, unlike your saying a relationship was too much stress, I have come to this for entirely different reasons. You don't really give your reasons, do you? I only know what I was told. But, please, for your own sake, not mine, get some help to get to the source of your incessant road rage. There's only unhealthy food in your fridge—it's like you are committing a slow suicide. Please get some help so that you can concentrate on writing your memoirs. (I know you write well—have read some.) And please, do not eat the very things that will make you sicker and sicker.

Yes, I have my own challenges (financial losses, weight to lose, my desire for a second marriage, FibroFuckingMyAlgia). But I have conquered many losses, with the help of expert practitioners, both medicines and talk therapy, and especially learning and practicing mindfulness. It's been hell, it's been difficult and exorbitant, but I'm prevailing against all the odds, at least on some days.

You deserve energy, happiness, and a good life. Go out and make it happen. Sixty-nine ain't so old.

Yours truly,
Julia

CHAPTER 4

The Ruby Ring Rediscovered

Littered on the sidewalk were a mountain of boxes and bubble wrap used in transporting, once again, all of Julia's possessions from the Fifth Ward loft to her new, student-sized rental apartment in Bay View, south of downtown, and known as the current hot spot for real estate. The neighborhood had not suffered Milwaukee's plague of Dutch Elm disease, and the trees on Superior Street were eighty feet tall. Superior was one block away from the glorious Lake Michigan, which brought cool breezes in summer and less snow in winter, the famed Lake Effect that dropped temperatures a degree every two blocks in Milwaukee.

The boxes and wrappings blew in the May winds, pushing up against resting places near porches and trees in the sunny neighborhood of Bay View, where Julia had no view of the bay. It was a neighborhood, formerly a separate city, that was settled a century ago with homestead plots and summer cottages reachable by street cars, and garages added later, detached from the cottages, some built two levels deep to the lake. Bay View had now turned into expensive real estate. (*What is fake estate?* Julia wondered.)

It was now 2010, two years into the Great Recession, two years dominated by Julia's illnesses, with no relief in sight and the same creepy "we don't know what to do to help you" said in identical words by her friends for life or new specialists on her interminable case. Or worse, silence, no return calls, no response to her letters, sent as emails. Who could be so sick and look so well and show up so often at arts performances or the grocery store was the riff on her, Julia knew.

"Julia is faking, she wants attention, she wants people to do things for her, she forgets we have jobs and lives." Julia had heard it all, or at least had heard the insinuations of her scientifically proven diagnoses of fibromyalgia, irritable bowel syndrome, and wretched feet. Oh well, as Wanderful reminded her often, they were not really friends anyway, and they would get what's coming to them. "Just be patient, Julia, what goes around comes around."

Milwaukee exploded that spring and summer with heat normally known only in large cities radiating from sidewalks, three to six savage shootings before dawn many days, and the continued Great Recession, so quaintly named the Jobless Recovery. Some of Julia's friends and acquaintances were working three jobs or scratching out a living in a desperate attempt to live by their wits, creating a sole proprietorship or "consulting"—ergo, they were looking for a job with health insurance. It was all maddening and paradoxical, for while there were so many without jobs, you couldn't find a cab, you couldn't find qualified health aides, you couldn't find a beauty shop that understood that if you were unable to drive there for your appointment, it was real, it was true, so they fired you. It happened to Julia three times. Three times! In little old Milwaukee, so fancy schmantzy now. But one of the hoity-toity salons in Bay View closed up shortly after banning Julia from coming—too many canceled appointments. She smiled every time she saw the empty storefront. *Deserved it,* she thought. Zapped them but good.

But, quite obviously, there were tens of thousands of jobs that needed doing. And not only the twenty-four-hours-a-day reconstruction of the Hoan Bridge, her beloved pathway to downtown from Bay View. Hal could never pass by it on her parents' regular, twice-yearly trips to Milwaukee without reminding Julia that it was named for Milwaukee's Socialist Mayor, Frank Hoan. Hmmm. A Democratic Socialist in the 1930s? History would repeat itself in 2016 when Senator Bernie Sanders, a democratic socialist, would win twenty-three states during the primary season, but not the nomination.

It was an America of Monopoly® money, where money and power were thrown around continuously in brazen, meaningless displays of winner take all. Being a millionaire was nothing; one had to be a billionaire, or at least a demi-billionaire to count for something in

31

Millennium World. It seemed like the whole country, watching dozens of media sources, getting more irate and even more confused, was sort of like Julia's medical case. These experiences were interwoven like a Rubik's Cube, one politician commented. Or like Julia's knitting skeins, kept around in case she ever got around to knitting again, if the "incurable" small nerve neuropathy in both hands ever went away.

Dear Reader, if you kept the news around your friends and loved ones at bay, you missed America's shift from connecting to those around us to a supreme connectivity to the immediate, intricate, interconnected world of electronic contact. These random touch points cannot be found online or in print, but seep into your mind surreptitiously when others call things by names of what they are not, by folks who daily invented a new lingo for the *crise du jour*. It was precisely in denying Julia's symptoms and diagnoses that others simply said she was "in mourning" or worse, crazy.

Naming things differently was known to Julia as Janespeak, a word her mother created, and it represented the struggle to speak differently, to grab hold of humor in the midst of aloneness, solitude, and singular suffering, experienced throughout Jane's middle age and her elder years. As Julia grew further away from Jane's death, she discovered the wordplay coming into her speech and out of her mouth. It was a way of coping, of infusing her morning of licorice- or passion-flavored tea leaves with something different, something stronger and more durable than the sixty-four ounces of pure water recommended by her doctors. It was tradition. It was family. It was the mother tongue of connection.

"Thanks, Mom. I didn't know you were a poet, but now I know it," Julia remembered having said when she read a birthday card or one of Jane's regular letters sent throughout her eighty-three-year life.

"You'll see," Jane assured her. "It will come to you."

The puns and nicknames had all started one day at the synagogue, when Jane admired a particularly well-groomed-to-the-max lady, perhaps in her sixties, perhaps older. The Fields didn't really know her or her family. But aside from the elegant suit, the *comme il faut* hat, and the gloves, there was something distinctive about this woman, especially for Waterbury in the 1960s: She was wearing false eyelashes! Unheard of. Only New Yorkers or actresses wore them. And so, Jane dubbed her "Fluttery," as her lashes fluttered with her every word or nod.

From then on, everyone had a nickname. Julia was Jules; people at restaurants or shops might gain instant nicknames, depending on how outrageous their behavior was. Many decades later, as Jane needed her attention and assistance, even when Julia was 900 miles away in Milwaukee or on trips with Ben to Italy or New Zealand, she was nicknamed Lady Jane. There was a hint of sarcasm on Julia's part, for Jane needed as much help as she could get others to offer her, day in and day out. Julia remembered how, with perfectly coiffed hair, a fresh pedicure and manicure, she went in for thyroid surgery, and not again to the hospital for decades until the congestive heart and lungs failure that put her under in a week.

On the way back from the alley dumpster to Julia's new flat (instantly dubbed "Mini Mouse House"), Julia found a small box on the lawn. It must have fallen out of the moving boxes. She examined it carefully—it was a Russian enameled box made of black lacquer with a scene painted in reds and oranges. Julia opened it and found a ring. But not just a ring—this was the ring her mother had worn to the hospital, her everyday wedding ring, the one with three small rubies and gold filigree, the one that had once vanished in the Hyde Park Hotel in New York and was found an hour later stuck in the bottom hinge of Jane's purse. Trying on the ring and seeing it did not fit on her finger, Julia put it back in the box.

What sights had it been witness to during fifty-six years of marriage and five of widowhood? Where had her mother replaced the ruby that had fallen out after an Ice Capades show in Boston? Who had taken the ring off the finger of a dead woman? A nurse who never knew Lady Jane, most assuredly, just doing her job. And now, Julia rediscovered the ring, amid the mountains of boxes and paraphernalia from the moving van. The wedding ring, a symbol of so much joy and connectivity in a young married couple in the 1940s, ended up smelted, the rubies removed and sold, as was the gold for astronomical direct and indirect medical costs, pre- and post-Obamacare.

Lady Jane, too, had suffered many pains of indeterminate origins. There was no scientific name in the 1960s and 1970s. There was no test. But it was clearly, in retrospect, fibromyalgia: Julia had the specific EMG test of excruciating pain administered at the Prospect Avenue Clinic by the infallible Dr. Jacqueline Carter, chief of neurology, and spent ten days in bed to recover from the nerve pain it caused. Jane's pain was treated with numerous downers, bringing on more depression and exhaustion. That was the remedy for housewives and women not only in those decades but into the twenty-first century. These pills robbed Julia of her mother's love and attention and gave her the wrong kind of inheritance. These pills gave her a mother who was numb through her day, forgetting many things that occurred, and, providing instead, a mother who was walking and, worse, driving around virtually stoned. It was the same for millions of women treated by male doctors. These women were frustrated almost to madness, their days relegated to volunteer or half-time jobs, college degrees dumbed down to housekeeping, wifing, mothering, all that was expected of them, except the scant few with professional careers as nurses, secretaries, or teachers.

A Journal Entry

June 1, 2010

This new home, cramped but colorful, is now painted in pink, purple, and lavender. I had to give away a great deal to suit small closets. And I turned an old junky Shorewood basement cabinet into a linen closet/ sweater armoire that takes up half my bedroom, geez Louise, and I put many more things into a storage locker. The three-

room hamster wheel is plastered with art, music, books, and photographs since childhood, back three generations, the erstwhile wedding photo, all of it I squeezed into four hundred ninety-five square feet upstairs, plus the large study downstairs.

Naturellement, *the bookcases arrived two weeks late, and the sole proprietor carpenter from out in the country got here tonight at 6:15 and told me first up that "the installation will take at least until ten." Stunning, his banging and banging are more than I can take.*

Vicious pains and the usual doctor meds plus my Bayer *are not doing much: FUKITOL. I am trying to drown out the carpenter with my* REO Speedwagon *songs.*

Read the Wall Street Journal's *article this morning, "'Til Forty Years Do Us Part," re boomers and marriage after kids. Today's paper, D1, Personal Section, with a nod to philanthropy: This is one of many articles I have clipped as part of my life's bibliography.*

Killin' this stinkin' landlord tomorrow, getting ripped off with a still-broken closet rod, two months after he promised it would be fixed before I moved in.

It's 11:00 p.m. now and he is still banging away. Haven't eaten yet. Got all kinds of food ready, if this guy will ever finish and leave me in peace.

Tummy terrific, bloating/ swelling (lymph?) going down, at long last, without exercise or change of diet, it just swells and unbloats, it seems, on a daily basis.

I think that the doctors forget and "forgot" in my case: Patients and people in general need love and support. Especially if we can manage twenty-five things at once, as some reflect that I do. We still need regular vacations, but how can we afford them in this economy, while working on gigs? This is all normal, not a psychological abnormality.

There is the every-hour stress from the broken down society, with so little community or compassion for the disabled, like me, who live alone. Everyone is creepily a power-seeker in Millennium World.

We, each of us, can fight and take back the country, even in small ways of being active. We must prevent apathy from letting fascism take over.

CHAPTER 5

Sundays Were the Worst

ady Jane was right: Sundays were the worst. The phone barely rang, emails were eerily infrequent, and once Julia had completed her errands and housework, she awaited the hours to pass for a concert, play, or movie, or sometimes two of them. As fall began, the frigid Milwaukee wind off Lake Michigan reminded everyone to pile the layers on. In an instant, summer was over.

Julia worked on her contracts, she worked on getting more contracts, she made lists in her calendar and duplicated them on a separate sheet of paper with more details, and she occasionally napped. There was no television, no idiot box, but she listened to Pavarotti or Enya or Eric Clapton while she worked, so as to hear human voices. Sunday, usually without sun in Milwaukee's fall and winter, was endless. It was forever reminiscent of her single years in New York City and, sure, occasionally there was a boyfriend in the picture. But as her neighbor, Patti, had said, they came and went like buses—there would be another one coming around soon. Julia was not so sure. She was particular; she wanted someone with kindness first, and that was hard to find. She wanted a guy who read, at least the news, if not her trove of literary novels. Julia sought companionship, and it was rare for women to find that with Boomer Men in the early twenty-first century.

Julia spent time remembering Lady Jane and Prince Hal, all their virtues and not too many of their vices. Unlike her mother, Julia could not eat an entire box of Social Tea Biscuits without gaining an ounce; she would gain five pounds by just looking at the box. But she did replicate her mom's eating in bed habit with carrots, apples, and almonds. Okay, maybe an occasional starch, such as oatmeal, but Julia found it necessary and comforting to eat and read herself to sleep, as she had since childhood, with a pink AM-only radio in her naps after kindergarten.

One happenstance boyfriend started out charmingly princely, with suits and ties that were classy; with promises of trips to Las Vegas, where Julia had never been; with mentions of evenings spent listening to CDs from her vast collection; of a trip to Chicago; of future trips to Wisconsin's state parks, as he had purchased an annual pass when they spent a mere hour at his first Wisconsin state park in June.

And then, the guy froze up. He did not call back. Her emails languished, unanswered. He claimed to work and work and work, but when she asked what he did on many weekend days, he said, "Nothing." It reminded her of *King Lear*'s "Nothing comes from nothing." He did not want to go to another state park or to Bayfield and sail the Apostle Islands, as she had done for many summers. He did not want to do anything except sit in his oversized easy chair and drink beer, or maybe wine. It didn't matter; it was all bad for his diabetes and made him even more depressed. Julia let him know this was not okay, "You must return my calls and texts. My God, I was in a car accident over the weekend and wanted to talk to someone and left you three messages. Do you not ever turn on your phone?"

And then, without a moment's hesitation, he invited her for coffee "to see her," but only for about forty minutes—hardly a date—he had to rush off to the barber, typical, and with great frequency for a beard and hair trimmed to perfection. But no, Julia must not touch his beard; it tickled him. Everything was an ordeal. He had to control everything. It was kind of like trying to please the implacable Lady Jane. Control freaks, these Boomer Men, raised in the postwar boom period, as were the women. But the guys were destined to go to college and more, become Titans of Industry. But, for the gals, the real agenda was not college, though they went and did well, also in graduate school. The main deal in the 1970s was to get married and marry well. There you have it: the success freaks vs. the brainy + homemaker + civically involved Boomer Women, an exploding conflict, leading to many a divorce or even two or three in one lifetime, now normalized.

Was it because women are not supposed to make more money than their husbands, ohmygod? Julia questioned. *Women are not supposed to go to their offices on Sundays. They are not supposed to travel for business and leave the children's care to the workaholic husband—or, if they could afford it, to the daycare provider.*

Mini Mouse Hospital—Journal Entry

June 11, 2010

Bronchial illness unremitting, IBS cured for days, maybe not for long, nothing seems to stay well for long. Music, soft lights, fresh air in Bay View in every room, even the glass block windows have tiny openings: and there's no dust every day in my new home = I can breathe without constant sniffles, was SUFFOCATING before in the Fifth Ward. I have a renewed hope since the advent of finding and retaining the purported best lawyer to win back cash and maybe also afford the necessaries for my health. The race for cash in the Jobless Recovery ain't happening via jobs, or even gigs, for many of us.

They did not break my spirit permanently, but in the darkness
In the ever-present physical pain
In the dark nights of unbearable agony in solitude
In the frigid mornings of dark, gray, blue, or snowy skies
They nearly drove me over the edge.

Where, at the time, there seemed no better place
Than to join my beloved parents, who exited stage left
Before their time, in great suffering.

All made far worse by behaviors, words, and actions
With malice aforethought
In cold blood.

Robbed of health, savings, and inheritance, and nearly
Of my spirit.

This is my argument
This is my case
Definitive, against the intentionally recirculated chemical toxins
Pervasive, inhaled, interlacing all cells. (1)

(1) High levels of methylene chloride and perchloroethylene were discovered in Julia's apartment vents. When she had trouble breathing in her new apartment, she scooped up the dust and debris in the floor vents and sent it to a specialty lab. Both of these chemicals affect the central nervous system and the immune system and have been vigorously lobbied against by the Environmental Protection Agency. In addition, the known carcinogen surfactant, found in the samples by the lab, was recirculated throughout the building, among its forty apartments, as no dryers were vented outside, a violation of the City Building Code. Many months later, these vents were redirected outside, but that was long after Julia needed to replace a brand-new HVAC system with one that worked, to the tune of forty-five thousand dollars.

CHAPTER 6

Julia's Mother

Lady Jane always wore impeccably fine clothes, always sported a fresh manicure and twice-weekly hair styling. Despite her intractable flirtatiousness, she was more often a reserved woman, except when she found humor in the moment. Then, her laugh was infectious, a silent giggle, or heaving as she shook with controlled mirth. Her sneezes were the same—a silent trembling of her nose and throat, barely audible, a learned response to her mother's "children should be seen, but not heard."

Raised in Manhattan, educated there, Jane was a city girl at heart. She left it all for marriage to a U.S. Navy Seabee. This was followed by a brief stint with the Tennessee Valley Authority in Norman, Oklahoma with the other U.S. Navy wives, gaining twenty pounds in six months from fried chicken and pecan pie. Then, onto a lifetime in

Waterbury, Connecticut she went, where Hal was born. Jane, as a new bride, immersed herself in learning to cook and keep house, never having been taught either skill in her upbringing in a pre- and post-Depression family with "two in help."

Jane forever missed the city—its stores, the Broadway theater, and the art world. As a small recompense, there was the Schubert Theater in New Haven, just thirty-five minutes away, where Broadway shows tried out before hitting the Great White Way. And if they liked the play, Jane went to the one and only Waterbury Record Shop to special order the soundtrack, which could take three weeks to arrive and might get scratched all too soon on their turntable, its unruly arm apt to skid from Julia's rope-jumping or bounding into the room.

Julia often wondered why her mother spent so much time alone in their unique, marvelous, brother Joe Fields-designed house, with a planter area encased in Brass City copper in the entry, the glorious curved wall in the living room, and the requisite 1950s piano—required in every post-World War II home. Leroy Anderson had played that piano at a League of Women Voters meeting hosted by Jane during the McCarthy era. The American Institute of Architects award winner designed a gorgeous, split-level house with two sets of stairs to the bedroom and "playroom," as they called the den, with their sole television set, which occasionally could receive programs from the New York educational channel. Hal or a workman was forever fixing the antenna, not quite tall enough to receive the signal from New York. *The New York Times* could not be delivered to Hal and Jane until they moved into their retirement home in Southbury, fifteen miles away and, finally, they were close enough to receive America's finest newspaper at their doorstep and WQXR FM, the City's classical music station. Hal and Jane listened to the Friday night service from Temple Emanu-El every single week.

In the late sixties, the house became an albatross. Julia noticed her mother's changed behaviors and isolation from everyone except dear Hal, her high school sweetheart. She became more withdrawn, even around Julia. Dinnertime became a prolonged, painful silence of thirty minutes as the gourmet food appeared, course after course, painstakingly invented from scratch, starting by 3:30 in the afternoon every day. The repertoire included weekly artichokes, long before they were known as a fresh vegetable on the East Coast. Jane served up crêpes suzette as lunch during Julia's primary school years. Jane's kitchen had not one shiny utensil or highfalutin' yuppie machine. She was *avant la lettre*, in this and so many other ways, imperceptible to others, as Jane hid herself in the house and her emotions in her heart, buried deep, until they burst forth in fury every week or so, prompted by a mere nothing—a schedule change, a sick Julia, or her childhood memories, bereft of the fabric of family: love.

Betty Lois was her real name. She was a math major at Hunter College, and before that, attended Hunter High School, where her classmates included Lauren (formerly Betty) Bacall and Bess Myerson. Her brief foray into the workaday world after their marriage was as a statistician at U.S. Time in Connecticut, renamed Timex® when American supremacy fell out of favor during the Vietnam War years, and later, as a substitute teacher in Julia's primary school. Like tens of millions of postwar moms, she devoted her daytime hours to child rearing, housekeeping, and occasional volunteer work. Lady Jane also studied the piano—show tunes, mostly—and became an expert knitter. Julia still occasionally wore the white sequin sweater, perfect in every eye-popping detail, with its deft separation of one thin sequin per stitch. It's one of a hundred or more projects that Jane made, and one of the only she knit for herself. Housewifery was Jane's tortuous, endless, secluded drudgery. The house, impeccable to the eye, required four hours a day of cleaning, perhaps to fill Jane's day and to keep her in a typical housewife reality, a rat race of a different sort.

Maybe not? Maybe it was Julia's allergies, abundant as a child and adult? Maybe the cleanliness was a mother's supreme act of love?

Julia's first apartment in the city was just six blocks from Jane's childhood apartment on the Upper West Side. It was the only real Upper West Side in America, or so the Fields believed. Julia swore she would live life differently, neither married nor a mom, neither a business executive working seven days a week nor an establishment life, but a writer of articles, stories, and poetry.

By the time this tale of memory began, Julia had worked for thirty-nine years since her first job teaching piano. And, against Hal and Jane's vehement pleas, she'd attended four years of graduate school at Columbia, not quite completing a doctorate in French Literature and Romance Philology. And, she'd supported herself with multiple part-time jobs. Julia's angst about the dismissive treatment of women and the less fortunate knew no bounds. This life of solitude was altogether different than her adolescent years, shrouded in self-imposed or punished exile to her very small, fuchsia and pink bedroom, whose colors she grew to loathe.

Had she even wished it were possible, Julia could not have reached Jane, for she was caught in the hamster wheel of postwar educated women who settled for the suburban lifestyle, with all its cosmetic procedures and expenses, riling up Hal—"What, you spent $50 at the beauty shop in just two hours? What could they possibly do? You are already the most beautiful woman in the world." That was not hyperbole, for Hal believed Jane was and always would be the magnificent fifteen-year-old across the dance floor, one blizzardy Saturday in the 1930s when they came to the dance with other dates but left together for the two-mile ride home across Waterbury's "Green," covered in eighteen inches of fresh, white snow.

Dear Reader, there is no perfect childhood; there are only gradations of short-lived happiness. *"But our good times are all gone, and we're bound for moving on; we'll look for you if we're ever back this way,"* in the words of Julia's camp song in the Maine woods. Julia's diaries from childhood were focused on leaving Waterbury for the big city as soon as she could, diving into its arts culture and bustling streets, teeming with many languages around her.

Motherhood is difficult, a balance of one's needs and the demands of the child, as one molds and watches the daily evolution of a unique person. These wounds were Julia's personal tragedy, reminders of times not shared, of thoughts not spoken, the wavering remains of her solitary adolescence and early adult years. The roles became reversed during Jane's widowhood, as Julia took charge of her mother's clothing and travel needs, and the inimitable Wanderful took care of Jane's home in Heritage Village in Southbury. The three of them covered all the bases of Jane's daily needs, medical and otherwise, leaving a few paragraphs of time for Julia's world. There are never enough hours in the day to mother, to show, to teach, to listen, or to explain. Invariably, some topics are left out, some conversations left unfinished, and invisible, unintentional wounds created. These wounds were part of Julia's unraveling tasks during her lengthy psychoanalysis.

To this day, Julia wonders whether her mother ever had the experience of hearing her own mother's voice in her years of raising Julia: that grandmother playing canasta with friends in the Alamont Hotel on West 71st Street, where Julia rented her first apartment, or in her subsequent one around the corner on West 72nd Street above Gristedes, where Julia could afford to shop only in emergency runs for coffee or apples or yogurt—her staples. Julia preferred Fairway on Broadway with its knee-high bins of copious varieties of produce and barrels of coffee beans. She watched Fairway grow from one storefront to three, with the same cheese man, Steve, profiled one day in *The New York Times* for his longevity and expertise in worldwide cheeses. When Wisconsin began to win international cheese prizes, Julia wondered whether Fairway had kept current. Julia found Wisconsin cheeses in stores throughout Jamaica and New Zealand during Ben's and her travels. As Jane began to suffer from incurable insomnia and Irritable Everything Syndrome, she frequently began discussions with a few nuclear bombs to start everyday critiques of this person or that, and that person was often Julia.

One night at dinner, Hal could not take it another minute. He went out to the shared company station wagon and sat for hours with the engine running. Julia's father explained the next evening that he could not tolerate their fighting another day, but the car was low on gas, and there was no all-night gas station in Waterbury at that time, so he had come back inside at midnight. Even as a teenager, Julia knew why he didn't leave: it was love. Hal had unending love for his teenage sweetheart and their daughter, but the generation gap arguments about clothes, pierced ears, or a ski weekend in Vermont with a girlfriend tapped him out after his ten-hour workday, despite a delicious dinner with new recipes.

Julia still hears echoes of Jane's voice and mannerisms and habits in her own activities, hobbies, and vacations. But her mother never spoke about her present inner life. She was often distant and self-absorbed, in too much pain from untreated illnesses, in a time and a place when housewives were stoked up with Valium and Xanax like candy by their internists. A whole generation stoned, driving carpools while under the influence, with no voice to fight back against the onset of the Pills for Ills, prescribed primarily by male doctors, and the weekly descent into more Pills for Ills, created by the prior ones.

Julia's friends Essex (a sisterly friend from their 1969 study/travel trip to Grenoble), Megan, and Wanderful carried the memories of Hal and Jane for her when times were rough. These friendships of decades proved the best, rare to have in middle age, when most had paired off, it seemed, except the 80 percent of the remaining world that appeared to be single women.

"You were the only one of the thirty of us who ever studied in Grenoble," Essex reminded Julia. "The rest of the group bolted straight to the patisserie once we checked ourselves off the attendance list."

"No way?! I didn't ever know that. I did my homework every night. I only tossed those notes when I moved to Milwaukee in 1987."

Julia's mornings often began with the special memories of Jane's raven beauty, as she passed the 1939 Central Park poster-sized photograph in the hall of her home on the way to make morning coffee. Jane wore two strands of small pearls, all dolled up, but not a drop of makeup for an afternoon stroll in Central Park with her Dartmouth boyfriend. He stayed at the Hotel Nevada on Broadway and 69th Street, and took two trains to reach Jane, changing in Bridgeport to a proper train after the forty-minute ride on the small Waterbury line—a drafty, dingy two-car, out-of-date wreck with no bathroom that moved with fits and starts along the antiquated tracks.

Each of Jane's deathbed words to Julia analyzed their lives with perfect accuracy, and the family prodded Julia to transcribe her mother's predictions in her journal.

"No question, go to Jamaica, despite your separation from Ben," Jane advised. "It was our favorite country."

"What?! You only went there twice and to Antigua about fifteen times," Julia observed.

Jane giggled. "We fell in love with the hotel there. But in Jamaica, it's the people, just as you wrote about in your short story." After years of keeping her creative writing to herself, Julia had begun to share final drafts with her mother, who had missed so much during her years in eclipse.

Julia arrived at her last visit to the Waterbury Hospital Intensive Care Unit after a ten-hour trip, four hours spent awaiting her flight due to a winter storm at Mitchell International Airport, ticket purchased quickly with travel miles. She'd packed in a half hour when she'd heard on her regular morning call to Wanderful that the ambulance was there. Julia spoke to the former internist, who told her Jane's congestive heart failure was at its very worst in five years.

Jane did not want to go to the Waterbury, or any other hospital, as she had told Julia when congestive heart failure and other heart issues were diagnosed at the walk-in clinic at Armand Circle, the shopping paradise halfway between Longboat Key and Sarasota.

"I wore her out," Hal ventured, after Jane's two-and-a-half-hour appointment complete with tests and three cardiac diagnoses, his face ashen, as he waited for Julia and Jane in the car, half napping, half fraught with anxiety. On their way up the stairs at Bayport, his pants stained after being trapped in the car all afternoon, Hal fell on the very last step. It was the only time Julia ever heard her father swear in her entire life. She ran to the office for men to help him up, as his swollen lymph had ballooned up his legs and made a caricature of his body.

Wanderful and the former internist, The Doctor Who Made Us Sick, said there was no choice: Jane must leave her treasured, romantic bed and get onto the gurney and into the ambulance. Jane had often told Julia that she would die in Southbury, in her own bed. Julia immediately sensed that her mother's first hospitalization since an urgent 1965 thyroid goiter removal would be her last.

On subsequent days, Julia arrived at nine, met with the pulmonologist, cleaned up Jane's room—pitifully small and ill-stocked by Milwaukee hospital standards—and awaited words of hope.

"The films aren't showing any improvement *yet?*" Julia inquired.

"I'm afraid not," the pulmonologist said in a dispirited tone. Her heart and lungs were in free fall, and Jane died at 9:18 p.m. on Wednesday, December 5, 2007, just six hours and eighteen minutes after her arm, too weak to fully raise, waved a fluttery goodbye to her daughter. This was nearly five years since the sudden onset of symptoms, diagnosed as three kinds of cardiac illness. That day, Jane ate not a morsel at their anniversary lunch, hosted by Julia at the Ritz. Julia had never suspected more than a low sugar count or transitory illness.

No one could imagine it had just been one week to end the death spiral, but Julia knew it was the end. She had the daily tracking reports, and she knew Jane was giving up. She was suspicious of her caregivers, she did not recognize her surroundings, and she had stopped getting dressed or leaving the bedroom. But still, Julia cried for hours when she got the call announcing Jane's death. Her first call was to Wanderful, who had reached out to her six months prior and said, "I cannot leave your mother." She stayed that night and every twenty-four-hour cycle of care for weeks, until her blessed daughter, Vicki, a schoolteacher at Hal's Crosby High School, took over the weekends. At one point in October, Jane confused the two caregivers and called Vicki "the other Wanda." No amount of explanation by Julia could clarify the situation, nor could she convince Jane that she was still in her real home, not a home that looked like hers, but wasn't really. Of course not, it had been a totally surreal home since her beloved Hal's death.

It was over. No more laughing at old times, no more reviewing Jane's mail and paying her bills, no more reimbursement checks for Julia's upkeep of the apartment—just in case the tests were wrong, and Jane came home, Julia wanted everything to be fixed up in perfect, Inspector General state.

Jane was no more.

Death's eerie silence prompted a flood of memories of their most recent conversations—reread from her journals at Jane's funeral—of that final week as a mother and a daughter. Julia provided what daughters do: safe passage to the next world.

Lady Jane's heart broke down after the medicine for her heart destroyed her lungs. The autopsy couldn't determine which came first as cause of death, as they were so close together—the ultimate chicken and egg scenario. Jane was reluctant to take those drugs, as Julia learned only at the *shiva* from Jane's lifelong friend, Joyce, who was to live in Southbury another twenty years. She was "ready to die" weeks earlier, but Wanderful kept Lady Jane going, refused to let her avoid climbing the stairs or miss their daily meals from the Good News Café. Wanderful spent every night "with one eye open," awaiting Jane's invariable screams from leg cramps or nightmares. Wanderful made sure that her "Betty Boop" got out of the house to enjoy what would be her last autumn in the stately and gloriously crimson, golden, and orange Southbury hills, lit afire in autumn.

Julia remembered their last trip to the city, as well, Wanderful in tow and holding all the medicine and assistive devices so that Jane would not be mortified walking into the Belasco Theater for what Julia knew would be her last trip to either the theater or the city where all her mother's memories had begun in 1924. Julia found out that Eloise, that mainstay of postwar girls, lasting into the Boomlet years of the twenty-first century, had so well chronicled the life in the city, that walking one's turtles on leashes really was a fact of life in Manhattan.

"What is your first memory?" Julia asked during one of their summer trips to Lenox or Montauk.

"My building on West 79th Street and neighbors walking turtles on leashes," Jane had replied.

"*Whaaat?!* I thought Kay Thompson had invented that."

The very next memory Jane shared was of 1926, a blizzardy day in Manhattan, and a visit from her grandfather. As Julia was the only daughter, so, too, had her mother and her grandmother been the only daughters in their families. Herman Stern showed off a purchase he had made while at work in lower Manhattan that morning before the storm arrived. He carefully opened the paper bag in his trousers and displayed a small, blue, velvet box. He handed it to his granddaughter to open.

"Oh my goodness, Grandpa. It's so beautiful." It was a shimmering emerald with two almost blinding diamonds, one on each side, and a trail of tiny diamonds down the flanks. It was a surprise for Grandmom for Valentine's Day. The ring became two rings—Jane felt it was much too "ostentatious" all as one. One day in Milwaukee, Jane presented Julia with the diamonds portion, unworn for years, as a fortieth birthday gift. The stunning ring was Julia's very favorite, carrying with it the history of Jane's family in New York. When Julia inherited the emerald solitaire, she had her jeweler, Cynthia, put the ring back together.

Alas, the ring was stolen twice. During the Milwaukee County's vast opiate epidemic, one of Julia's licensed health aides stole it while Julia was in the tub, in a vain attempt to pawn Julia's most cherished ring for drugs. But the *ne plus ultra* Milwaukee Police Department, District 4 convinced Jewel Thief to put it back in the red Jetta she had also helped herself to on the previous night. Jewel Thief would face ten years in jail for grand larceny, the police told her, and she thought better of her behavior, also returning fifty bucks for groceries not purchased. Julia insisted that the police officers hand over the cash—but there was no way she was going to face Jewel Thief, who had walked off with all Julia's keys, taken her car for a spin to sell the ring fast for cold cash, leaving the car askew in parking space number 9.

Sadly, Jane's grandpa died three days after the ring purchase, a victim of the great New York influenza epidemic. Jane forever thought that his exposure to the blizzard and coming to see her had made him susceptible to the prevalent germs.

The final theft occurred the following year one afternoon in Jamaica, during a working vacation in the off-season, along with Julia's prescription medicines. They were heisted while Julia was on an emergency visit to the hotel's medical center. She had rushed out of her room to meet the doctor at the end of his shift and forgotten to put things in the room safe. Julia wore it often as a pseudo engagement ring to dissuade guys from hitting on her. The medicines? Their street value in Jamaica was astronomical, in a country where an aspirin costs one American dollar at the pharmacy and where neurological medicines were generally unavailable, as Julia learned when she tried in vain to replace them.

Letter to Prince Hal from Julia

Dearly Departed Dad,

My swearing comes from my incessant pain. And compared to in New York, I am mild-mouthed. But you would be telling me to watch my mouth. Mom would be in horror, too.

Maybe I should move to Jamaica, where you can grow your own ganja, the best way to stop pain, as many states are now offering medicinal marijuana, but not yet Wisconsin. That is definitely not happening. I love it here on South Superior Street, the fourth house south of Bennett on your right, yellow and white, in bad need of paint, purportedly "right away" when I moved in months ago. These landlords will tell you anything, even in fine neighborhoods.

Jesus was nailed up by false speakers like this jerk, my landlord, who remarkably changed his arrogant tune after using my Julia fakestern, low voice for one half hour from Hayek Pharmacy's parking lot, explaining that I was having someone install a hammock and not imperiling his nonexistent backyard lawn.

Here is the phone conversation I had with my internist today:

"Coughing and chills—did you take your temperature?" Dr. Ted asked.

Oh my God—for this they go to med school?

"If you have 99.1 or higher, that suggests you have a new infection, possibly pneumonia. Antibiotics are usually recommended if a person has a fever."

What?! Antibiotics every month for years destroyed my immunities. Are you sleeping when I talk to you? "I am using the new medicine you prescribed last week."

"Did you feel calmer? If you didn't notice a benefit in two days on that dose, I'd recommend not using it tomorrow. The fibromyalgia and stomach pains seem to be the worst part of it for you. You stated it well in one of your letters—no surefire cures there, sorry to say."

Great—shall I just throw myself off the balcony?!?! I cannot take this pain and the pain-in-the-butt that is the American disease Uncare Unsystem another second.

"You sounded 'okay' on the phone this morning. Did you get more anxious about anything during the day? I am not one of those who assumes anxiety is the cause. So, if we're thinking stress plays a part in your fibro acting up, what's the evidence? If so, then there might be a reason to consider a stronger tranquilizer."

Dad, I need a tranquilizer like I need a trip to Mars. How can I focus or get down to my work with drugs he knows just make me stoned and fatter, twenty pounds in two weeks? He then sent me a list of plausible medicines by email with this note:

If you go through this list and want to try a different med, see if you can find a drugstore open and have them call my office before six.

I replied:

I shall lie on my two heating pads and pray, instead. Drugs, schmugs, they do not help one whit.

Dad, you would be having a fit. You would repeat what you said in your final days of life: "We put a man on the moon a generation ago, but no one can help me." 'Tis sadly also now true for me.

Wish I could talk to you right now. I also wish I had not inherited your quick temper. People don't tolerate it in women.

Love,
Pipsqueak

CHAPTER 7

Julia's Remission, More Diagnoses, and Remission

There were many true and false recoveries that year. The initial scourge of Julia's fibromyalgia relapse that began in February had slipped away by August. Its crippling lightning strikes of pain interrupted Julia's thoughts and activities. Fibromyalgia was difficult to pronounce, and even more difficult to explain, re-explain, and deal with, especially with the 5 percent of the medical profession who did not believe it was real, despite the excruciating full body EMG neurological test to diagnose it.

Julia continued working and her many emails reaching out to friends and colleagues reflected her new energy, describing her newly recovered walking and tennis, a propulsion of activities and words, often without proper vetting, words spilling out in emails and in private conversations. She was happy to have licked fibro, at least for the present. Her emails overwhelmed Julia's friends and—upon rereading them— were hurtful, but she wrote a torrent in an attempt to connect worldwide and elicit a response—a card, a visit, or even a phone call on the solitary weekends in Millennium World. The promise of community was why she moved to Bay View, but aside from a parade of passersby going to the Saturday Farmers Market in South Shore Park, people pretty much kept to their lawn mowing and dog walking, when they weren't decorating their lawns and porches for Memorial Day and the Fourth of July with all manner of electronic and lawn sculpture displays.

The inexplicable onset of depression close on the heels of fibromyalgia's withering away was the most painful of the year's illnesses. It crushed Julia's thoughts and hopes. It eviscerated any moments of quiet, turning them into storms of self-doubt, anguish, and pain beyond words. Depression lacerated even small joys, such as eating a meal or having a haircut. It cut into a walk in the park, turning it into an endurance test, or worse, a fear of failure, of the pains making the walk home impossible.

Recovery came in tiny, fragmentary pieces. There were hours to notice recovery, but just as much evidence of backtracking into pain and the total isolation of depression, even at a party or holiday celebration. The pain of depression was worse than fibromyalgia and more acute. It was ceaseless. It knew no boundaries, neither during sleep nor wakeful moments. The simple pleasures of eating, talking to a friend, or laying down to rest were scuttled with depression's powerful scythe, with soulful anxiety about many aspects of her life, and trauma about the anxiety: Would it *never end*?

Julia learned from her first psychoanalyst that she had post-traumatic stress disorder, a diagnosis she had never known could afflict civilians. "You have severe trauma, and from a very early age," Jim, the Renaissance Doctor, said. It was their task to delve into this, into the origins of her trauma, that began with her surgeries in childhood for tonsillitis, two ankylosed teeth, and missing an entire month of school for rheumatic fever at age ten. As a child, spending ten days alone in the hospital after the tonsillectomy was the start of Julia's trauma around illness.

One day, a crack appeared in its strangling darkness, and Julia saw a glimpse of daylight. The colors of Mini Mouse House had a new radiance. The taste of food became pleasurable. The sound of a friend's voice was restored to its kind timbre. The doctor noticed. The new friend noticed—he was following Julia's illnesses and treatments closely, and he researched each new medication, much to her amazement. Dreadlocks was the guy next door, which in Bay View meant they could practically shake hands from his kitchen window to her bedroom. Didn't he realize that if their windows were open, she heard his every word, his screams to his business partner, perennially late to work, with the *mal mot* to trigger Dreadlocks' shouts, day or night? Dreadlocks was a kind man, single seemingly forever, a double engineering major, jobs eclipsed by the recession. Instead, he took on healing roles for his aging parents and was the very best uncle Julia had ever seen, playing sports and taking his two bereaved nephews to movies and ball games now that their dad had died. The boys lived across the alley, which was a shared driveway in Milwaukee. Julia's Mini Mouse House and Dreadlocks' shared a pathway to their garages and their backyards functioned as one large play area for the boys.

Unfortunately, Julia took the medicines for healing as prescribed, without questioning the docs. Years later, she wondered why she hadn't heeded the words of her 2008 published essay on the falsification of psychotropics by three Big Pharma companies, as reported in a front-page story of *The New York Times*. It was a big mistake and derailed her case for many more years. The bottles from Hayek's Pharmacy, each one of them, came with disclosures that taking this pill could cause further depression and suicidality. And there were multiple bottles, up to eight at a time.

The doctor who originally treated her with some meds to ease the autonomic nervous system pain of Fibro*Fucking*MyAlgia knew his two nervous systems. But there were many doctors and onlookers who thought these were for her instability, to tamp down her full-bore energy, manifested even amid the pains. Julia was still very active, writing a book and completing work for her clients seven days a week. In guys, this was seen as leadership, prowess, putting the irrepressible pedal to the floor. For women, *still*, in Millennium World, they were supposed to temper their enthusiasm, not work on the weekends. Just show up, dolled up in business suits with hair and makeup perfect, and don't make too many leadership suggestions. Women's words and ideas were often copied or stolen outright by their male colleagues. *Tough shit,* Julia thought, *I am who I am, and I have perseverance in bucketsful, and I will continue working from bed, even from my hospital beds.* She cut a deal with the doctors so that she could continue working with her mobile phone and copious pages of notes and edits of her clients' materials, even with her depression.

As her depression was evaporating, a fourth cervical disc erupted in blazing pain. It destroyed sleep, Julia's left arm motion, her concentration, and activities. The symptoms of depression and fibromyalgia slowly returned.

But this time, it was not deep depression. It did not shake her courage or self-image. The disc was merely a garden variety of hell, bound to respond to physical therapy, traction, cold packs, massage, and caffeine delivered by Milwaukee's own roaster, Colectivo, now a national chain of coffees and teas, with the world's best veggie sandwiches and twice-baked oatmeal, which Julia enjoyed at meetings with clients and friends.

The seven months of relapse would slowly slip away to a memory space in Julia's mind. They had included fifteen in- and outpatient hospitalizations, dozens of bottles of pills, thirteen ECTs, psychotherapy of varying worth, and two visits to the Mayo Clinic. The second visit, to the fibromyalgia three-day clinic, perplexed Julia. She was the only one working and exercising. Was it *really and truly* fibro? Or were the doctors once again mistaken?

The Mayo Clinic performed exotic tests to determine the origin of Julia's nerve pain.

"You will need to lie still in this box," the nurse explained, after applying a purple powder to Julia's torso. "We have a selection of music for you to choose from. And we can talk to you during the procedure."

"How long will it last?" Julia asked.

"Probably an hour."

"Okay, I'll choose the reggae music."

"Are you ready to start the test?"

"I guess so." Julia gulped, as the temperature in the three-foot-by-eight-foot box rose to 105° and sweat poured off her. The promised music did not play, and the team monitoring Julia tried to fix the audio but could not. Julia imagined she was walking on a beach and collecting shells, counting them up to twenty, then thirty.

"Are you doing okay in there?" the technician, a man young enough to be Julia's son, asked.

"Not really. It's pretty claustrophobic."

"Yes, I realize that. You are just one-quarter the way through the test."

Julia decided to count more shells and then pieces of turquoise and coral glass, scarce on beaches. The technician told her the heat would rise now to 108°, the hottest she would have to endure.

It was now just halfway through the test. Julia decided to count her favorite beaches: Terry Andrae near Sheboygan, the beach in Via Reggio, where she and Ben had spent May Day, a beach with thousands of parasols and tourists that perfect weather day, and the secluded beaches that she and Essex visited on the north shore of Oahu many decades before.

At last, the test was over, and the medical staff took her off the gurney.

"We will have the results sent to you," the technician explained.

"Did you see anything that you can tell me now?" Julia asked.

"You seemed to have a lot of nerve damage in your hands and feet, but it's best to wait for the doctors to report on everything at Mayo in one report that will be given to you in the video conference in August, some weeks hence."

It was a year of medical trial and error by doctors and nurses who often spoke before they thought, who acted before learning, reading, or listening to Julia's long case (trained medical personnel who dwelled on computers more than facial expressions or words). And then, they looked at Julia with dismay if she asked whether they could return calls a bit more promptly.

"Uh, patient service is customer service, godalmighty. And no, your nurse did not fill my prescription before the weekend. I spent three days in utter hell, and how is it she can keep her blasted job?" Julia inquired.

The GI doctor had no answer. He offered a lame apology.

Julia was the patient impatient for full recovery. It was a year of trying to create a time and place without illness. It wasn't cancer or heart disease, but those illnesses always received great concern and respect from friends and family, as though her illnesses were trivial. That made her suffering all the more painful. *But fuck it*, Julia thought. *I am getting better, and now my work life will fall into place.*

Alas, Dear Reader, it was not so easy to find gigs in Millennium World, despite the need for experienced writers. The workplace was laden with inside-out and upside-down behaviors and crimes right under managers' noses, employees coming to work late, leaving early, researching Saturday night's restaurant while at their desks, texting friends, or being ill themselves, with a myriad of environmentally caused sicknesses. Some called in sick just to use up their sick days while they were on job interviews or taking a mental health day at the movies.

Managing her case while living alone was Julia's second job. Being the nurse and the patient was Julia's hardest challenge.

Poem for a New Day

Awakening by sunrise
As if on flight, colors
Spread deep across the horizon.

This view, so well defined,
Gone now
Except in memory.

All senses awakened by my newly washed brain
And loving the sunrise and the day.

Finding strength and courage
Finding beauty
In a face like a Botticelli
Like a rainbow painter.

In his face of fierce and handsome beauty
With compassion
With a writer's hand and brain
With an admiring smile.

There will be hundreds of thousands
More sunrises and sunsets.

But there will never be ones
Like this beauty,
This straight shot on sunrise over water,
This city Milwaukee, a gathering place of the waters.

A place of glory and inglorious actions:
Having found a breathtaking view
Bought it, made it a home
Wherein toxins ripped two neighbors apart in disease,
Our neurological systems shredded
By deadly chemicals stashed in the air passages.

And us to hospital upon hospital

With the ambulances and blazing sirens
Of emerging emergencies.

The sun will rise in a new home
And set as well
From my writing perch
Rising on a city,
Asleep.

Morning colors cascading
Over the Great Lake of Great Beauty.

Painted forever in my mind:
This scene: plenitude, crashing waves on one side
And nineteenth century rehabs
And the sunset on the other.

My home, poisoned, is a rape of sorts:
It is a tiny slice of
Greed.
Health shredded

The sunrise is forever.
All else fades, is gone, dies.

I wake up, cannot breathe
Strange acrid smells
Open the windows
Put all exhaust fans on:

THE SAME THING OVER AND OVER UNTIL I SHALL GO MAD.

And no one addressing the obvious stuff
Of environmental illnesses far too complex
For old answers.

CHAPTER 8

"Sunday with Momma"
A Short Story by Julia

Just like every day at four o'clock, the children waited at the bus stop. Their green uniforms, pressed in perfect form each morning, were now limp from the afternoon humidity. The sun, scathing and ubiquitous, showed no mercy that day.

When the bus arrived, the children bounded on. At least they had a roof to block out the sun now. The driver greeted each student by name, reminding one to close her backpack, another to sew on her missing button by Monday.

It was a Friday in January 2001 and Winsome looked forward to the weekend. Even though Momma had to work, she had told Winsome that they could go to the water park on Sunday afternoon. The island's first water park had just opened, and Winsome would be the first of her friends to try it. Being first meant something to her, something special.

The bus clanked along on the decrepit old roads to each child's home village: Barrettown, St. Mary's, Falmouth, towns that followed each other seamlessly, hilltop to hilltop. Winsome sat on the same side of the bus every day—the one closest to the water park. She had watched a scraggly field transform in a matter of months into a serpentine swimming pool, replete with whirlpools, waterfalls, and shiny, yellow inner tubes. She had always assumed that this was not going to be a place for *her.*

"They've got day passes," Momma said the previous evening after dinner.

"What's that mean?" Winsome asked.

"We pay $20 U.S. (because Jamaicans also call their money dollars) and can use the water park for the entire day. We don't have to be guests at the hotel." Her mother saw Winsome's face light up. She didn't even have to ask whether she wanted to go.

"Momma, could we really? You know, I see the hotel from my bus every day. I saw that slide go up. But I never thought we could go. Can we really?"

"It's a lot of money for us. But I can splurge, just once. Now, don't you be anticipating this every week."

Winsome hugged her mother. The thrill of a day at *that* hotel, the one where so many of her mothers' friends worked second shift, was almost too much for her to believe. Would they look at her bathing suit, her only one, and find it odd? Old fashioned? Would she have things to talk about with the kids in the pool? How would she get by without spending any money on snacks? Could she sneak in some bread and fruit?

"You look puzzled, child. What you be thinkin'?"

"I don't know. I am so happy you said I could go, Momma. But do you think it'll be right when we're there?"

"Right?" She knew Winsome's fears. They were also hers.

"You know. We are not staying at the hotel. We gonna be wearing old-fashioned island clothes. What would I think if I were one of *them?*"

"Oh, honey, you be thinkin' too hard. Suppose we skip the whole thing?" Momma said the last part with a twinkle in her eye, with no expectation that Winsome would go for it.

"No, Momma, no. I be all right."

The weekend passed slowly until Sunday. Winsome and her mother proceeded on as so many other weekends, Momma leaving early on Saturday to work in the hotel adjacent to the water park hotel, Winsome tidying up their home and yard.

Saturday lunch was always special. That was when Winsome played with her cousins, all twenty-eight of them, at her grandmother's home a few blocks away. Saturday lunch meant everyone helped out, everyone brought food, everyone stayed until the last dish was finished and the last plate cleaned and returned to Gram's cupboard.

Today, it was Winsome's turn to bring the fruit: seven pineapples, three papayas, four plantains, fruits of small size and mottled color, all organic always in Jamaica She stuffed everything into her backpack and set out for Gram's just before noon, walking slowly under the weight.

Thoughts of tomorrow swirled in her head. She knew it would be difficult to sit through church, waiting for the end of the sermon, the end of the service, hair in bows, feet in stiff dress shoes. Momma said they could get there at one and stay until it closed. What if she didn't like it, after spending all that money? What if she couldn't swim as well as the other kids?

Winsome's daydream was ended by Gram's voice, welcoming her back after a week's absence.

"You lookin' so pretty, Winny."

"Thanks, Gram. You look wonderful, too."

"Oh, I'm just an old gramma, that's all. But I have you kids to keep me young. Keep me crazy is more like it." Gram laughed a loud, deep laugh. She hugged Winny close to her.

The cousins played outside, mancala, braiding each other's hair, a brief game of tag. Winsome was trying hard to get the attention of her favorite cousin, Josie, who lived two villages away in Barrettown. But Josie didn't seem to want to talk to Winsome, not today. She was flirting with their cousin, Timmy, the six-foot-six basketball star—the one everyone was so eager to see succeed, maybe get a chance to be the first cousin to go to college, all the way to Kingston.

"Hi, Josie," Winsome tried again.

"Hi, Winnie. Whatcha up to?"

"Not much. The usual at school. Momma's working awfully hard. But she's giving me a big treat." Winsome smiled.

"What's that?"

"A day pass at the big hotel, for the waterpark."

"Wow! You *are* lucky. Luckier than me." Josie pouted.

"Maybe we can both go next time," Winsome offered.

Josie smiled. "That'd be swell. But Winnie, are you *sure* about this? I mean, well, you know."

Winsome knew but didn't want to discuss it then. The being different part, being an islander, not a tourist.

Winsome and Josie wandered off, giggling about Gram's desserts, spread out on the picnic table. Gram always made six dozen cookies for Saturdays and served the same three kinds on identical platters. The girls snitched several and went to sit under the only trees in the backyard.

Sunday began with a huge rainstorm, pelting Winsome's bedroom windows before dawn. The island's beauty was showcased best at the end of a storm, when the sweet smells of flowers mixed with the refreshed air. This particular morning, Winsome slept late, not aware of the storm. She woke up to the smell of her mother's biscuits, another weekend ritual.

"Hi, dear, did you sleep well?"

"Sure, Momma, just fine. And you?"

"Never do too well after I put in those extra hours."

"Extra hours" meant Momma worked two extra nights plus Saturday this week, in addition to her regular eight-to-six schedule.

"Momma, we goin' today!" Winsome exclaimed. "I almost forgot."

"I don't think you could forget that, darlin', not for one measly second."

Church was special today, with twin boys having their baptism. Momma always cried at a baptism, even if she was not friendly with the family. Winsome didn't know why, would never know that Momma cried for her unborn children, three lost in pregnancy before Winnie came, healthy, full term.

On the way home, Momma walked slowly.

"You okay, Momma?"

"Sure, darlin', just tryin' to get this crick out of my neck. Feels like I pulled a muscle."

"Sorry, Momma. Maybe I rub it for you at home?"

"Sure, sure. I know what we are doing today, and neck rubs are not on that list." Momma chuckled.

The drive to the hotel seemed interminable to Winsome, but it only took ten minutes—less traffic on Sundays. Momma bought their tickets, and the desk clerk fastened an orange band to their wrists, indicating a day pass. It made Winsome feel important, a part of something special. She moved quickly to get in line for the water slide.

Slowly, the line progressed, mostly two at a time. Winsome reached the top and took a tube. The assistant helped her, explaining where to sit, how to hold and balance herself.

With a surge she had never before experienced, Winsome's tube whooshed forward, careening off the sides, splashing into the pool. It was not as she had expected, not at all. Winsome had no idea she would move so quickly along the tube's twists and turns. She lay back and was surprised when the current drew her toward the pool bar and its barstools.

There was a gradual turning of heads as hotel guests noticed this child, a native, drifting toward them. Winsome looked up, saw a woman in a broad-brimmed, white hat, their eyes catching each other's.

With each ride, her confidence built and what had initially seemed so fast became routine. Winsome had never spent a whole afternoon in a swimming pool before. She walked to the fence and spoke to Momma through it. She sat on the other side, knitting.

"Momma, thank you," she said as she approached. "This is so much fun."

"Really, darling? I looked over at you a few times, and I couldn't reckon if you were scared or laughing."

"Sure, I was scared, but I made it through."

"Yes, you did, honey, and I'm happy for you."

Winsome continued up the slide's stairs and down into the pool until five o'clock, when the pool closed for cleaning. Packing up her things, Winsome thought, *So this is what it would be like if I were staying at the hotel. This is how they see my island—a little piece of paradise.*

All the way home, Winsome said nothing, and thought about the lady in the hat, her stare. Icy, intimidating. It was good to have gone once, good now to be going home.

CHAPTER 9

Bayfield—Sails Aloft

Julia spent one summer weekend in Bayfield for decades. It was a seven-hour ride from Milwaukee to the shores of Lake Superior. At first, it was just a place to go, but it became a touch point for Julia—the kayaking to the famed sea caves, the day trip on a sailboat, and the walks around town, its population swollen from 585 to thousands on summer weekends.

"Hi. Can I sail with you today?" she asked the tall, curly, red-haired man, who was removing the blue wraps on the mainsail and jib.

"All booked today, but how about tomorrow at nine o'clock?" he asked.

"Sure, that works! I love sailing, I was once a sailing counselor in the Adirondacks, but there was seldom any wind on Paradox Lake, so I spent most of the summer teaching knots."

He laughed and stuck out his hand. "Niibawi's my name. What's yours?"

"Julia. It's my first time to sail on Lake Superior. I see there is lots of wind here."

"Oh, yes, it's a good day today. Remember to bring your own food and drinks. I don't provide them."

"No problem. I have a crazy, restricted diet in any case. Niibawi, such an interesting name!" Julia noted.

"Yes, it's Ojibwe. Well, I've got to prepare my boat."

After paying for the ride, Julia waved goodbye and set out to explore the orchards on the hills beyond town. They offered all kinds of berries—raspberries, blueberries, and blackberries—and Julia purchased a basket to pick her own. The apple orchards offered opportunities to pick your own in the summer and fall. She picked for an hour, paid for the berries, and went back to her B&B for a nap.

Niibawe greeted Julia the next morning with a smile.

"Hi, there, Julia. I see you brought a windbreaker, good idea. We're going to have a blustery day out there. She is blowing pretty darn good."

"Fine with me. I prefer it when the wind is up," Julia replied.

"You might get a bit more than you bargained for," Niibawe warned.

"That's all right. I read your brochure, and I see you spent twenty years in the Coast Guard. We probably are not going to tip."

"This boat? No way," Niibawi said.

They spent nine hours sailing that day, stopping at Cranberry Island for lunch on the grass near the lighthouse. There were times when Julia was at the wheel. She was thrilled to be able to sail on Lake Superior with its strong winds. Niibawi prepped her for their route. He pointed out the spot on the lake where you can see three states: Minnesota, Michigan, and Wisconsin. He admired Julia's prowess sailing the thirty-eight-footer, the largest boat she had ever skippered. As they talked, Julia wondered: *Can this guy be for real? He seems to have it all—a teacher in the winter, a sailboat business during summer vacation.*

Niibawi was single, widowed a few years back. He was eager to learn more about Julia and her life in Milwaukee.

"I am sure you've got a boyfriend or two. You are so attractive and interesting."

"No, no boyfriend for quite a while. I'm divorced a few years."

And so it began, their friendship and courting, the old-fashioned way, through letters via email and phone calls long into the night. They talked about his students, his growing up in an orphanage, and the books they were reading. Niibawi was his assumed name, after he'd been adopted at age eleven by a couple from the Red Cliff reservation, just north of Bayfield.

CHAPTER 10

Letters to Niibawi

Early morning, June 11, 2010

Dear Niibawi,

It is coming to an end. I am finally leaving the hotel at the end of the month. My three-day stay has turned into three weeks. Since the bank turned me down for a mortgage, I am moving into a small rental apartment for a year, just to be settled somewhere immediately. Unlike you, I am not the least bit handy, so I will hire my new neighbor, "Dreadlocks," to paint it in pinks and purple, with an eat-in and cheerfully sunlit kitchen, many odd crannies, and just what the doctors forgot to order: comfort, clean air, and relaxation for work and home, in a neighborhood of families. It is a home with dark woods and coved archways reminiscent of the 1904 period when it was built. The German industrialists here built their summer cottages too close together, but the bungalows are charming, have character, have possibilities, if I can squeeze in all my art and books.

Hope all is well with your job and everything else.

Hugs to you,
Julia

———

June 30, 2010

Dearest,

I had incredible narcolepsy all afternoon yesterday, on the telephone with bookkeeper Dan, in person with the framer Mike and the kid Kevin, packer and unpacker of my books. So embarrassing. I keep falling asleep in mid-sentence, even when I sleep well at night, plus requisite naps.

Intense paresthesia in my hands and feet (simultaneous numbness and tingling, if you can believe it) lasted all afternoon and evening, somewhat better when moving around.

I am throwing the scale off the terrace immediately: now weigh twenty-nine pounds more than three months ago, at my shocking annual physical.

How will I deal with all of this with you 365 miles to the northwest? When can you come visit? There must be a long weekend in your school schedule sometime soon. I don't think I am well enough to drive to Bayfield yet.

Hope to hear from you soon!
Julia

———————

July 2, 2010

Niibawi,

All my paintings and photography collection are still not hung up here. It is awful to see my life in boxes again, as I had said I would live in that loft until I was taken to a nursing home the day I moved in. Oh, well, wrong again.

"They did it to the wrong person," Wanderful says nightly. No kidding.

It is CREEPY to remember all the beautiful things left behind, especially the paint colors, carpet, and draperies I chose so carefully, now doing that all over again just two and a half years later. What a waste of money.

JF had NEVER spent two yrs minus two mos without a man in her bed, not since age eighteen, when still a virgin.

UNFUCKINGBELIEVABLE BREATHTAKING NIGHTS WE HAD TOGETHER HERE. You are the best listener, rare in your generation of Boomer Men, and you are so well read in so many different subjects. I am glad that you are not scared off by this crazy time in my life of death, abandonment, illnesses incorrectly and correctly diagnosed. That's probably because you knew me healthy, you knew me with abundant energy and health when I was just your customer on a sailboat ride last summer in the Apostle Islands, so heavenly, my very favorite part of Wisconsin.

HUGE HUGS,
Me, Julia

CHAPTER 11

The Death of Lady Jane Recollected

"Julie, you're a doozie," Jane rhymed in her stellar widowhood, as they traveled, traded clothes and jewelry, laughed through the night, talked incessantly when together and when apart. Julia had made the late-night decision in February 2002 to accept her mother's apology about the origin of their decades of fighting.

"That was a long time ago," Jane confessed, hugging her on the bed, amidst Julia's unstoppable tears the night the surgeon called with the god-awful news about Hal's status as "a very sick man" with four concurrent antibiotics for his split open intestines. The emergency room had proclaimed it "pneumonia," but it was nothing of the sort, another false diagnosis. Jane never cried, and Julia's unstoppable tears were enough for both of them. It was late in the game but later, as they talked through the night, theirs became a deep friendship, absent in many ways for their first fifty years. Julia had found the love letter, secreted away among Jane's organized greeting cards, looking for one the previous night in Jane's immaculate desk drawers.

"*Him?*" Julia screamed and hollered. "The doctor who made us all sick and forgot to check Dad's prostate?!"

Yes, Dear Reader, even on a dead-end street, in a dead-end town called "that sooty industrial city" by *Life* magazine, at a time and a place when Waterbury was the Brass Center of the World, all of it gone in the 1980s, jobs outsourced. It was possible, Julia learned later in life, to love two men at the same time.

After many months of solitude, Lady Jane emerged from widowhood triumphant, a lady to the end. She merely waved goodbye, her arm splayed, lifeless, against the side of the mattress. Julia had an urgent need to leave Waterbury Hospital, right after the lurking Doctor Who Makes Us Sick assured Julia the nurses in ICU would help her mother drink and eat, now that Jane could just barely lift a can of Sprite, but could still not leave her bed, on what would turn out to be her final night on the planet.

Lady Jane only lived six hours after the innocent wave, until 9:18 pm, as Julia was about to get into her drawn bath in Jane's pink whirlpool tub, rarely used, as she feared falling, despite Wanderful there through the night to assuage Jane's fears and ever-present needs. It was the exact same minute when Ben had proposed to Julia, twenty-one years prior, on a carriage ride in Central Park.

Lady Jane did it all with grace and charm and abundant wit: the spectacular, brilliant, mathematician mom, Lady Jane to Wanderful's Betty Boop, a moniker only Wanderful could use without recriminations.

That is the way it was in Heritage Village, Southbury, Connecticut. A different time and place, with four hundred daffodils in spring, each one planted by Hal, her dearly departed husband, a hill of daffodils enjoyed by the entire cluster of homes, where he was the only guy, bringing groceries to the single women in bad weather.

Incomparable parents, in deed and in fact. That's her story, Dear Reader. It does not mean *perfect*, Julia explained often; it meant that fights were part of love, that piano lessons, sports, Hebrew School, community service projects, and cramming a lot into every day were part of the drill, part of growing up. Travel was part of one's education, as were tennis, skiing, and learning every imaginable sport, even scuba diving in murky North Pond on Maine's Belgrade Lakes. Julia learned to enjoy all the sports, but sailing and tennis became her lifelong favorites. And when Ben arrived on the scene, playing bridge became one of Julia's favorite pastimes.

Jane and Hal loved Ben: his tennis and bridge prowess, his brilliant and nationally recognized prosecutorial career, his investiture after approval by President Clinton, with a stunning buffet lunch in the Federal Building on Wisconsin Avenue, the prototype for many buildings in America, including the United States Post Office Pennsylvania Avenue, later turned into a *shopping arcade?!*

Not in Milwaukee, boasted Julia, we have gorgeous amber marble in our atrium, and an exquisite ceremonial courtroom for the November investiture, with three of their four parents there to witness it. Senator Herb Kohl had nominated Ben, and he had passed the U.S. Senate confirmation in September as the United States Attorney for the Eastern District of Wisconsin (comprising two-thirds of the state's population, including Indian Country).

Julia remembered his long nights of studying federal law at their kitchen table, despite his lime-green study in their 1928 Shorewood Tudor home, nicknamed "The Mansion" by Lady Jane. It had two staircases to the second floor, just like Julia's great-uncle Dave's, in Paterson, New Jersey so many decades before. Julia fell in love with the house immediately, but Ben was more cautious, worried they could not sell their first home during the winter.

"It's in great shape, on the corner of Menlo Boulevard and Downer Avenue, in front of the curved brick wall," she countered. "It will sell in two weeks." And so it did, snow and ice not intervening.

Lady Jane died four weeks into their trial separation.

Splat went Julia's world. Jane would have patched things up, Julia just *knew* it, but she was gone to be an angel, to her beloved Hal, who also adored Ben, the man who had it all, who understood Julia's ferocious energy and wit, derived from Hal and Jane and rarely missing a beat or a pun. They lived in a time where there were many chances for reconciliation in pre-Millennium World.

A Poem from Julia

There are no winners, save in tennis, that great love match of
good manners.
There is yet union
In a holy or unholy communion
In this sterling Jane Perfect Blue Skies/No Wind Day.
Be seeing you soon, the impatient patient,
With my usual tote
Filled with books, memorabilia, articles, and rosebuds.

We were a constellation of strength,
As Orion, our mutual fav, since childhood.
Are the stars now aligned
A symphony of perfect pitch
A Botticelli painting
No monkeying around?
"Tora Bora Lei, Tora Bora Laddie,"
Peace unto you, my lad, peace unto you, my lady.

Sweet reconciliation plays my sound machine.
Go to it, Eileen Ivers, New York beauty of words, sound, and
instruments.
On this good planet Earth,
Tiny spinning orb in one galaxy of God's good measure.

It is a tale of greed and consumption gone mad,
It is my story:

We tested our love
And it went out to sea.

Sweet reconciliation,
Indeed.

CHAPTER 12

They Call This Friday "Good."
Jesus's Last Meal Was a Passover Seder.

An incomparable rebel with a cause could not stand the hypocrisy of the synagogue: neither can Julia, who returned to her Orthodox roots, from the Pale of Settlement, as were Grandpa David's parents and Ben's great-grandparents, who came to Wisconsin and went to Arpin in the early twentieth century as part of a failed farming community—there were rocks in those fields in Arpin. Ben's grandfather then turned to plumbing and heating supplies. What a riot for them on their first date. *Oy vey! Both families were in plumbing supply businesses started by their Lithuanian grandfathers.*

The worldly and wise Rabbi Michel Twerski listened to Julia's tale of Lady Jane's last months and understood her grief, penetrating and apt. "I cried every day for a year when my father died," he confessed. His Hasidic garb recalled memories of her great-grandfather's from Lithuania. His speech in English knew no off-color words, which were saved for Yiddish, that inimitable connector of the *shtehl*, a secret language in the ghettos of Europe, slightly different in each country where Jews lived, hid, or were burned up in ovens, two-thirds of Europe's Jews, during the prior century.

Julia had her dearly departed great-grandmother's name; from her, she had also inherited Julia's black hair. Lady Jane insisted that her aging grand mother-in-law come to cook in Jane's kitchen for several days, so that Jane could measure out every ingredient and write down the some of this and some of that into her thrown together recipes for *ruggelach, blintzes, geflite* fish, and chicken soup. Jane presented these unique compilations for Julia and Ben with a cookbook as their wedding gift. Julia never attempted these heart-killing recipes during the twenty-one years of marriage and post-divorce but was glad to have them on her kitchen shelf. Julia wore the distantly passed Julia Grossfield's wedding ring, charm bracelet, and watch and kept the scarlet and orange Oriental rug in the very same place, by her own bedside. The brilliant colors stitched together more than a century before graced her bedroom. Julia thought of these as good luck and continuity with the past, with her ancestors' struggles in their immigrant lives.

The wedding band was just a plain, white gold band, no jewels, so unlike the ornate jewelry handed down from Jane's side of the family.

It was on that day the anniversary of Julia's arrival in that fair city of Milwaukee. It was both Passover and Good Friday. It had been a gorgeous couple of decades, until the last year. "Remember," Julia said to her overwrought Former, "Tomorrow is April fourth."

"Huh?" he replied, reaching for his third Diet Pepsi of that visit to her marital home.

"It's going to be April fourth tomorrow. Don't you remember why that's important?"

"No. Come on, Julia, what is it you're trying to say?"

"It's the twenty-third anniversary of my arrival in Milwaukee, just two pale blue suitcases and the stunning engagement ring from 47th Street." The ring, now a pendant around Julia's neck, had to do something with it, god almighty. She had come despite no job, no friends, just the proverbial "shoeshine and a smile" of Willy Loman.

"That's right," Former acknowledged. "It was April fourth."

"Yes, four four, my lucky number squared twice. Remember when we were counting the years until Milwaukee would be the city I had lived in the longest?"

Now at the kitchen sink, washing a piece of fruit, Former said, "Yes, I do. Now let's get on with this. You said you wanted to look at some things you forgot to take."

Julia winced inside. Can't we spend three more minutes on the past? Can't he ever slow down and think about the good ole days, the days of the special bond since their first date, blind in every sense except that it was a romantic big bang, bringing two single people to *the chuppah* in fifteen months, nine days? No, Julia remembered, he cannot slow down. He will not slow down. The present moment is what angles his thoughts, his meticulous work, his tennis prowess, his fears, his every sense.

Julia noted that the table was turned and that she was sitting in Former's usual seat, and he in hers. *This time, I hope our karma will be good. Let's find some things to agree about, like Jenny and Joshua's progress in college, politics, something!* This was Julia's determined response to the situation for three months now: have a peaceful divorce, be friends, even in separate lives.

"I want to talk about my health," was her opener. It was a kind of bold, extremely difficult salvo.

Former groaned with his eyes. She knew it would be tough sledding, but she went on. Julia tried to explain what fibromyalgia was. He smirked. She commented. He had his own diagnosis, and she blew up. He had gone to law school, not medical school, and it was her right to have a physical disease. Wrong. Former and Former Other Friends denied her that—everything must be a crazy woman, a scorned woman, a woman without reason. Julia took the challenge he had lain down. She was valiant. She explained fibromyalgia was a physical diagnosis, with telltale signs, and she explained why Former's diagnoses were all wrong; they were gratuitous, and there were no tests in any respect for them. Her psychiatrist had told her so. It was all libel in emails and slander in phone conversations, with phones crashed down on Julia's ears in a Milwaukee minute.

It was all slander and maligning 24/7/365(6).

IT WAS ALL WRONG.

"Do not call me that," she insisted. "There is no test for that, and you are not a psychiatrist. The stress you are causing makes my FibroFreakingMyAlgia and post-traumatic stress disorder worse."

Julia walked through the rooms, noticing a book here, a CD there that she had forgotten. The mood lightened, and they breezed through it.

Next, she took on Ben's health, his stress for three years, his undying mother, soon-to-be dying, and what he would do. He would fly to the town, that pretty college town in Idaho, but there would be no service, no memorial for his mother, *her* mother-in-law, and in life.

Finally, the subject was not roses; it was about the peonies, and since they had not yet cracked through the surface, no, Ben said, the gardener *par excellence,* they could not be dug up and transplanted to Julia's terraces. One thing led to another, and Julia told Ben the story of Jane and the turtles that day for the first time. There were turtles on leashes, and Jane had been a part of it. She was walking her very own Skipperdee on West 79th Street in the heart of the civilized world: the Upper West Side of Manhattan, in the twenties, the thirties, and into the mid-forties. That was when her teenage idol walked off a United States Navy warship in San Francisco one day in January 1946, got to a telephone, reversed the charges (naturally), and called his bride-to-be only to learn: "We are going to get married on Valentine's Day."

Isn't that amazing?

Ben had listened carefully, but Former could not respond. The moving van from Hernia Movers arrived a half-hour late, and books, cameras, and Julia's remaining clothes were all safely loaded into the van. No one had died, and while it was stress upon stress, *vahz mehr* upon *vahz mehr*, it was another step on the road to friendship after divorce. Another step after twenty-two years point five years minus two weeks of a fairytale romance, a marriage made in a plumbing supply showroom and a teak furniture store, some of their many instant commonalities.

Julia did have proven scientific diagnoses, whether or not the non-physicians believed it.

Julia's spirits were strengthened by the visit, by reclaiming some of her possessions and by explaining the correct diagnoses in detail. The peonies would have to wait a few more weeks. Ben promised them to her with his goodbye hug and good wishes.

CHAPTER 13

A City Divided against Itself

A guest had called up Julia in 1988 to thank her for the invitation to Ben's and her New Year's Day party and offered these words of praise: "There were so many different kinds of people at your party—black and white, Jews and Gentiles, single and married, young and old. We don't have parties like that in Milwaukee."

Not much had changed in the past decades. Julia gave a Spring has Sprung/Julia's Back Party in her first post-marital apartment, the loft. Twenty-five of the sixty who had RSVP'd showed up. No one called to say they or their grandkids were sick, they had a relative in the hospital, their cat died, or that they would be away on business. Those who came had a blast. They did the *hora* and Julia's choreographed backward step, invented two years prior in her solitude. The great Great Room was some dance floor, the city to the north and the west of her. Lake Michigan's turquoise-to-gray palette splayed out to the horizon.

Ben and Julia, who married at thirty-five and forty, had always had all kinds of friends.

"In my solitude, I have the same. We have got to get Milwaukee moving," Julia responded to her friend. This town is SO BEHIND. We are dissing women and minorities before they open their mouths. It is all wrong, and it is easy to fix up. It's more fun. People like different kinds of people, if they get the chance to talk to them."

Her client Jim had stayed at the party for seven hours. He met current and new prospective donors. At Julia's insistence, he sent those two eighty-five-year-old female doctors handwritten notes the following day. *It is correct etiquette, but many moms and most employees don't model that in Millennium World.*

Julia's secretary fled for her life the same week as the party when gunfire enveloped her car with her two children in it on Silver Spring Drive and 61st Street. Quoting her, "Our neighborhood is under indictment." *Indictment*, Julia thought. *It just needs the basic standards of any neighborhood: dentists, fresh food, playgrounds, daycare, and the ever-elusive J O B S with benefits.*

"Nope," Julia said. "There are now only gigs. There are only jobs with benefits for the 1 percenters, maybe the 30 percenters, if that."

Letter to Niibawi

Hi there—sending this overnight mail to you,

Please reconsider our work on the book. You are busy. We are all busy. But this is part of our friendship, isn't it? But you are unwinding after school and I am, après nap, winding up. Also, in my robe since 3:00 after a 7–3 writing day. Exhausted.

You know my feelings about healthcare and re the brain care I have chosen to use. It is all wrong and can be fixed up, if society would understand how much cheaper it is to attend to these things on the front end. So, my recommendation is that we NOT abandon the work we have begun. It would GREATLY distress and depress me, as I would not have asked you except that you are a wonderful, talented writer and that we think alike in so many ways.

Please stay the course and finish the writing. I will find the funds. You have promised a good publisher at Bellevue Publishing in New York. The book will be a smash, and we will have fun at all the signings, with all the media, and with new media, not available before.

LTY (Love to you),
Mlle Julia Fields

CHAPTER 14

Whither Milwaukee and the Married Doctors?

Milwaukee is no big East Coast city, not a big anything city, but it is Julia's favorite city in America, as it was her incomparable parents' favorite city, once they found it on the map. In the eighties, no one from the East Coast knew or visited anything west of the Hudson River, except maybe Chicago, Denver for skiing, L.A., San Francisco, and, after the technology bubble, Seattle. Her friends in the City always confused Minneapolis with Milwaukee on her visits to see Ben: "You aren't going to *move there*?" they asked. "You betcha," Julia replied. "Milwaukee is fun, it has great culture and architecture, and it has a terrific lakefront."

Julia had experienced a period of twenty-nine months of unbearable hell of one sort or another—hospitalizations amounting to ninety days out of three hundred and sixty-five during 2009 and 2010. It was her tragedy of epic proportions, and she was at the epicenter of the decline or outright demise of these American institutions, having become totally UnAmerican activities: Health UnCare. Lawyers who protect the perpetrators, not the innocently harmed. Banks of Ill Repute. Real estate developers mired in corruption. Merchant thieves in spas, in stores, in every type of store in Milwaukee. The telephone system, no matter the vendor. Even the corner pharmacy started flubbing up.

Oh my god, Julia thought. *Is the whole country coming apart at the seams? Maybe it's not as bad as it seems....*

Amidst all this, Julia adopted the theme and purpose of life as loving kindness, with all the rest clamor and a distraction. Some days and in some places, she got her message across to her friends and clients. At other times, she was talking to the wall, but not the Western Wall. There was not a prayer with relief of any sort. Julia prayed regularly during these hospitalizations for relief from her incessant pain of one sort or another, and her psychic and physical exhaustion. Two left feet were killing her and her left knee from hell was cracking up. FibroFreakingMyAlgia felt like inserted knives of torture, incessant and totally incapacitating. Many nights she could not even get up to brush her teeth or retrieve the bedpan. Wetting the bed at fifty-seven? *Ohmygod, what has become of my life?*

One day, she had a new thought: ask her leading physician about going back to the pills that worked so well the prior year. He thought it was a fine idea, but these Lamictal pills (also beguilingly having a French name,

Lamotrigine, in Julia's favorite language), they take six weeks to take effect. For nerve pain of all kinds, emotional and physical.

Six weeks? Julia shrieked. She had forgotten. And yes, Dear Reader, it was six weeks to the minute that Julia's pains were gone with the wind. They evaporated into the early Milwaukee spring air, air at 75° in late March and throughout early April. It was incredible. There were flowers everywhere, flowers like her best friend, Susan, meaning flower in Egyptian. *WOW*. Flowers in Milwaukee in March?! Now that was something to write home about.

The loft had been given away at the interminable four-hour closing, with the collapse of real estate ("What is fake estate," she asked?) for 210,000 smackers less than she paid for it, plus the necessary $50,000 in retrofitting "a furnace fit for a trailer park" as proclaimed the chief investigator, "None of this passes code. Someone was bought off." Hal's daughter knew it was specked wrong, for her father had taught her many things about HVAC. She had no choice but to spend it to give herself clean air, eliminate toxic mold, and have air circulate without incessant drafts, so she could breathe in the fucking place.

Dear Reader, $210,000 was nothing, a mere fraction of the more than $1 million pickpocketed from Julia during those years of unimaginable HELL ALLOVERTHEPLACE. She was determined to get it back. She was the daughter of a U.S. Navy Seabee. Hal had designed bridges, roads, and desalinization plants straight across the Pacific, from Manus to the Admiralty Islands and, finally, to Okinawa, Hal's last location before THESE UNITED STATES would have invaded Japan, with a prediction of one million American soldiers lost. He had survived, and so could she.

NEVER GIVE UP.

Not only personally, but never give up on one person. Keep an open mind, find the time and the patience to talk and listen to others, to wrestle these differences to the ground, to grind out the falsehoods and errors, and to live in a new way, body broken down, but live nonetheless. It was not easy, it was not fun. It was the worst thing imaginable. In the age of technological easy connectivity, no one was connected to anything or to anyone—not to family, not to a common culture, not to manners.

Julia was ready to explode, to commit heinous acts, but she had nothing more dangerous than her canes in multiple colors and her red Volkswagen Beetle key, which popped out like a tiny weapon. The German engineering was perfect, it was brilliant, and yet it hearkened also to hope, to people forgiving the Germans of the twenty-first century for the Holocaust. These new Germans were not alive then, they did not push Jews, gypsies, and homosexuals into ovens...it was time for a change, even Julia's dearly departed dad had eventually purchased Siemens and Nikon products from the people we went to war against. And that was decades earlier. But in the fiercely taut emotions of Millennium World, it seemed that no one was forgiving anyone.

Julia rejoiced over her tofu salad, slowly eaten, of course, due to Irritable Bowel and Everything Else Syndrome. The doctor, of sorts, more of a leading man wannabe, gave her a salad from his office's buffet one day. Julia, with her jewelryoholic nature, her wardrobe sporting everything from a twelve-dollar pink Target shirt to Jane's old full-length mink coat, was not in the least bit a "cheap date," and don't tell the doctor, but she really wasn't attracted to him, but fine, free lunch in his office, great.

This lead physician had eyes just like another doctor, it was uncanny, it was **unheimlich**, it was crazy. It was as though they were the same person. *Godalmighty*, Julia thought, *am I going nuts, too?* And the other doctor, administering ten perfect shocks that reassembled Julia's brain and washed it clean—he, too, with more blue eyes. *Hmm*, she thought, *line 'em up and do 'em one night after the other*. Nope, they are all married and harried. Forget about it.

Letter to the Kindly Octogenarian, Julia's Psychoanalyst

Dear Doctor,

I wasn't asking you for any money. I just would like consideration of a reduced fee, as I have little income and have already cut and re-cut my expenses, as you know. This character I am writing about, a "doctor of doctors" in Milwaukee—the smoking Renaissance doctor, like my mom and dad both did for a time—he reminds me of an old boyfriend, keeps his head down, knows all about his specialty, studies and teaches and practices it, teaches at the University of Chicago, and perhaps elsewhere. But across the way, a related sub-specialty? Not so clear he keeps up on that, whilst seeing thirty-two patients a day, a huge stack of files to start his every day.

I don't understand why doctors are experts in your fields only?! In our crazed specialist of specialist age, a doc last week checked me for carpal tunnel and actually said I do have large nerve pain, as well as small, which the latter he does not treat. Huh?! No referral, as a tried and true neurologist, so am I to hang myself? No alternative treatment? Not in an entire department of neurology?! Geez Louise.

There you have it. Five minutes' worth of writing, not a second longer.

I will see you when you return from vacation.

Sincerely,
J.F.

CHAPTER 15

Julia Loves Big Sur

J ulia first visited Big Sur in 1985, on an eighteen-day, 1,800-mile car trip in California, primarily on the coastal highway, that ribbon of road going north from Venice to San Francisco. She went to Big Sur three times, though never to Esalen or to the Henry Miller Library, but she climbed the canyons and walked the state parks. She bought all the books about Big Sur that she could and winced every time the news told of a mudslide, shutting off Big Sur from the outside world. There was a pattern to Julia's travels—a combination of adding more countries to her list and revisiting many times the places she loved the best: Paris, Jamaica, Costa Rica, Italy, Israel, and…Big Sur.

It was more than Lawrence Durrell's "spirit of place"; it was, for Julia, the feeling of people or of her being instantly at home, even when away. She organized every hotel room with her treasured things—the tiny reading light, her reading glasses, her laptop, and her clothes, all out of her suitcases in a New York minute. Julia was comfortable this way, or as she explained it: "Think of me as a blind person—everything has to be in the same place." This meticulous nature was perhaps expected from an engineer father and a mathematician mother.

The confluence of so many writers in tiny Big Sur amazed Julia. Robinson Jeffers, Jack London, and George Sterling made frequent visits there in the old days. Some rode on horseback, all the way from the Valley of the Moon. Julia met a writer, a latter-day hippie, on her first visit in 1985. A friend had told her where to stay: Deetjen's Big Sur Inn, with incomparable blueberry pancakes and the best coffee she had ever tasted. Her room was "charming," as in you could barely step on the floor when you got out of bed, the bathroom requiring acrobatics so as not to bump your elbow or trip on the way into it. During her first meal at Deetjen's, she met Robert Greenwood, a former television writer for *Gunsmoke*, who explained this history. He, like many in town, were dropouts, folks who had left other jobs and places to live in the solace of Big Sur with all-seasons spectacular views, from the canyons, creeks, and views three hundred feet down to the roaring, mighty Pacific Ocean. Big Sur continues in linear fashion along Highway 1, without street addresses, without side streets. It is a whole life lived along and alongside the main thoroughfare of ever-present tourists, stoners, and dreamers.

Robert's cabin was secluded and without running water in his favorite Pfeiffer Canyon, with bare metal kitchenware and an inoperative woodburning stove. September was chilly, but after the three-hour climb to the cabin, there was no need for heat—just drinking as much as possible from the gallons of water they carried in two massive backpacks. The daybed had a few musty blankets he used for sleep. The racoons and stray dogs did not bother Julia but going to the outhouse and seeing a black bear.... That terrified her. She braved it and told Robert in the morning.

"He's harmless, but just don't feed the bears when you get to Yosemite," the grand finale of Julia's trip, timed for Rosh Hashanah, seeking spirituality among the mighty redwoods. Robert was massively strong, the size of a football player, but with a gentle spirit, teaching her all the names of the trees and the fauna in the canyon, his occupied and by *force majeure* home for a decade.

Later, in 2010, Julia thought of Big Sur as her new escape plan, not accessible except for the strong of heart who can drive Highway 1, with its manifold twists and turns, breathtaking views of mountains to the sea, and secluded canyons and thick forests. It was all of nature atop one's head, in a continuous drum roll, softly in one's mind, of a simpler life that called soulfully to Julia. There are no affordable long-term places to stay in Big Sur, except for the three or four campgrounds. Camping? Julia had done it for seven summers in Maine, and that was O V E R.

115

Julia had a fervent need to write, to chill out, to rethink the hundreds of false starts, of a marriage wistfully ended, of people collapsing from anxiety, lies, and the creepy fall forward economy, knocking many for a loop. *Ah*, Julia thought, *Big Sur in the years ahead, where frosty mornings give way to temperate climes and mists of thick and sauna-like dampness, replenishing the dense foliage, and her spirits.* She dreamed of sitting for weeks and reading her childhood and early adult life journals, lined up for two solid bookshelves, a world perhaps too frightening to uncover, disabled now and home alone in the city that Julia has called home since the very first weeks of a Big Bang romance, in which happily ever after was the question one hour after her and Ben's first meeting.

Julia bought a Jeffers book on her third visit to Big Sur in 2010, soloing again. Afterwards, she went back to Stanford Medical Center to see Beardog, bro-in-law or in fact, now awake, shaved, and totally alert, and to the airport for her first miserable and therefore her last red eye to Milwaukee.

"You missed Ben."

"Ben was here?"

"Yes, for five days. We both flew out last week. You were in a coma, airlifted from Petaluma Hospital in a helicopter. You were barely alive, hemorrhaging, but Stanford found you have hepatitis and removed a tumor, and your surgery went well. You look great."

"I have cancer?"

"Yes, a bad tumor in your liver."

116

Julia would not reveal to Beardog what the doctors had told her—it was their job to tell Beardog that he had but one year to live.

Julia arrived in Milwaukee on July 2, her move-in day to Bay View. She had a huge job ahead of her, to sort through furnishings for a storage locker near the airport. Julia would never be able to find this location again on her own, after the home furnishings that did not fit were stored there. One day, years later, the kindly Gregg disposed of everything at Goodwill.

CHAPTER 16

A Summer Weekend, 2010

I t was an unusually beautiful weekend in Milwaukee, and Julia was nearly finished unpacking—just seven more boxes of client files and books left. Absolute deadline, could not be missed, was 8:30 p.m. on July 3, had to get the place ready for friends on the Fourth of July, celebrated for a full week in Milwaukee, with the highlight of the hour-long fireworks over Lake Michigan on the third. Julia's friend Bill, whose back actually worked, had planted hundreds of flowers and herbs for cooking, fixed up the deck and terrace to perfection, flowers and shrubs everywhere, wind chimes galore.

Julia bought a hummingbird feeder at Downer Hardware, which has the smell of bins of nails and couplings and all sorts of things of an old-fashioned general store. The reliable checkout guys would carry everything to her car without question, "Of course, Miss

Fields." Her new and old outdoor furniture fit together perfectly, in a summer of abundant sunshine, of harmony of 4:30 a.m. birds waking her up, and of gorgeous sunsets from the Divine Deck, with planes landing at Mitchell Field continuing until eleven o'clock.

Many aspects of Julia's life had fallen into place, Dear Reader, into places of Good Repute, into crevices of her mind, unimaginable things, wondrous things, and all of them quite unthinkable a mere sixty days prior. It was a cascade of hope, of rejoicing, of people helping, of people celebrating her fifty-eighth birthday, from near and far, friends of newfound friendship, friends of sixty seconds prior, and special East Coast friends, especially Essex, from June 29, 1969, Amsterdam, and "The Graduate."

It was a collision of camaraderie, of elegant, witty, and gorgeous gifts, for her birthday and for her housewarming, but which house had little warmth with the cool Lake Michigan breezes and ceiling fans to hasten the flight of the air around Mini Mouse House, her small rental apartment.

Still, our heroine moved on, whose heroic efforts at thrift, at work, at play, at romance were bringing home the dividends despite a divided family, a divorce, the death of Lady Jane and Prince Hal, and the confluence of others going totally berserk and blaming her. In fact, it was their own actions, reactions, but especially their inaction that had won the day...or so they thought, and Julia was still trudging forward.

Julia had lain in her sleigh bed from northern Vermont and thought and twisted in absolute pain since early 2008. *Get me some healing, get me some satisfaction. Christ, what are these doctors here for, anyway?* It was all nonsensical: the patients pay their salaries, and the physician assistants and three layers of clerks before you see a medical school grad. They are treating us like a nuisance to protect the "doctors." Ohmygod, Lady Jane would have started right then and there with the nuclear weapons. She would not have waited either a New York minute or a Milwaukee minute (which could last a week and a half) to repeat for the millionth time her birth date, her phone number, and to tell an utter stranger why she was calling—nope, no way, not happening. Julia needed medically trained professionals, not clerks.

• • •

The good times were rolling. Julia was deeply in love. He was handsome, he was cool. They had crisscrossed the same continent for forty years, not in the Egyptian desert, but having lived in some of the same American cities. Kind of crazy. They found each other at long last, but it was not simple, it was not apparent, in the ethernet, in the safety net, in the fishing net: it was Kismet. It was *beshert*, but Julia had a lot of Yiddish to teach Mr. Right, as he was not Jewish, but a wannabe. And, like Ben, it was a long-distance romance. This dude lived three hundred and sixty-five miles away, six and a half hours speeding at

121

eighty most of the way, plus a ferry ride. Niibawe lived in a log cabin on Madeleine Island, part of the Apostle Islands, off Bayfield, Wisconsin, reminiscent of Julia's New England roots in a tiny town of 545 or so residents.

Bayfield had it all: an astonishing, well-stocked bookstore, a used bookstore, a health food store, a dock filled with sailboats, quiet inns, pottery stores, berry- and apple-filled orchards, and clothing stores with fashionable and dowdy clothes all in the same store. There was a maritime museum, a performing arts center, just in summer, the Big Top Chautauqua, and H I L L S! They entranced Julia the most, hills like her native Connecticut. But it wasn't just the city of Bayfield, it was the setting on rich, navy-blue Lake Superior that captivated Julia: velvet blue water eight hundred feet deep, and the very same practice, as in her beloved Jamaica, of pleasing every tourist, without whom neither Bayfield nor Jamaica could survive.

Customer service was aglow in Bayfield, in all the bed and breakfasts, in the elegant Rittenhouse Inn, in the mere motels with kindly Hmong owners, at the casino nearby, and at the curiosity shops. These plentiful stores offered every manner of hand-blown glass, pottery, and souvenirs, things to remember a visit, or in Julia's case, twenty visits in thirty years. Topping it off was a jewelry store with necklaces designed and made by a Minnesotan psychiatrist. It seemed that Julia could not escape them, wherever she traveled.

After awakening, Julia took her used, pumpkin-colored-interior sports car out of the garage at 5:00 a.m. and detoured to see the lake, feel its cool breezes, where people had been picnicking for weeks already, as spring came early that year. There were sailboats aplenty. There were chicks nearly naked. There were studs all studded up. Julia stopped by her marital home to pick some of her prized perennials—part of the marital separation agreement—perennially gorgeous, in all shades of purple, her favorite color, a healing color, and the favorite color of the Renaissance doctor's secretary, who was not one who made access difficult, thank the Lord, and pass the schnapps, for which he had a penchant.

The bouquet was varied, of lilacs, peonies to be forced open, star-studded pink and white flowers, sweet williams, oh my, and tiny blue whatevertheyarecalled.

Julia dropped some flowers off at her friends' home—their best friends, who stood up at their wedding some twenty-three years prior. It was, ironically, their wedding anniversary the very next day—number thirty-seven.

Even the fine people of Milwaukee get divorced. It is a worldwide epidemic. Julia thought about this a lot. *Why now? Why so many? Why so many on third marriages with triplicate doses of kids, enough alimony and child support payments to drive a person out of his or her bank account? Why is everyone so eager to give up the ship, to get divorced?* It was imponderable. It was difficult unto tears. There was no easy response.

But, for Julia, it had been a glorious courtship, marriage, and the redeeming powers of life in the Midwest.

On that day, it was sad—tearfully so.

It was nice to pick a bouquet that was so hardy, colorful, and remarkably early in the day, but color and hardiness were most important to Julia in people, how they dressed, wore their hair, what clothing they chose or which car they drove, or to be determined by their degrees or salaried positions, with or without stratospheric bonuses, this was mere icing on the cake. The interior was the *real life*, in real time, it was fine, it was time for thought, passion, compassion, all blended together in dreams, waking and sleeping ones. It was an interior that was different for each person, a stretch to make the leap to understanding, but vital, Julia believed.

Otherwise, Lady Jane had the right tactic. You may as well start with the nuclear weapons. Line 'em up and shoot them nasty letters. It was not, according to the Good Book, the death of sinners that the Almighty sought, it was that they turn from their sinful ways and live. *Please*, prayed Julia, *let them turn inward and change their ways. Let there be peace in families, in friendships, in offices, in shared mourning for Lady Jane, the most magnificent, finely clothed, well-groomed, fragile-as-a-snowflake-but-sharp-as-steel mommy I could never have dreamed of.*

Let there be peace, but there was no peace. Not in Milwaukee, not in New Haven, or in the City.

There was no peace in the Gulf of Mexico.

There was no peace in *Eretz Yisrael*.

There was no peace in the Palestinian Authority.

There were just sincere and diligent efforts, in the foreground and in the background, to have dialogue, face to face, to listen and be listened to, to right the wrongs of years or decades, and centuries—and in righting this Ship of State would come a better Millennium.

Everyone married is harried and divorcing.

Everyone young is worried about the entire cosmos before they grow up.

Everyone old is terrified of having no money for healthcare and older and older old age.

It was a sight not to be seen. It was frightful, it was terrifying.

And Julia had been in its depths, but on this Memorial Day weekend, there was abundant light and especially grace at the end of the tunnel. Not the Lincoln Tunnel, in her former City, just the tunnel of the mind.

CHAPTER 17

A Journal Entry from Julia

July 19, 2010

It is Friday night and I am, as per usual, alone. As I light my candles, I think about the questions we might ask at such a time as this, a quiet Shabbat evening on the terrace.

Some of my very favorites are in Deuteronomy. "Thou shalt love the Lord thy God with all thy heart, with all thy soul, and with all thy might. And these words which I command you this day...you shall teach them diligently to thy children. Thou shalt speak of them when thou risest up and when thou liest down, when thou walkest by the way, and thou shalt bind them upon the doorposts of thy house and upon thy gates, that ye shall remember and do all my commandments [there are 618 in Judaism, not just ten on one scroll] and be holy unto thy God."

This is the prayer inside the mezuzah.

No one can follow my interminable medical morass—now with enough nightly sleep most nights, I am cookin' with NUCLEAR ENERGY. Julia's back?! Or too soon to know? A great weekend in the Apostles may not mean anything re my strength level or this relationship.

Damnit, just coughed, sounds like croup. Never had it as a kid, just hundreds of allergies, reconfirmed in that 1989 visit to the allergist. They are all back like gangbusters this spring.

Whatever.

———

Another Journal Entry from Julia

What have I accomplished with all this introspection, my third and perhaps the most important psychoanalysis?

1) Brand-new Julia: rarely yells, as it didn't get me anywhere.

2) Have a soft, husky fake voice down pat—give it to those who deserve a bit of scorn heaped on their heads.

3) Cannot pay current, much less old, medical bills on my gig earnings. I am too weak to leave the house for more than three hours. Exhaustion is my norm, but I am not accepting that.

4) I have figured out the cause of my feet and back problems: packing in the evening, atop strenuous a.m. workout, five days a week, preparing and serving dinner amid the angst of Mom dying and the end of a marriage. The Fields family's abandonment of me mirrors theirs of Jane during her later years with Dad's estate settlement and $100,000 of totally wasteful legal fees, which wrecked her health with anxiety, atop the abuse and neglect of simple medical issues, some occurring just before she was admitted to the hospital and would die in seven short days.

The reason for my left calf/left leg traumas stemming from...? We are not sure what. Hormones? Over exertion tout simplement? *It is the normal size leg, but it hurts because it is bearing more of my weight. I lean on it while washing dishes or at my standing desk.*

I see that rarely in Millennium World do people want the intensity of deep friendship, of examining one's inner life, of stretching the boundaries of knowledge. I am up for anything, all the time. Not a big deal, where we eat, where we live. It's what's inside that I care about: values, character, kindness, empathy, personal history, conflicts, difficulties, allofit. The old-fashioned stuff I love, as in writing in my journal every day or maybe twice a day.

Here then, is the punch line:

I met my priorities set in January. Soon, I will have zero short-term debt. My continued figuring out of what went wrong, so terribly wrong, producing Julia-cidal depression—it was my guilt re having a beautiful home which was in a denuded state for the eight months of the realtor showing it, and the requisite sale/just gave it away at a stunning loss. Guilt re not paying off damn credit cards, the misery at "living" on the same amount as my 1992 fee income, misery with no new friends in my client work, the first time in J.F. history. I always met one fella at work and plenty of gals, like for decade—I am too exhausted, in too much in pain, too behind on my bookkeeping, housekeeping, reading, writing, piano, knitting, sailing, allofit, to have the time it takes for new friends.

Therefore, I ask again the question: What to expect that can change by talking and writing? I am on the top of my game in my head, shoehorned into Mini Mouse House, made it gorgeous. I'm really into this gig with some satisfaction of a regular check, but, hey, it's something. I have enormous confidence in the future working out. I have such renewed psychic energy. I can focus again—the laser focus people know in me. I let little stuff go. I respond now in real time to instances where folks are taking advantage of me, using the fake husky voice.

I realize now that I need to be among more generous, empathetic, sympathetic, worldly ones, not to mention literary ones.

But the world came at me and also at most Americans, not just the 2008 economic collapse, but the moral and the psychic, with so many losing so much in all spheres of their lives.

I adore life and really love it here in Milrideee, an honor to a kid from a backwater town and a truly cut-off, dead-end street. I have a need to fly, to be in present time, to find a permanent home.

As I have said to all guys, the way to my heart has always been through the mailbox, now email and text box. I can fall in love talking, my very favorite thing, and from that, the ease with which I write, even a difficult journal entry like this one. I am confident of my abilities, emotional stability, and surviving the physical shit. Analysis cannot solve it. Kindly is managing thirty residents and his private caseload. He may not be totally immersed in my case and all the medical teams I refer to during each session. It is not the end of the world. Depression went away before, and Kindly Octogenarian will help me through it again when it inevitably arrives.

These years of precipitating illness have given me newfound strength and faith in myself and my judgment about people, about business, about my parents, about The Doctor Who Made Us All Sick's role. As an internist friend in the fifties, he had many intersecting health roles with medicines he never should have been able to prescribe to my dear mother, so over medicated and yet untreated at the same time. I understand now my father's devotion to the stunning New York brilliant lass; my mother's devotion to him, her missing him, leading her to dying...of a broken heart, truly, really. I will always believe that.

It is "unverifiable fact," per my teacher, Muriel Rukeyser.

• • •

How can I possibly thank you, Niibawi, except with tiny gifts, cards that thrill me to write to you, against the backdrop of my beloved Bayfield & the Apostle Islands? I will be here in Brew City, have made the decision to stay and suck it up when I run into those who left me for dead, in excruciating pain, or from the quaintly named Jobless Recovery. They'll find out one day what it is all about, I expect. The creeping and creepy economic collapse seems to envelop a new discipline, year by year.

I have learned that my chronic and unremitting symptoms are too much reality to handle by those in good health. Chronic pain bears no resemblance to "pain."

About the weight thing: I may never weigh 106 again, as I did last December, before my ECTs, but you know, pounds make me crazy—girls made me cry through the night at the Maine camp for over-privileged girls, who also teased me re being from Connecticut, the only one of two hundred twenty-three girls.

Geez, when I see or hear how most of my house helper guys behave, I feel I am running the School for Husbands with the bevy of chronically late, ADHD goofballs around here. Wish you lived closer.

Love,
Jules

CHAPTER 18

The Battle Hymn of the Republic

"The Battle Hymn of the Republic" was one of the songs to enliven Julia's morning—driving her visitors crazy, played in a continuous loop for up to half a day.

Julia thought obsessively about how to win the many battles since Lady Jane's death. These were fierce, unexpected, and often moronic in their stupidity, wastefulness, and yes, corruption of our fundamental American values of life, liberty, and the pursuit of happiness. They corrupted Jewish values of charity, deeds of loving kindness, especially to strangers, and the previous fifty-seven years of her life experience.

It was a nation gone upside down, inverted. Ordinary people were acting insane with greed and consumption, with malice aforethought all over the place, with tentacles of interference into her simple wish to move to a loft in the Fifth Ward and later to escape its toxins of methylene chloride in polyurethane dust left in HVAC and perchloroethylene in paints and coatings affecting the central nervous system and immune systems for Mini Mouse House, where the damages persisted throughout her body.

Had nearly everyone forgotten their education and the spirit of community, not to mention valuing family? Where and why did it all evaporate when Lady Jane died, an unquiet death, full of tubes and machines, against her expressed wishes, told in simple, declarative English to the ER staff at BurytheWater Hospital and stated in her will and by her volition and in accompanying codicils and amendments.

Christ, are we writing a freaking Constitution, Guilford? Julia asked as she was preparing her own estate plan, codicils, and amendments in the following years. It was designed to benefit the community of Milwaukee, whose population of desperately poor, uneducated, and jobless had surpassed by 2010 that of the first Great Depression, according to the *Milwaukee Journal Sentinel.* People had been ignoring all the signs or were overwhelmed with the minutiae in their social media feeds.

Julia realized it was just a coincidence that Jane's death and the collapse of the economy a few months later happened with ferocious intensity for her. There were only theories why she suffered so much, no answers. Prince Hal, too, would have been up late at night, trying to find a method to this madness, with Lady Jane crying from leg cramps or a myriad of other afflictions. Insomniac City reigned in Julia's Family of Origin. "You'll sleep when you are dead," Julia comforted Lady Jane, who benefited from Julia's jokes to get through the pains when she called her during the night.

Suddenly, Julia had developed incurable pains allovertheplace. The tennis player who walked two and a half miles every weekday could now not lift a bag of groceries unless they were previously weighed on a scale not to exceed five pounds. The train doors between cars on her recent ride to see Guilford about legal matters (from New Haven to Gotham) were too heavy to open, and with irritable bowel syndrome, Julia's trips to the bathroom were emerging emergencies allthetime and allovertheplace. "Buy stock in Charmin," she told her friends.

The pains came back in bucketsful, like ferocious waves at lightning speed, waking Julia up at 1:00 and 3:00 a.m. They were there in Hamlet battalions, far from single spies. What could she do? She tried Bayer: nothing doing. She tried a muscle relaxant: slow going. She tried writing to her oldest friend, Essex. She tried a dozen things. Eventually, she fell back to sleep, awakening at 7:15 to a brilliant Milwaukee summer morning.

Uh oh, Julia realized, reviewing her calendar, *the Inspector General comes today*. Not really, but it was how she had termed Lady Jane's visits to her apartment in the City— everything must be tidied up, it must be in order, it cannot

135

look like a hurricane just passed through fifty-two seconds ago.

This time the inspector was Seal, Julia's childhood babysitter, who stayed overnight when Hal and Jane went to California or their first-won USA sales trip to Europe. Ninety years old last month, looking sixty-five, the original Monopoly (™) player, the incomparable chef, who taught Lady Jane to make beef wellington when everyone used pots and pans, not kitchenware and costly cooking classes for which one must take out a third mortgage at the bank.

Dear Reader, the Banking System in THESE UNITED STATES was collapsing left, center, and right in the 2010 year of our Lord, Christ Almighty. It was a hurricane of an economy, men with college degrees having worked hard to help Julia pack up in a hurry at the loft, then packed her up at The Pfister Hotel, while she had a veritable emergency, to go to Beardog's bedside at Stanford University Medical Center—these men having or not having a job in years, only gigs, and pleased to have $15 an hour for such heavy lifting of Julia's 1,500-volume library, which amazed even the desultory Jim, the part-time bookseller at Renaissance Books at the airport, the best bookstore of used and new books.

Yes, the packing and unpacking of the lives of Hal and Jane continued, compounded by these illnesses of indeterminate and genetically determined origins. It was unfathomable, chronic and persistent, the worst imaginable scene. Julia was soloing again and *ZAP!* gone her health, AGAIN, gone her savings for retirement, allofit alloverthepiace, to the doctors, lawyers, and merchant thieves with which America was replete in the Millennium World.

It was a battle of epic proportions. It was a battle on which many of Julia's friends and business colleagues had already given up, refusing to read a newspaper, a news magazine, *The New Yorker*, this journal or that one.

Everyone was rushing around, but no one was making any visible progress, not here and not there.

"Glory, glory hallelujah, His Truth is marching on," sang Joan Baez that Sunday morning of the Vast Clean Up of Papers and Photographs in Bucketsful. Seal was coming for ten days, and she could not start off with a terrible impression. That would simply not do.

Yes, a terrible swift sword must be applied to the love seats, purple and red, to rid them of torrents of paper and thousands of Hal's and Julia's photographs, some dating to the early twentieth century. *We survived those two world wars,* Julia thought, *but now find ourselves in a war of epic proportions, to reclaim our air and water godalmighty. To remember whence we all came, the insidious "birther" question of an honorable president. To reinstate true family values. To Honor Thy Father and Thy Mother, for God's sake, even and ESPECIALLY IN THEIR ABSENCE. Nope, none of it happening, everyone going nutso in a hand basket.*

Why had Winnie Careuso fought Prince Hal's Estate? It had literally made Lady Jane sick, the more than two years of worrying about the outcome of that legal case. What would she stand to gain? Was it jealousy of her dad?

Was it her toilet training, Julia's shrink/shrank/shrunk asked her? *Whatever*, Julia had thought at the time, *it is a colossal waste of time, which is all we have in the end. It had been something monstrous. It was horrifying, it was wasteful, it was greedy, and it was exactly the inverse of what Prince Hal had exemplified his entire life.*

Dear Reader, it was also unending, and its memories were deleterious to Julia's now fragile health alloverherbodandsoul.

"As they died to make men holy, let us die to make men free."

You got it, Joanie, sterling voice, marvelous face, a figure for the sixties and for the 2010s. Rock the roof off. Julia had seen Baez in live performance four times. There was no better voice validating human struggle.

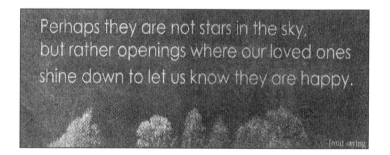

Perhaps they are not stars in the sky, but rather openings where our loved ones shine down to let us know they are happy.

Inuit saying

A Letter from Julia

To my medical team, physical therapists, and legal eagle team:

I am going to make a break, been in bed a week with intolerable pains, many sleepless nights.

The docs and clinics have managed this case for thirty-two tortuous months. There have been weeks when I felt fine; mostly not. Some of you with Chronic Fatigue Immune Deficiency Syndrome, cancer, or other horrific pain illnesses understand the wholesale disappearance of lives as we knew them before getting so sick. Not to mention the wholesale disappearance of our life savings, a horrid depressive event in and of itself.

Please fight for change: We cannot recover as a society until people are allowed to get well and go back to work.

The origins of these illnesses have been amply described. The knockout apartment that knocked me out as it did my neighbor, also named Julia, also fifty-five, who moved in the same week, both of us to brand-new lofts in a Walker's Point former industrial warehouse that was insufficiently cleaned out. Developers, for no reason, chose to give us homes fit to kill. We were the only two who both lived and worked there, so the effects on us were far more severe.

And OMG, are you kidding: Mold in other apartments? Glass showers crashing down into thousands of pieces? Cracked brand-new double marble vanities? A window broke my Handy Handyman's five fingers. Dear Kathy got a horrible knee injury on the unsalted ice. And I also had a severe concussion, from a large kitchen window falling inside onto me, rather than opening out.

In the words of San Francisco poet Lawrence Ferlinghetti, "I am waiting for my case to come up And I am waiting for someone to really discover America and wail."

Very sincerely yours,
Julia Fields

CHAPTER 19

Julia Puts Together a Wee Bit of Her Case

Julia put many aspects of her case together, in ways that no doctors could or would. There is little coordination of care in Millennium World for complicated cases. She realized that her vast neurological wipeout was located at the precise entry point of her stabbing wound from Central Park in 1974. It was a more minor wound, located under her left breast, the wound that she found herself at Roosevelt Hospital, with their attention focused solely on her two-point-five-centimeter wound near her right kidney. As Julia thought about the "minor wound,' she explained to her Renaissance doctor: "It is right near my heart."

In a sense, the creepy or kindly people also went like a knife for Julia's heart and soul with illegalities, trivial pursuits, disregarding her doctors' diagnoses from scientific tests, and their devotion to Lady Jane's nemesis:

the idiot box. No one read books or newspapers very much any longer. Julia was forever cold in those years and would have died on her simple walk to work, but for her Kelly-green suede jacket with a zipped-in lining in October 1974. Hal showed her the blood covering two layers of the garment before he threw it away.

It made sense to Kindly that laying in Roosevelt Hospital at twenty-two was a BIG TRAUMA, mirroring her many other health traumas during childhood and adolescence. Some of Julia's family actually said it was all her fault, for carrying a purse in the open. Jesus Christ. The trauma of chest pains from toxins manifold, seven ambulances in two and one-half years, fainting twice while alone, falling asleep in the tub—it was now clear that so ill with fibromyalgia, irritable bowel, and her two left feet that wouldn't walk that Julia would relive this Central Park trauma throughout her life, when her sense of security was literally first sliced open. New York, on an Indian summer morning, had given way to terror, trauma personalized to Julia, trauma of early hospitalization at five, trauma of being expected to perform always and forever at warp speed, to overachieve, illness or not, economic depression or not.

It was now twenty-one years after the onset of being sick in Gay Paree, no diagnosis there except sciatica, which did not explain all of her pains, but it was the only thing that two weeks at La Salpêtrière and a week's workup at Yale could produce.

Julia Drops the Bomb on the Bank of Ill Repute

March 4, 2010
Mr. Max Intrudesky
Loss Mitigation Negotiator
Bank of Ill Repute
Mail Code: Max Intrudesky ASC-CP

Dear Mr. Intrudesky:

I am writing to request forgiveness of my $200,000 note on apartment 622 at the Walker's Point Milwaukee Lofts building and the elimination of the debt thereon. I wish the bank to take ownership of this property and its lessor. I formerly ran my several small businesses there. This apartment has been leased out since for a period of twelve months. My businesses did not survive the recession and are inoperative. It has been marketed by three successive realtors, with no offers. I marketed it extensively on Craigslist twice, and last spring, I secured Mr. Jerkanzxi at the lease rate of $1,100 per month. I also wish to assign this lease, which ends on May 31st, to the bank.

I have been quite ill since 2008, with a myriad of crippling diagnoses. My indirect and direct medical costs exceed one million dollars. I have aggressively sought alternative employment, despite my ill health, on a daily basis. Therefore, and in accordance with the accompanying forms you requested, it is no longer possible for me to fulfill the obligations of this note.

Very sincerely yours,
Julia Fields

143

P.S. My former husband and I were happy customers of the bank for twenty years, but I am certain you will agree that the terms of the note, made just prior to the near-collapse of the American banking system, were gravely flawed. The bank gave me this note with just $5,000 down, and to an independent contractor, without any income guarantee. Thank you for your consideration.

Julia's Letter to the Editor

August 2010

Letter to the Editor, Milwaukee Journal Sentinel:

It seems to me that one person can influence another with an encouraging conversation, a helpful hand, a visit to an ill friend, a surprise on a birthday or anniversary, even a humorous email; or by letting the other person go first at an intersection, in a cashier line, at the bank, in all the places where we displace our rage and helplessness in the society we have become, mired in consumption and greed. What happened to our country?

Together, we might raise the level of civility, and in so doing, everyone could calm down a little bit and get back to the real work of figuring out solutions to complex, decades-old problems.

Sincerely,
Julia Fields
3021 South Superior Street, lower level
Bay View, Wisconsin 53207
414 217 1292

A Letter to Lady Jane

August 4, 2010

Dearly Departed Mom:

HAPPY BIRTHDAY, Momily! Today is your 86th birthday, and I am going to celebrate with Dreadlocks, as it is also his birthday today. And President Obama's, too. Three great people, all having birthdays on August fourth. Dreadlocks and I will raise a toast to you, Lady Jane, as you enjoy your birthday with Dad in heavenly spheres, and we will unfortunately have to skip the presents, now that you are gone.

Hurrah! At last, there is no limitation on health insurance for preexisting conditions, thanks to Obamacare, but will it last? Some influential lobbyists are gunning for it from the get-go.

Lady Jane, I tried as hard as I could but did not get to purchase the gray and white duplex facing the cool waters of Lake Michigan, with its view of the sailboats splendiferous, and with the view of our annual Air Show, soon to begin. No mortgage in the gig economy.

Back in the eighties, my first analyst had warned me that in Milwaukee, she knew that Jews were separated from Gentiles. I was incredulous, as Ben's friends were a mixture, as have mine been always. Here, though, I must say, religion is often attributed by others to my lack of finding work. I loathe tagging it as anti-Semitism. Of course, being a woman does not help, as you often said, "It's a man's world." Our city is increasingly a segregated town, with intentionality, with third and fourth generation wealth displayed in eateries and $3 million downtown condos unthinkable a decade ago. Even Heart Throb now has deep lines of weary, wizened age, but yet not quite

145

sixty. Perhaps it comes from Boomer Males figuring they must run, get the next promotion, must work out daily, cannot stop for a minute, cannot share power with us in a true sense.

It could be hard for you to understand a family withering, as most people never knew your generation's generosity. They never had to face the disabilities I did as the "good daughter," taking you to doctors in Longboat Key and in Milwaukee, even on vacations in Lake Placid or Jamaica, you were often sick, and I was the presumptive caregiver from adolescence forward.

It was like my recently published work on Inversion Theory in another sense: You were supposed to be taking care of ME! But I was taking care of you, as only a daughter can muster the effort and the time to do. Of course, we have the largest share of home responsibilities and our own careers atop taking care of ill parents and children, arranging childcare or daycare to permit us to take on work and community activities.

You know, Dearest Lady Jane, I have never had patience for the economic marriage, where the wife lives the life she does because of the husband's salary and prominence. It never made sense, sort of like suburban prostitution, but no one likes that when I name it what it is.

The other two things that I am trying to catch up with that sit on my desk: Deadhead Redhead, whom I may just have to send packing.

Here in Brew City, as you well know, we run into each other, old lovers, current lovers, lovers' lovers, we are one step away from catastrophic Revealing the Truth, but oh no, it is the Midwest. We must button it up and not say too much. You can meet your former best friend of years at the store, at a funeral, or in the shoe department, and she will profess not recognizing you, after walking, or talking, or

146

having done a billion other things. Yes, while I love Milwaukee, it is called "repression" for a reason, and we have it here in glorious rhymin' time in the Second Great Depression/Recession. Or, if you so much as annoy the friend's husband or the wife, by being your East Coast friendly, bear hug self, ohmygod, the friendship can go up in smoke in an instant. Or if you mention your education and travels, people think you are making it up: no one can have traveled to thirty countries by the age of fifty-five, just earning modest salaries. I did, before and also with Ben, travel the world, year by year.

My second nap of the day was very therapeutic. Had a strange dream, set last year, when I really was in eclipse, like no fucking kidding around, too many pills, too many ills, no sex drive (doctors like repressing that, it seems, while opening up the Memory Bin). There was no drive for excellence, no combative spirit, few hobbies to concentrate on, even when sailing with friends. I had no recall of many terms learned in the sixties, sailing upon North Pond, part of the Belgrade Lakes, in central Maine, where we learned all sports imaginable, and some weird ones, like scuba diving in a murky damn lake, with hardly any fish. But mostly, we learned to live and work on projects together, without swearing or false critiques.

The people brought up in "Trashville" follow the laissez-faire *theory, so well-named by you, Lady Jane. It describes their abject refusal to set standards or guidelines for their children. She who is gorgeous and lazy. She who is wealthy and greedy. This plague of laissez-faire parenting has created a society with no moral focus— with selfish and narcissistic creatures, barely human, without regard for Landlord/City Regulations/Marital/Estate laws. Seems I have encountered all of these folks since you exited stage left.*

You would be screaming bloody murder in Millennium World, Mom!

Imagine this: we now have to pay in advance at all the doctors and dentists, whose tardiness goes unmentioned, while we are losing our ability to work for hours of waiting. One surgeon, even with having made the wrong diagnosis, gets "bowled over" by me on the telephone, listening to all my accomplishments of late. With a diagnosis very correct—you have seen where I came from—it is Post-Traumatic Fields Family Disorder, and you could maybe rewrite the PDR in your spare time in heaven. Leave 'em laughin' for having known your mastery, in absentia, *of this case from hell.*

I have high regard for people with firm intentions, as well as a softie side, which probably people cruise to their advantage. We are supposed to be all tough and all business allthetime. It is rare for professional women to have both moxie + loving kindness. In that, I feel, I am a rarity, mentoring others to take care of their health, family, community obligations, and jobs, in that order.

I wish you had been well enough to come to see me get the TEMPO mentor award in 2003. I am now going to trundle to my tulip sheets, snuggle up, and as often, fall asleep with phones aside me, or in my hands. Lousy day for Yard Sale, just watching Superior Street promenade by, only about $150 of furnishings sold for food and medicine in the richest country in the history of the world. I'd expected a lot more sales, but nothin' doin'.

I have to cut down on salt and substitute some "permissible" snacks. My weight gain is intolerable and grotesque. Damn it!

Love,
Julia

PART II
THE BEAT GOES ON

CHAPTER 1

Moving On, 2014

Julia was emerging from the years of emerging emergencies, in Janespeak—the divorce, the death of her beloved and beautiful Lady, the deaths of two dear client friends, and others, simply sick of her illnesses, despite these illnesses having precise names, tests, and diagnoses. The disappeared were incapable of seeing Julia looking so well, with a stylish new 'do, with a fine complexion, with a trove of good health indicators, and believing that she was in any way ill. There were no mysteries—these diagnoses, some of 'em, were new in the Millennium World, with toxins everywhere, which had grown copiously in her Milwaukee loft, ate up her inheritance, and prevented her from paying bills many months. Yes, Dear Reader, one could be incapacitated and still look well, even with cancer or heart disease.

"I've had months of bed rest, and I know how to camouflage my exhaustion and pain," Julia explained. Julia had always wished to be an actress, with perfect hair and makeup, with the ability to change personas, to use different voices, to fool the crowd. Some bought it, others trundled off to their own narratives of broken bones or pending surgeries. Julia longed for a comprehensive medical protocol, something that would not sporadically and chronically upend her days, while appearing *sans* care at a cocktail party at the Lakefront, at intermission during the magnificent Milwaukee Symphony, or during a client meeting, all the while pushing through the feelings of knives in her hands and feet.

Then, there was the excess problem of her weight. Julia had devoted her entire life to escaping the calumny of ever again being called "chubby," as Lady Jane had termed it; she did 150 sit-ups every morning until her fiftieth birthday, when, for an hour and a half, she weighed in at 120, as in her Sarah Lawrence sophomore year. She had done it again, without trying, in the Year of Living Frugally, still eating, but alone, Julia had less of a dinner, and the pounds flew away. Her feet felt fine; she played tennis and worked out many times a week. But then all systems that were go just went to pieces. Julia's feet were killing her, and she and the Renaissance doctor, who had taken over her entire case, at his suggestion, with her primary primarily missing in action—they had decided it was perhaps time for the foot surgeries, already postponed for six years. A simple pre-op physical, no sweat, go to her internist of twenty years, over in a New York minute. Not so easy. The minute he laid hands on her for the pre-op physical, Julia yelped and wept. It was excruciating. There were no words to describe this sudden, surreptitious, and sickening return of FibroFreakingMyAlgia. Quickly on its heels, her guts twisted with every molecule of food, and even water hurt going down. Here we go again, and another $70,000 of direct and indirect medical costs were sitting on Julia's plate, along with three pieces of celery, as fat is not in, it is not appreciated, it is a detriment to Julia's day, it is totally terrible. Celery followed the Susan Stein diet, so it should have been working, but no, it cannot be easy. Could it be MenoSTOP rearing its ugly, F A T, bestial self?

The fibro, the Irritating Irritable Intestines, the excruciating welter of bills, heaps of them, these did not depress Julia this time. She had made it through this before, and so she would again—Prince Hal and the United States Navy Seabees had seen far worse, as he had reminded her vigilantly. It was a miracle that they escaped an invasion of Japan. And she, he told and retold her, was resilient. She would be back on top. He told her this constantly, until his death on March 8, 2002, at 6:35 a.m. in hospice, in a crapola nursing home five miles from his beloved and bewitching Lady Jane. Resilient? Julia questioned how much more internal and external crap she could possibly take. How resilient would he have been, as he always said that the four worst things were to be ill, alone, poor, and old. Julia had racked up three-quarters of this bundle of misery. Was there an escape? It was not easy, there were monstacles knocking her down, the corruption of real estate, the simple estate gone mad, the fake estate of everyone gypping everyone all day long. The situation was terrible.

It was all terribly wrong, Julia thought, *wasting one's time and effort on such goofiness, such sheer stupidity, such nonsense, when folks could be walking, playing stick ball, playing gin rummy, inventing new medical cures for fibro. Get rid of this stinking gene. Just blow it up. People could be making love and not war. People could be minding their own fucking business and get back to work and put their country back to work. It would only take a little ingenuity.*

Whenever Julia thought about it, she sensed there was something ineffable in the Milwaukee climate—it was not seasonal, it was pervasive, and it had nothing at all to do with the weather. It was as if the sixties, seventies, eighties, nineties, and first decade of the Millennium World hadn't happened—at least not for women. What is this craziness of women being kept down and out of power in the city? What is the damn thing about a woman being firm, resolute, and a leader that so frightened the people around Julia? Why is this still going on in 2014? After hundreds of hours, making lists of pros and cons, Julia had made up her mind. Her Milwaukee stint was coming to an end. It was time for a new location. She would move to New Paltz, New York, for a quieter life with less stress. Ah no, a real move, far away from her fabulous and tortured Milwaukee memories.

This went over like a lead balloon with Niibawi, her beautiful friend of ever-lovin' hippiedom. He had his students, and they always came first, students with disabilities, and his summers for sailing and his clientele, and his daughter part-time, and a whole lot of time-consuming contraptions around his house. He claimed he loved Julia, but he wanted her at a distance. He said it flat out.

Ohmygod, was Julia's response. *He actually said it.*

Yes, Dear Reader, there are times when singles look around and there are only babies, gay friends, and the harried and married, you see them all around, they are uncertain of whether they are married, why they got married, how to stay married, and they were always falling in love with Julia, since age nineteen. It was not necessarily her wish, but she had a *whoosh* effect on people, a resolute woman with a Renaissance woman's command of the facts, the whole facts, and nothin' but the facts. But, these were coupled with what her first analyst had called Julia's "exquisite sensitivity." It was exquisite, but the stinkin' fibromyalgia, an acute sensitivity to all the senses, all the pains, and to all the losses of Julia's life of recent date— this exquisite nature was sometimes a fucking pain in the ass, one of the few places that never hurt.

Hmmm, Julia thought. *Gotta have a plan. There has got to be more than waiting for Niibawi to jump ship, or sailboat. There has got to be more than living squeezed into a student flat, with a trillion nightly interruptions of ambulances and motorcycles on Superior Street. There has got to be more, and where would that be?*

155

Why New York, of course, as it was both new and old, there were friends of forty years in the City, there were a couple of thousands of hippies per square block. There was also Vassar Medical Center in Poughkeepsie, the homeowners proudly told her, boasting of their recent surgeries and their cures. *Forget about hospitals*, thought Julia on a day trip up the Hudson just to see what was to become her home. Forget about doctors and their pills for ills, which cause more ills and more pills, in an Alice in Wonderland of repetitive mirrored images, of her insides coming out, and her outsides feeling as if she were 108 years old, but she was only sixty-one, a babe in Niibawi's arms.

"I get very sad when I read you are going to go to New York," he wrote in their ever-present emails. *Me too*, Julia thought. *I am about as sad as I could be to leave the best friend I have ever had.* And it totally sucks to start in again with Mr. Not So Right, as she predicted would happen for a long time. You cannot go from man to man, her analyst had cautioned her when she said she would never marry again. He was correct, but come on, no sex for the rest of her life? No one on the other side of the dinner table? No cuddle bunnies? *It cannot be this way forever. Even overweight by 8,000 pounds I look pretty damn good, folks guessing I am thirty-eight, forty-two, all sorts of ages.* Niibawi was some kind of special Daddy Long Legs. He could have been the Jolly Green Giant, too, all rumpled up in his ever-present turtlenecks of green and on alternate days, there was more green. *Ohmygod, does he sleep in them every night? Does he have no sense of variety? Of color? Of people reacting differently to different colors? Is he ever going to change?* 'Course not, you never change 'em. Julia knew better than to think that at the ripened age of sixty-one.

You can lead them, but these Boomer horses do not drink, except if it is Pinot Grigio, then they don't stop drinking. Or Red Stripe, from Julia's Jamaican jaunts via its Pennsylvania brewery. Or endless Colectivo coffee cups by the quadrillions. Niibawi was some special dude. He read to her, he wrote for her, he warmed her cockles, he sent her roses in bucketsful, he picked her apples from his Bayfield trees, he made her triple berry pie, he did all these things, but he could not possibly tear himself away from his students and the stinking boat, *Animiashi*—Let's Go Sailing—his beloved thirty-four feet of splendor in the Apostle Islands on deep dark blue Lake Superior.

Niibawi Schmiibawi. I gotta get me a life, Julia decided. It was not going to be easy, more monstacles around every corner, more Milwaukee/Millennium emerging emergencies every day, and more people totally bereft of work, comfort, cash, and spare change were even becoming a problem. It was ceaseless, it was untoward, it was moving toward a total collapse of These United States, and it was at this moment that as the country went down, that Julia went up and planned and dreamed of her home in the woods, a home of perfect solace, a home in which she would continue her career as a writer, and where, who knows what might happen?

157

But Niibawi? It would be difficult to have the last meal, to say the last goodbye, to depend on email and an occasional phone call. And even with Skype, there are no goddamned hugs, there is no twisting in each other's mouths. The twisting of ideas cannot happen in the same way in pixels, picking apart one's solitude at all hours, smart phones being nothing like the strawberries he brought to their bed and fed her one at a time, till she would start caressing him, laughing like a teenager, and they would talk and make love all night.

It was apt to be a very apt decision, but these decisions made alone, in one's home, in one's solitude, they basically suck the big one. They are creepy, they have no backdrop, they have no foreground, they have no reflection—they are all in air, in space, in a museum of her mind—where she would go, whom she would meet, what would become of her, how could she leave her very best planetary friend, the orb of her life, in her brain like nobody's business. Niibawi was a friend for all the seasons of her mind, of her psyche, and of her soul, now nearly healed from the traumas of the emerging emergencies. There was not one thing Julia could write about Niibawi that did not bring tears to her eyes. He was sublime, he was subterranean—as in she barely saw him. He was superbly the Man of Many Magnificent and Mellifluous Moments, and he would remain so, in the pixels, in the cards, on the telephone, from his antiquated BlackBerry to the blueberries in the pies he would invariably overnight to her...but it could all stop one day.

It could, but it was unlikely, for in Niibawi, Julia had found herself, her wings, her equanimity in a time of torture of illnesses deciphered but not understood, in a time when life was cruel to love, and there was no more time, but flight.

A Poem from Julia to Niibawi

"Love"
A Poem of Hello and Goodbye

Listen.
Warmed silence of winter come home.   Free.
Go on with me if, for a second:
The second of birth
And the seconding of life fleet:
We go by unawares,
Caged and unfree.
Selves, slaves to an image of half-dried beginnings
Mirrored distortions
Of endings, births, loves—
In a time of all seasons sliding
Of all dreams awakening in a burst:
Fright   fantasy   fury.

In and over our one being
Our one need, love.

There, waiting

The filled platter of life goodies
Come home neither to be nor to boast:
Left alone to fight a world decrepit
Weary of toiling
Scared of ending
Having never begun.

Songs in raptured time.
How can life be cruel to love.
It is a novel's plan: attack the living, slight loving people.

Be a comfort; be there for me.

I am here   waiting
Distance is place. A way is in the heart.

Be free from fought fears
Of the friend I am for you.
Life of a wonder, my friends,
Soar with me
As I am yours.

Love the water, the rushing, calm, maddening gaze.
Be a lark, uncaged in time.
Being is now and there will always be a way

A way from life to love
Catch me
As time falling heals

On the last wink
Be there.

II

Quiet is a death
A fear of no one   nothing
Answering.

Placed alone
No one   nothing exists, is there to touch

Neither comic nor tragic
Lost and afraid to cry
Reaching for you   I find words helpless
Find walls existing
See mountains of valleys between.

I cry a tearless tear
I lift
Only to fall.

There is no peace in silence.
There are no hopes, only illusions
There are only silences around us.

There will be no reprise
No wistful memories
I try

161

This solitary day of blue.

Peace like a river of golden darkness
The fight to free has begun
This is the end   I flee now.
I exit alone   I cry for you.

I search for you in every alley
I leave out nothing I open all paths.
Fire and red   the silent embrace and the noisemakers subside
The earth grows weary of noise.

Be an echo in time
As I leave
As I wait for you
This is the end   There is no ending.
Let ends merge, comic muse into tragedy.
I grope, blinded by life, joyous in love
I search   again.

Time unhalted falters
Falling in the space of places past
After touch passed.

My love is strengthened
In an essential way
In a holy honor of you.

Soft shadows, crisp farewells, vibrant embraces merge and flow
forward.

There is no fear
There are no questions of the heart.
In places distant
Are no regret   no reproaches
Flowing to freedom   Time forsaken.

Graceful locks of hair tumbling   sheltering us
As one without fear   As never foreseen
I forget
How I began to cherish your hand
When I heard your voice
Or where it all happened.

Here, time echoes silence.

One is two are one we two.

I am escapading away.

We meld through time in space refined
As my last hope   Rushing
In cascades are praises of you.

After billowing
The wind leaves no one behind
In a day of sad joy.

Time hollers for freedom and love to collide and live.
Let it be love!
Be the reason for life
Under all   be there.

Be my friend as you are.

You lay here by my side
I feel, do not clutch backwards:
Middles dissolve dissolved by time.

III

We may find beyond tomorrow
Silences again flowing and fleeting
Time without touch.

Presents fade for future hollers
Without time in this space
Stringent walls appear—
Something of love licks walls.

I will aim toward you as I take flight
A way to see is to love.
To see invisibility
To be prince like
To stride astride oneself:
There are no differences

We are two are one are none
Of these words
Of these thoughts
Or are all.

As cherished is faint
As held is lost
As we are one in mind's space
Be us two now.

Never forget to remember
Every cord of a chord of love
Every whine of a pain too real
Every whim of a winter love.

Where there is fear be also: joy!
In silences create new vigor to fight and conquer fear.

Immersed
I must now leave
Must undo the present
Must pinch time   Fight pain.
Love is falling
Delving
Into the deep sunshine
Of an ending winter
Of pain too real
Of real too false

Of no time for love.

My mind of time is nothing now.
Love can vanquish
Can disperse   fleeting minutes
When there is place
For no more time.

This is no battle, no blood is shed.
This is no hell, no devilish powers.

This is real fire
Of urgent embraces
This is a love for a love
Now   parting.

Simply taught, casually sensed
A longing for life is a need for love

A source in time without time
A monstrous flight away and toward begins.

You are away
Or is it I?

There: It is the place of holding time.
Each feature: joy

Each minute: delight

Each kiss: love making.

Months of glory to share:
Did I give   did I share   did I love enough   or too little?

Questions, beget no answers—
In a time when life was crude
Joys enclosed in minutes
All touch   passed.

There was no time—
But   flight.

A Journal Entry

December 18, 2014

THESE PEOPLE, WHOEVER THEY ARE, WHO DO NOT VOTE, WHO DO NOT VOLUNTEER, WHO DO NOT PAY TAXES….

FUCK THESE MORALISTIC PEOPLE WHO HAVE NOT A CARE FOR UNWANTED BABIES….

FUCK THIS PURITANICAL SOCIETY THAT IS OBSESSED WITH PUBLIC OFFICIALS' SEX LIVES MORE THAN THE POLITICIANS' WORK ETHICS OR MORAL FIBER.

167

CHAPTER 2

Julia Learns about Susan-cidal Depression

Julia's very closest friend, Susan, had been a friend since the sixties, since summer camp in Maine—a pretty camp with all the trimmings, all the sports, all the skills of learning to live together with people from near and far. It was a far cry from Millennium World and couch potatoes allovertheplace. This was a camp with spirit, with songs nightly, where girls wrote songs on the way back from every camping trip and sang them in the dining room in front of two hundred and thirty-four girls and counselors. The counselors were women from the South, mostly, and they were fine, they were great pals, they were strong as steel, they had values, and they valued their cabin as though these girls were their very own daughters or younger sisters. Susan was different than Julia, but they were instant best friends. They played doubles and won every match on the camp circuit, they told each other secrets, they visited each during the winter, they counted the days until the New York City reunion each March. They counted the seconds until the date when all the girls would be back at camp, making new friends, living in the woods without gadgets except hair dryers, without any contraptions except spirit, feeling, new places to go, new bike rides, new canoe trips, new paintings and sculpture in the arts and crafts barn.

It was just about heaven on earth, a camp on the Belgrade Lakes, a lake that Julia and Susan swam across when they were fifteen, seven miles in one day—*keep going, do not stop, it will be great to finish, it will be a miracle, it will be a memory for the rest of your life*—that is what Julia told herself during the last impossible mile. She almost did not make it up the long walk up the hill from the waterfront, half dead, no dinner that night, just sleep and more sleep. Julia and Susan both did it, and it was characteristic of the times. People did not give up left and right. They did the right thing, they followed rules and prescriptions, they read their summer reading books at night by flashlight, and they set hundreds of candles to float on their cove in North Pond two nights before the end of camp. It was a sight, it was serene, it was Julia's and Susan's favorite night, but it beckoned the end of summer, the parting of friends and counselors, and these friendships were strong, they were real, they were indivisible. Even through distance, they were assured for the next summer. They wrote letters to each other, with a rare phone call, as long distance, even from seventy-five miles away to Westchester County, cost five dollars.

Later in life, Julia heard regularly from Susan, about her college days, about her boyfriends, about her parents, beloved by Julia, and about when their next get together would work out: Susan looked forward to visiting Julia in Waterbury, Connecticut, even though their visits were infrequent as they grew older. Lady Jane made incredible gourmet meals, there were tennis games, there were all sorts of things that made life more predictable every day, and these things were often free, they were sitting and knitting by the fireplace, they were planting flowers and trees in Julia's backyard, under the watchful eye of Prince Hal. *They were easier times for people,* Julia thought in retrospect. There were hobbies and pastimes notable for their simplicity, for the ease with which one could have fun, maintain a long-distance friendship, write long letters, be in charge of one's feelings, not feeling that every microsecond one must respond, one must check one's phone, one's email, or multiple emails ninety million times throughout the day. During college, Susan stopped writing to Julia, and this was cause for great concern. Susan was called the "best letter writer" by Prince Hal, and for good reason, as her letters to Julia were lengthy, frequent, written in great happiness, and with ample details of her favorite people in her world.

After waiting her turn (thirty minutes for time at the dorm phone), Julia called Susan up. No response. That was all one could do; there were no cell phones. There was one phone for ten rooms, but people managed, they stayed in touch, they were connected. Weeks later, Julia finally heard from Susan. The letter was horrific. It was the worst letter Julia had ever received, scorching in its depths of woe, something Julia had read about but had never experienced ever before in her life or her family or friendships, except with Lady Jane, from another generation of women. Susan described her depression as a total nightmare all day long. It was impossible to focus on anything, in any place, in any way. Reading was impossible, writing was excruciating, getting dressed was an issue, there were no dates at college, there was simply hanging out and going to bed. It was before AIDS, it was all very open and Grecian, everyone having sex all the time allovertheplace, in the dorms, in their teachers' offices, in the glades, or in cars.

Susan had tried to kill herself.

Julia gasped. *How could this be? How could my very best camp friend for years go down the tubes? How could this happen among fine people and in such a pretty campus as hers in Virginia?* Well, it did happen, and during the years to come, Susan continued to have problems about once a decade with this horror show of an illness, which, in her fifties, she called "Susan-cidal Depression." She said it in jest, but it was not funny, it was very real, and it was painful to the max. There was no getting away from it, as Susan wrote to Julia during their continued email correspondence as middle-aged women.

The drugs never worked. The therapy was often clueless, as Susan explained to Julia, these doctors and therapists live lives with families around them. They have no experience with capital D Depression, they are mostly treating people who have routine anxiety and depression, not that their problems weren't real, but they were really different from Suicidal Depression, as Susan explained to Julia. It was a totally different kettle of fish, and these fish weren't flying, they weren't growing, they were...dead fish.

Susan pushed on through, and Julia found that she could be helpful to her lifelong friend, despite the long distance between Princeton and Milwaukee, despite Susan knowing the best shrinks in the city and in Princeton, despite all these things, this lurking, surreptitious Depression of the Soul never disappeared. It marched across her life, through the day and through the night, whether married or divorced, whether with children or grown children, whether with parents living or parents gone. It was not curable, though there were some palliative cures. There was hospitalization, which Susan felt was a mini vacation. Hospitalization provides various helpful and kind people around to relieve you of panic, to take care of you twenty-four hours of the day, even though these people themselves did not really absorb it. They never had Depression with a capital D, and they had not attempted suicide.

Susan wrote one time about a miraculous cure. She had gone to a hospital for ten treatments of electroconvulsive therapy, despite some people saying it was too extreme, it was too dangerous, she could lose her memory, she could end up having no relief, and amazingly, *she could die during the procedure.* But with no alternatives left, Susan took the plunge, and she did it. It was painless, it was simple, it was 2,000 percent more effective than pills with more side effects than main effects. It was simply the living end, a way to live without Susan-cidal Depression. There were many things Julia had known about Susan since age ten—they were friends for decades, they loved their camp memories, they were forever in touch, it was almost as though they were the same person they had so much in common. But Susan wrote often that she was jealous of Julia. Julia had Lady Jane and Prince Hal; she had parents of diligence, of merit, of humor, of many distinguishing characteristics. Susan's parents were fine, they were good people, they cared, but they were not Lady Jane and Prince Hal.

As Julia reconsidered it years later, having her parents was a blessing. It was unusual, it was serene, and even when they left this mortal world, she lived with them in her head and her heart. She thought of them throughout the day, when reading the *Times*, when sailing, when swimming, when playing bridge, when playing the piano. She would not let death overcome these memories etched into her like inscriptions of love, of cherished times, of fights like hell, of reconciliations, of trips to the Cape, to Washington, D.C., to Jamaica, to Vermont, and day trips to ski the Berkshires with Hal on Saturdays, these were treasures that no one, no illness like fibromyalgia and PTSD could ever erase. These were her vaulted memories, and as with camp friends, those memories are forever.

174

They are clear. They are the finest things to think about before sleep and upon awakening. Like chimes in Julia's head, they rang clear and true. Susan's proclivities for Susan-cidal Depression did not ever disappear, they were still there, especially after her father died—they were strong, they were mighty hard to escape. But, as Susan wrote to Julia—*I will win this battle, I will knock this down, I will overcome this plague*—and Julia believed her. She knew that Susan was serious about business, about her life, about her family, and if she said she would win, conquering depression, then she would.

CHAPTER 3

Fall to Winter, 2015

J ulia wondered when her pains and the grief of mourning would end. Would they ever end? Would her parents' legacy and their world of conviction, morality, steadfast devotion to friends, loyalty to workers, and so much more, would this world reappear, even in just small portions of Millennium World? It no longer kept Julia up at night. FibroFreakingMyAlgia and its exhaustion took care of that, and its companion disorder of irritable bowel syndrome, tell us about it; just invest in Charmin post haste. It was incredible, it was not to be believed, that all the elements were still in place, not elementary, my dear Watson: this is advanced, advancing middle age, and it is not in the Middle Ages, but in Millennium World, with the whole nation fixated on their most recent text or email message, without a context—often without a clue, it appeared.

The symbols of Julia's past were all around her. The cosmetics inherited from Lady Jane? They lasted Julia for three years. Her sweaters and scarves were making their eighth appearance since Lady Jane's death. They were tumbling out of boxes, out of bureaus, out of armoires, and yet, Julia had given so many away to erstwhile and continuing friends—to the Handy Handyman's wife, to Megan, to Lefty's wife, to just about anyone who had a birthday or a special occasion.

There were lakeside sunrises on Julia's short morning walks in Bay View, and the mammoth deck had a great view of the orange autumn sunsets, but it was not a loft with floor-to-ceiling windows; it was just a view from Bay View. There was community, there were neighbors who interacted, there were glorious old trees lining Superior Street and, for that, Julia was thankful. She dreaded all the attendant anniversaries of late fall, the splitting up from Ben, leaving the multiracial and multi-ethnic Shorewood community, living in a 1928 Tudor home with all the fixings and all the series of Foley & Lardner attorneys' families who had fixed it up perfectly before Julia found it one December day in 1993. It had been a beautiful life in all respects.

Julia had made few visits to the East Coast since Lady Jane's death. She went religiously to visit Jenny in Manhattan and to her Brooklyn art studio twice a year, sometimes thrice, and to Boston when Joshua began college and stayed on for journalism work. These trips were but three days long—hardly enough to satisfy Julia—but they were intense, talking all day and way past Julia's normal early bedtime. They brought her deep satisfaction that both children, despite the unexpected and searing divorce, were well launched, had lots of friends, and were glowing and most of all, kind and independent thinkers as young adults.

Having only intermittent emails, texts, and mobile-to-mobile overlapping telephone conversations was short shrift. It would do, but it was tough, no doubt about that. Wanderful, the saintly caregiver, and Julia talked about the old times during their daily phone calls—the Fields' perfectly appointed home, the small gourmet meals, whether made by Jane or, as a widow, brought in from Good News Café, and Wanda's incessant vacuuming and washing of each towel every day, Jane had to do it. There was no stopping her. There must be an immaculate reception each day. Even if no one came by, we must be ready, she told Julia ninety million times. As with the clothes, lovingly stored in seven closets after Hal died, all perfect but mostly unworn, with the price tags still on. Jane's arthritic hands had trouble doing small motor tasks with scissors.

"I must have something to wear in case the occasion comes up," Jane explained.

"Where would Dad put his stuff if he came back?" Julia often asked, with a twinkle in her eye, matching Jane's glamorous hazel eyes, never more sterling than on the afternoon prior to her death on Wednesday, December 5, 2007. The losses of Julia's clients, their deaths in mid-projects, was another blow to the jugular. Others could and would come back, Wanderful encouraged Julia. But, the country was in free fall, coming apart now in a more uninterrupted fashion, with longer and longer lines at meal sites for the Friday boxes of three-day supplies of emergency food, people of all ages, with all manner of dress, with no cars or decent cars, it was the Second Great Depression allovertheplace.

Kindly, the gracious, mellifluous voiced psychoanalyst, saw Julia evolve, kept encouraging her writing, her growing, her getting a grip on these complex illnesses, and the incessant stress allovertheplace—her own depression mirroring the economic depression. As if it were not enough, there was a third depression: a tropical depression had come to Jamaica and ravaged the sands of Negril Beach. But Jamaicans were different. They knew that September brought hurricanes and such. They would rebuild immediately. The beach vendors would continue to eke out a living selling newspapers, fresh coconuts, mangoes, and pineapples. Folks would be making bamboo hats, wood carvings, and the braiding and beading of hair would resume immediately. Tourists would resume their customary custom of bargaining for the indelible $10 cotton print dresses, shorts, bathing suit wraps, and t-shirts. It would all continue, in the land of One Love, One Heart. Having a slogan, having a spirit, that's what Jamaicans had, though they knew interminable poverty, they worked hard, mostly seven days a week, many of them doing two jobs, but they hung in there, they prayed for economic recovery in America since, as the hair-braider Ann reminded Julia, "As America goes, so goes Jamaica." It amazed Julia that a woman supporting three on a beach vendor's income could understand so much while reading no news; it was all oral transmission from her regular customers, who sought her out every year on Negril Beach, one shack among hundreds, no address, no marketing, not even a sign.

Kindly listened to Julia's grief, her losses of so many people, her loss of a marriage, her health sucked out of her, and the cyclical resulting catastrophe of catastrophic medical bills. He was there, he smiled, he laughed with Julia. Even though they had never spent more than forty-five minutes together at one time, it was real devotion, and it was not just some medical thing. It was a supportive relationship, more so than with parents, spouse, or children, as it skipped the stupid stuff and went deep into what mattered. Julia was very grateful that, since meeting Kindly in the fall of 2009, it had all worked out. Wanderful was right, with her uproarious laugh, amid her broken down body, she kept Julia laughing and soothed her tears, the tears of FibroFreakingMeOutMyAlgia. "It ain't goin' away, so you better learn to live with it," Wanderful said, as only she could say it, as words of encouragement, from her learned experience in the hood in Waterbury.

Julia's Journal Entries

November 2014
Recovery

Recovery requires a large measure of faith, beyond the dozens of bottles of medicines and vitamins. I wait a long time each week in waiting rooms, followed by the invariable poking and prodding by physicians' assistants and the physicians, who barely give me twelve short minutes.

Gradually, the pains have melted into an ever-present, low-range throbbing, my spinal neck injury radiating down my arms, yielding a fierce tingling in the fingertips that prevents small motor activities, like putting on earrings. (This would be diagnosed much later as two hands full of carpal tunnel.) *Dressing is difficult—zippers, buttons, snaps, and necklace clasps, two of my treasured grandmother's royal blue Cape Cod glasses slipping from my hands and breaking in the same stinking evening.*

Recovery was elusive. It came, it vanished, it reappeared. The medical team could not define the best course of treatment, but they tripped over each other's recommendations, leaving me with perplexing facts to sort out. My primary never followed up on Mayo's forty-three pages of analyses and necessary protocols. How could he keep his job when his job was to follow up on Mayo? What was the point of going to Mayo?

Chronic pain is so different than recovery from a surgery or an accident. It will never go away. Mine is degenerative, and while it can be controlled, all the medicines have side effects, which seem to me at times to be the MAIN effects, while the pain subsists.

182

People doubting you, calling you crazy or faking illness was the worst part. For so many years, seemingly lost forever.

It was, to quote Lady Jane's father, "Hell on earth."

Faith in recovery was an erratic thing. My medicines often failed to make a difference for weeks and sometimes collided with each other. I longed for a chart to bring along on all medical visits. On it would appear meds, therapy, exercise, physical therapy, social life or lack thereof, my work life, and recommendations for a resumption of healthy living. It would be difficult to diagram these overlapping illnesses. Some were in eclipse, while others took an ascendant path. And they shifted positions without the slightest warning.

Prayer

Meditation

Mindfulness

Wanderful and Seal, both of whom I can call in the middle of the night.

They are my new quartet of support, never suggested by doctors, not even the high and mighty doyennes at Mayo.

Imaginative cure—uses of steam, massages with hot stones as an expensive but terrific help, or unusual brews of tea, and Dr. Singha's nightly mustard baths. But when these did not work, it led only to greater frustration, anger, and others' dismissive name-calling, common to us autoimmune sufferers.

Hospitalizations—a pervasively sterile, white on glass on white atmosphere, with their mass production ways of treating all patients the same way, not correcting for our individual histories. Medicines are dispensed routinely, even when lacking visible results. There are no stop dates, just refills on the bottles.

A Journal Entry by Julia

February 2015
Recovery of Mind and Spirit

After months of diagnoses and treatments, I have begun to recover my physical health, but close on the heels of physical renewal arose a crippling depression, worse than any I'd experienced since my first in 1972. It brought ever-worsening symptoms: lack of concentration, hopelessness, insomnia, and withdrawal from activities like tennis, sailing, and morning walks. Taking a shower was a big achievement and a shampoo even more so. Getting out of bed was the first step toward despair—despair of the day and its obligations, too daunting to fulfill. I realize now that each one of these would eventually be a step toward recovery, just the mere act of getting out of bed.

My doctors seemed not to understand that depression affects the ability to think straight or to figure out problems, low-level or complex. Mostly, they were in the bubble of the twenty-first century 1 percent of Americans who knew not the evaporation of two generations of life savings for direct and indirect medical costs.

"Here, K. Look at this. I showed him my empty calendar for months going forward. How would you feel if you came to your office and there were no patients?" I asked him.

In a microsecond, he said, "I would commit suicide."

The medicines did not move the despair dial. An interim therapist, revered by some, made the symptoms worse by trivializing possible recovery routes: "Bake cookies. Get a job cleaning toilets like I did to have some money to start my practice. There are thousands of free things to do in Milwaukee. Go find things to occupy every single hour of every day. Bring back your list next week." This is actually verbatim and horrifying that it passes as "therapy." Glad I left her.

———————

March 2015

Like my friend Susan, I opted for electroconvulsive therapy. The Renaissance doctor has made all the difference. He began to listen more and stopped interrupting me. Wow! A Boomer Man who listens! Quel *rarity. He offered some genuine or faked praise for our work together.*

ECTs were treatment of another sort: a five-minute procedure, with slow but vital impact. They melted the dire grip of depression. So widely misunderstood, so feared, ECTs are today administered often as an outpatient and a tried and true century-old procedure developed in Italy. It may have first seemed as though there was no impact, but I listened to the administering physician: "It takes time." How would he know, I wondered, clearly never having been depressed, with his Beemer, a trove of patients to last until eventual retirement in his late seventies, a bratty nurse, precocious young'un, as they used to say, which turned out to be his wife. Uh, yes. They thought they were putting everyone on, but I had to ask—are you really close colleagues, or are you fooling around? Ah, the pregnant pause on the telephone. "Yes, we are very close, because she is my wife."

The Renaissance doctor provided much more than mere office visits. He gave me hope. He provided great psychotherapy, despite having had just a few courses in med school. He filled in the gap when Kindly was unavailable to take my call, when the clinical staff "forgot" to give him messages, or when he was on vacation.

I need to talk. A lot. My world of an upper-middle-class life has disappeared—no weekends away, little paid work, and the Millennium World of Everyone Out for His/Herself, Cowboy Country, gunshots nightly in Milwaukee and in many other cities, 259 opiate deaths in our county in THESE DISUNITED STATES in one year?! Yes, that was Milwaukee's count: 259 lives lost to street or prescribed opiates or purchased on the Dark Net with untraceable addresses and with Bitcoin, our twenty-first century monetary "system."

The Bay View homes and front and back terraces around me have been dolled up from Thanksgiving weekend on for Christmas, with a lone menorah down the block. There was snow I might fall down on, with numb feet and shoes that were too tight, as the inflammations continued or even grew. Size ten?! You have got to be kidding—I have worn a size 8½ shoe since '68. This is crazy and also expensive, buying all new shoes, boots, and slippers. Sad, getting rid of stylish heels and shoes with fronts that are too tight for my damned swollen and arthritic toes.

Lady Jane warned me from her deathbed: "Don't let anyone cut your feet." So, I have suffered through plantar fasciitis and three Morton's neuromas, the first diagnoses made in January 2008.

———

March 11, 2015

With the snow and frigid weather, I ironically somehow became symptom-free for the first time in months. My physical therapist, stunned by the impact of our mutual work, is ready to discharge me. I will soon cancel the neurosurgeon appointment—there was nothing left to discuss.

Solitude morphed into frequent loneliness. I dutifully practiced deep breathing, mindfulness, and an EMDR exercise as antidotes, to focus on the here and now and the business and personal friends I was in touch with and gradually filling up blank pages on my calendar. EMDR used eye movements to desensitize and reprogram feelings. It was a new experience, tossed into the mélange *of remedies. I even signed up for an eleven-week class on* Mindfulness in Everyday Life *right down the street at the stately former St. Mary's Academy, now a center for nonprofits.*

Gig interviews kept coming up. What they were seeking was obtuse. What I needed for fulfillment, aside from cold cash, was how to process the words of emails, texts, and the occasional in-person meeting, and keep the processes moving: my goal. Mostly, it was a sit and wait game, responses taking weeks to arrive, or simply not coming at all. Rejections were direct, by letter, and indirect, when I heard someone else got the gig, and frequently, they hired a novice or an MBA with no experience in the field.

Seeking clients creates piercing anxiety about my age, religion, and leaves too much time to stew over the outcomes. Many millions of Boomers are in the same boat—unemployed or underemployed, fiercely angry about seeing their dutiful savings going to everyday or astronomical medical costs. It seems to get worse each year, as though people are giving up their job searches, giving up on marriages, just plain giving up.

Jobs and gigs are most difficult for "women over fifty." It seems like I am continuing to follow the trend set when I arrived in Brew City, a copy of Newsweek in hand, the cover story proclaiming that a thirty-five-year-old woman had a greater likelihood of being struck by lightning than of finding a mate.

Proved them dead wrong. We got married two weeks after my thirty-fifth birthday.

But work? It will have to continue to my dying day—long after turning fifty. My savings are nearly gone.

Kindly sees and hears two Julias—in front of him, talking, and the one he vaguely knew from a distance. This multi-layering is probably useful—he knew of me as a healthy person, has those images to guide me toward, consciously or not.

CHAPTER 4

Sails Allovertheplace, Spring 2015

J ulia returned one glorious spring Sunday afternoon to her special spot at the Sailing Center, where she had often parked between client meetings and called Lady Jane to check up on her during her widowhood, but also to talk about Julia's clients, their progress, their problems. Lady Jane got it—she knew people so well, she psyched them out. They would talk for hours, from Tuscany, Auckland, Jerusalem, from the cities Ben and Julia had visited during a marriage of travel to countries of near and far fields. They spoke in Double Dutch, words of comfort or instantaneous puns overlaying each other's sentences, every phrase, every clause, because of course: this was love. It was mother-daughter love in its ascendancy, it was obdurate love. She *had never felt anything like it before, maybe never would again*. During her confining pains of

FibroFreakingMyAlgia (they weren't going away, just like they hadn't for Jane), she thought about things like this.

The exhaustion marred each day. It was overwhelming, and even Niibawi—the Jolly Green Giant, with his soul of manifest confidence—had never been exhausted like this. It was incredible, and Julia just got freaking used to it, eventually, in Year Nine of Illnesses Visible and Invisible. She had new hair, a new home, she had a new great love; Julia had it all, she was new head to toe, but the pains continued their march across her life. They were there, and that was that. Jane would have been sorry, she would have empathized, she would have sent weekly boxes of fruit or flowers, but then, that Jane was one of a kind.

So, too, were we all unique, but in Millennium World, it was different, everyone was texting and emailing to beat the band, but Jules, as she now called herself, Jules kept the old customs. They would serve her well in the end, in life with Niibawi, sails allovertheplace, in Bayfield, Negril, or Lake Michigan, all sailing was sensual, it was sporting sex, it whooshed by, it was ethereal, it was real, and in these realities, Jules believed she would find her new life.

A Poem from Julia

Being home is remembering old patterns and creating new ones,
Being with friends of forty years or new ones,
Finding a way in a brand-new and still-same world allatonce.

The ultimate home is in one's heart and mind,
With the turmoil, the peace, and the new spaces.

Homes shift, crash, stifle under weight
Genetic homes sting, burn, slice to the quick
And when there is no family, there can be no home.

Being home is acceptance
Making moments of peace,
Laced with memory,
Coupled with newness.

With faces facing the new, radiant sunrises
And pictures of those gone forever
Like the sailing winds.

CHAPTER 5

Julia's Trips to Fields Far and Close

People said in Negril that Julia was a Jamerican, with twenty visits to the island nation since age thirteen. She took a quick trip one winter, a long weekend, hastily planned to get a last-minute bargain with her travel agent, Sue Reiter, who was righter more often than she was wrong. On arrival at the secluded rocky west-end beach, Julia inserted her Simon & Garfunkel CD on her song played in continuous repeat during the trip: "For Emily, Wherever I May Find Her," the song of dreaming and searching, of seeking love.

Julia had visualized for months the scene: pushing back in her seat on the nonstop to Jamaica, to the village known as Lucy's Reef, at the tail end of Negril's West End. She kept an image of Jamaica in her mind most days: Julia loved the people and the music sometimes even more than America. When she switched on CNN, she was distraught to learn Congresswoman Gibbons had been shot during Julia's flight to Montego Bay, while speaking on a sunny Saturday morning to her constituents. Not dead, but very wounded. Julia never truly left America, wherever she was, she kept up on the news, but usually just once a day. *A Congresswoman shot in a shopping mall?!* That was over the top, it was unseemly, it was an invasion of democratic ways of connecting in person with one's supporters, and it overtook Julia's five days in Negril. She was glued to CNN, tracking the news of Guns Run Amok, the very same thing that had happened prior to the arrival of the young Illinois United States Senator for a rally in the Milwaukee Theatre. "No balloons or music today," the candidate explained back in 2007. "I cancelled them because of what happened today at Virginia Tech—thirty-two students shot dead. Instead, I am going to talk about Bobby Kennedy and violence in America." That got Julia's vote—a politician with flexibility, who revised his planned rally on the train up to Milwaukee, who connected to the forty-two hundred attendees. Julia begged Botticelli Daughter and the Shorewood High School crowd to come downtown after school let out, and she spotted them across the vast auditorium. It was important to get the next generation involved, but it was even more important to elect a president who could unite these Disunited States of Violence, not for a pristine future, but for public safety and for treating true criminals as such, white or blue or pink collared-ones. The candidate did shake hands at the end of his speech, a heartfelt one, put together by aides to fact check and get him the exact quotes. Would he survive a presidency, as a serious contender for the nomination, as an African American of mixed parentage? Or, would he end up like the Kennedy brothers and Martin Luther King Jr., slain at a young age?

Julia's Email to Two Doctors

To: The Renaissance doctor and to my neurologist:
Re: Microdose Therapy for fibromyalgia syndrome.

Hey, Dr. No finally returned my call, and I gave him my fibro update. He had not heard of its linkage before to curative ECTs and was open to learning more. Oh boy, I can hear you now: "Julia, you did not go to medical school." Yes, but if I don't research my case, we make little, if any, progress, even with you, the best docs on my case. Keep the pressure on D.C. Give us REAL healthcare, so that we are no longer forty-sixth in the world, an abject nightmare of epic proportions. Why must we who are sick also worry about food and medical costs? It is worse than Third World countries. By the way, those purported discount prescription drug cards don't work at all.

Yours,
Julia
Class of 1970...where did forty-six years go???
Oh my

CHAPTER 6

Recovery

Julia was counting the months, ninety-six of them since her feet went kerflooey, and they were interminable. There was scant healing. There was no grace from people in near and far fields. There were no jobs in Depression America of the twenty-first century. Everyone was pretty much tearing their hair out, or the balding ones were positioning the few remaining hairs. It was a collapsed country—2015 in Milwaukee. But there were a few things that Julia set her mind to, and they began to make a miracle cure, one suggested by no doctor, no nurse, no hospital, or no pharmacist. These were the things she began to do so as to return to her life as she knew it. They were scattered, they did not happen every day, but when they coalesced, it was a good or even a great day in MilRIDEee, where Julia swore as a newcomer in

1987 that she would walk to her Shorewood errands and did. Once.

In the end, Julia decided against the purchase of a home in New Paltz, as she believed that re-establishing a team of doctors who understood her case would be too complex. Also, it would be a four-hour commute to Jenny, not close at all, and some 1,000 miles away from Joshua in Chicago, with a long commute to LaGuardia Airport.

Obesity reigned in Brew City. Her camp friend, Susan, had written a book about sensible eating and exercise. Julia reread it. *What am I doing wrong? None of these miserable pounds or inches are coming off. They are stuck like glue to my hips and waist. This wasted wardrobe can't be replaced. Been there and done that after the last miserable weight gain from FibroFuckingMyAlgia.* Something obvious occurred to Julia: like the *These Are* **Not** *Your Husband's (Boyfriend's/Partner's) Portions* book says: smaller portions! Drown yourself in water! Exercise more, much more, even in five-minute stints, if that is all your worn-out legs and feet will permit. Just fucking do it. Every day. And throw the scale into Lake Michigan. Size is all that counts, for women and for men.

What a miracle! Julia's clothes started fitting better allovertheplace: she could wear the long line bra that kept her waist and tummy tucked in, which of course, she couldn't wear to get those advantages when she was too large (what a great piece of lingerie—when you need it, it's no good). She drowned in water. Even Niibawi complained that she was constantly peeing, but it was good, Julia explained, that water was attacking the calories, and

it was what Susan had done for forty years of success, so
it has got to work. Just kill it; go overdose on this crap, and
guess what? Dear Reader, all Julia's clothes started to fit,
which made her happier, which made her have more energy, which made her happier, which made her good times
better...and the sad times, they were there to stay, but became a little softer, less of a crash landing, more contained.
So, what gives? How does a person get well? Is it nutrition?
Is it rest? Is it having the knowledge that fibro ain't goin'
away, so you'd best figure this stuff out, especially because
the medical profession has taken a pass, has been hijacked,
is totally unwieldy and, of course, the offices close at 4:58
p.m., like a corner store. Lady Jane would have been
screaming bloody murder. "**They call themselves doctors?! What do they know? Are they women? Do they
know what a period or childbirth feels like? Do they
cook and shop for twenty meals a week?**"

Nope. In Millennium World, doctors are technicians,
they are merely keeping up with the tide of patients. They
might be nice people to go out to dinner or to bed
with...but *cures? Remedies? New ideas*? You can forget about
that. In Julia's home, she resumed doing 400 ab crunches
a day. **"WHAT?!"** her friends exclaimed. "Are you kidding?" No, Julia was *not* kidding. She was dead serious, and
this Fibro & Irritable Everything Syndrome, it could just
go straight to hell. She was not ever again giving up a play
or a movie or a concert or a trip. These afflictions, they
were dead on arrival. "Get out of Mini Mouse House,"
Julia said nightly. "Get out of the Almighty's world. Just,

plain and simple, GET THE HELL OUT." This collapse of Julia's body was repetitive and mind numbing in its repetition of the repetition but forget it; it has disappeared before, and it will leave again. The doctors cautioned Julia: "Don't get so fierce about it. You know that fibromyalgia is incurable, and medical knowledge is not there yet. Just do what you can." Some of the docs were kind, but the men had no idea of what Julia would do. She would do five thousand ab crunches a week and drink three gallons of water a day and dance the night away to zydeco or Jamaican music—she was going to KILL her disgraceful waistline and hips. And once she did, she would show it could be done, that even though Niibawi was a teacher and a sailor up in the Apostle Islands (where there were never any apostles whatsoever), she could be tough as nails in a different way. She could not sail his large boat, though she helped. But she could and she would get well.

And he'd be seeing her triumph soon enough.

Niibawi was a comely chap. He wrote real postage stamp letters and emails every day. Their emails crossed in the ether at the same second. They were pals for life, but as you've read, Dear Reader, the guy was married to his students and his boat. When Julia got well, she would move to Bayfield, she would get some sort of a job, and they would hang out like two hippies. Or maybe not.

The Ojibwa culture of Bayfield County descended from Canada into Wisconsin. They name themselves *Anishinabeg*, translated as "True People" or "Original People." Other tribes in Indian Country called them Ojibwa, referring to their moccasins sporting puckered seams. The Ojibwa people were fervent believers in guardian spirits, to call upon for protection and guidance through difficult times in life.

Julia studied about the *Midewiwin* or "medical communal religious functions" for those seeking health and long life. The Ojibwa remain on just four reservations in Wisconsin, after selling most of their central Wisconsin and Minnesota lands to the Federal Government. The Red Cliff reservation is adjacent to the town of Bayfield and great poverty persists there—amid land loss from massive sales to lumber companies, up to 90 percent of the tribal lands.

The twenty-one islands of the Apostles are a world apart from the reservation. Much remains national park property with historic lighthouses on Old Michigan and Raspberry Islands.

A Poem by Julia for Valentine's Day

Sleep Sliced Through

Sleep sliced through with drenching sweat
It is merely four good hours.
Why walk away from engagement
From simple discussion of the situation at hand.

We are here to love one another
Not to confuse happiness with envy,

201

Not to chill out from engagement.

We are here to be a little lower than the angels.
It is our right to talk and be listened to.
We are crowned with leaves of mistletoe or of so much more
We are the children of this moment in time.

We are not animals of prey
We are animals of praying powers.

We are here to love one another
Not to confuse happiness with envy
Not to run away from engagement.
On this eve of St. Valentine's Day
We are on the cusp of an early spring
In a winter of icy winds and snow
Of frozen hearts
Stuck in time past
And without benefit of counsel

Who, as the rest of the nation,
Are unavailable to take our call.

One answered it and flew to my side
A woman of valor, crowned with jewels
A saint of a lady
A ladylike saint.

Another has answered the call
In the night of pain intensifying

Of many nights of pain unrelenting
Morbid thoughts and no rest.
From suicide ideation without cease
Without hope
Without a prayer for recovery
With intensity of psychic wanderings
In a desert of thorns
Of no one hearing the call.

It is the eve of St. Valentine's Day
It is not right
It is not fair
It is not just
It is not true

To tell the patient "too bad"
"I must run, you were late"
You were this and you were that.

It is the doctor's role to heal
To be available
To a person in need
To a mother in grief
To a lady of valor.

We are here to love one another
It is a commandment
It is a responsibility
It is a need
And it is a call to answer.

We have only each other
There is so little time
Seeping through the hourglass
Through the day
And into the night.
Where pains prevail and
Where fierce winds rage
In a time of recovery
From all times past and passing
Or mourning
The marriage
The mother
The children gone off
The night chilled to the bone.

TO MY MEDICAL AND LEGAL TEAM
A Letter from Julia

First, physicians and lawyers shouldn't perhaps "practice" on us; they should be accomplished already. Hey, what an idea? A little joke before the real reason I am writing to you. Secondly, when symptoms arise, seemingly out of nowhere, they should examine what is different (new home, standing so long to pack up your life quickly, a toxic building and location near the Menomonee Valley, reported yesterday as the worst in metro area for inhaling deadly toxins), MenoSTOP, and not go straight for their playbook, one size fits all, all that jazz rammed down my throat for years now.

My whole case can be easier if people would realize: this patient's health is inverted insofar as weight, stamina, humor, ability to earn income, and a very supportive life, instead of looking first to the PDR. She hasn't really changed her eating habits, her work style, her outlook, but maybe the things around her have altered radically? Maybe we should get to the core issues more quickly? Her economic challenges? How to achieve less stress? With more kindness? I am going to stand on my head and tell the country: Inversion Theory: Making Sense in an Upside-Down World.

This theory showed up in a prior letter to you. I await hearing from you or seeing you in the office.

Sincerely,
Julia Fields

CHAPTER 7

Surprises for Niibawi

Dear Reader, there are few jobs for any senior professionals in Millennium World. The place is freaked out and getting weirder by the week— serious students can't stay in college due to debt and the stress of several part-time jobs. Businesses can't find trained employees. People can't become fathers or mothers, since they can barely buy groceries, gas, and pay for an occasional manicure. It was something terrible, another Milwaukee company closing or being bought out, like Ladish and Bucyrus, both were sold in the same week and would move operations out of state. Julia thought that people might start jumping out of windows soon, and not just stockbrokers. She had predicted the economic collapse in early 2008, before anyone had talked about it. One day amid the holidays, she had talked to a few dozen of her closest colleagues and predicted riots in the streets across the country during the winter of 2011—people frozen out by no heat, as was Wanderful in Waterbury. People losing their homes and businesses, as Julia had hers.

"It's all nonsense," she told Lefty, her trusted financial and social advisor, a pro about these kinds of things. He was a degreed expert in investments, law, and accounting, a total whiz kid. But he was worried for his clients, and it showed. He was losing weight without trying (Julia prayed for such a problem on her fibromyalgic torso). He had many clients now over the edge.

It was a total collapse of trust, of ingenuity, of people no longer using their minds for ingenuity, which had built Milwaukee, home of the nation's first kindergarten and creation of the QWERTY keyboard. There were, instead, so many fears, which perpetuated the downward spiral, as very few walked away with tens of millions of dollars or perhaps two hundred or more million dollars, from jobs in which simple buttons were pushed and for which trading on insider news was rife. They say that Milwaukee won't lose any jobs because of these colossal mergers, and it's false, and they know it's false.

All the white-collar jobs, these companies gonna keep duplicates? Julia asked Niibawi, her ever-present scribe, confidant, and captain of her ship of state, whereas Lefty dealt with her real estate, shrinking monthly.

Julia wrapped her mind around these ideas. It was winter. It totally sucked. The sky was dark at 3:50 p.m. People's fingers were falling off from dryness. Her vaporizers allovertheplace barely helped. "Okay, now what?" Julia asked herself. "It's 7:00 p.m., I've eaten, the mail is done, my clothes are out for tomorrow (especially the special underwear for Niibawi's scrutiny), and now what?" She'd read all day. She'd talked all day in meetings and on the telephone. She could call up her friend, Susan, but she'd probably be depressed about something—the weather, her fingernail breaking, her job, her lack of a boyfriend. Holy shit, Susan could really complain.

No, Julia thought, *I'm going to surprise Niibawi at his educators' conference, at a hotel in Sheboygan, just an hour's drive from Mini Mouse House.* She could probably drive that far or stop when tired on the highway, as needed. Julia decided to spring the big one on him. Years before, she had bought a lace and satin nightgown and robe, something incredible, like Greta Garbo wore, and she had never once worn it. She had bought it when newly separated, and it still hung in her closet years later. She had planned to wear it to a friend's office, just to get some fucking use out of the thing, purchased at Marshall Field's in downtown Chicago, on a whim. Their Milwaukee store was long gone, prior to the collapse of retail during the Second Great Depression. So, Julia got in the car, a shiny red VW Beetle, drove to Sheboygan, tricked the hotel clerk into giving her an extra key, and whammo, bammo, got into Niibawi's room, where she tucked herself in and took a nap. *This guy is going to go bonkers. He's not going to understand why I drove in twenty-degree weather for sixty miles to show him a tightly clinging ensemble during his annual conference about children with learning disabilities.*

It was simple, Dear Reader. Julia was going to surprise him because that is what love is: surprises, nestled among the good and bad times, flowers on Friday, dandelions on Saturday, diamonds on Tuesday, conniptions on Thursday. It is a whole series of serious things, but these things could be fun, they could produce his special, toothy smile, only for Julia, and it would be a terrific night, one they would never forget.

Twisting and turning, their lovemaking was of another world. It seemingly went on for hours, during which they consumed each other in embraces both fierce and tender. As Niibawi touched Julia, scenes of their other pleasurable delights, graced by the afternoon sun, played in her mind.

This particular afternoon, they twisted over each other's bodies and swerved into new, acrobatic positions, over and over, until Julia's mind was blown to ecstasy. No sounds but their movements on the sheets, it went on and on, and when she thought Niibawi had stopped, it was only a pause, and then more caressing of her large breasts, more sucking them, more orgasms and more orgasms. When they came to an end, Julia happened to glance at the clock. They had been together in bed for ninety minutes, precious time laced with memories for their future. Nothing like this had ever happened to Julia. *Not even remotely*, she thought, as she drifted off to sleep in Niibawi's arms.

Awakened by talking in her sleep, Julia laughed as Niibawi asked, "What?"

"Oh, that's a new thing I am doing. I wake myself up by talking in my sleep. It's crazy, I know."

He laughed and hugged her so tightly that her small diaphragm hurt. Julia's body and physical sensations reverberated amid their conversation and munching protein bars and potato chips. The lovemaking continued in her mind, the splendor of it, of him turning her over, of her moving up and down his torso, long and lean. Niibawi had climaxed twice, like a teenager, with shouts of joy. He was a venerable animal in bed, and cuddly, warm, and voracious—sometimes all of them simultaneously. He dug her. She dug him. It was late boomers' love. Simple as that.

"Let's take a shower together," Niibawi said.

"Great. I love doing that with you."

They arose from the tired bed with joyful smiles. Julia followed Niibawi into the bathroom. He handed her two perfectly folded almond-colored towels, one for her long tresses, the other for her body, which he usually dried off with random kisses. The hot water from a rainforest showerhead drenched them, one after the other, in long moments of cascading water, punctuated by using the hand-held spray and mock water fights.

"I just adore this shower," Julia said. "It's powerful, like you."

"Do you ever stop talking?!"

"Not even in my sleep."

He did not disappoint her, toweling Julia off and drenching her with kisses. Her travel kit included her favorite mix of perfumes—Trish McEvoy #9 and L'Air du Temps, a relatively new fragrance and one from her teenage years. As Julia sprayed herself, Niibawi began to kiss her lips and fondle her breasts, nipples taut and erect. He led her to their bed and climbed on top of her, ready again for their transcendent lovemaking. She realized he had decided not to go to the four o'clock session of the conference, and as the afternoon waned, he insisted that he only needed to make an appearance at the dinner and that they would order room service.

"I adore room service," Julia said.

"I rarely do it, but I really don't want to spend dinner without you. I am so glad you surprised me with a visit."

It was, sadly, to be their last time together, as passion's flames die just as surely as they arise.

About the conference: This man, this twisting-in-the-wind guy, he could never stop learning, he had read about ten thousand books, he knew hundreds of poems by heart, he inhaled these writings, he also wrote lovingly to Julia, and he drove from Bayfield in the dead of winter to LEARN *more*! To become a better pro with his students and to become someone more gifted, more talented, and more enlightened. In a time when daylight was scarce, when enlightenment was more scarce, when resources were drying up, when marriages were hung out to dry, this guy, he was something else. He was one for the books, and boy, had Julia booked him up. It was like he was an alternative psychoanalyst, and she couldn't stop talking or emailing, not for a half day, and he appreciated it. And he loved Julia for who she was, not who he projected onto her. And that, Dear Reader, is all the difference. It is love to the max, to a googolplex, as her adorable son Joshua used to say, "I love you, Mommy, to a googolplex times a googolplex, out to the galaxies and back billions of times." He had it right. That was love, unending, infinite, knowing no boundaries.

CHAPTER 8

Julia Remembers Prince Hal on His 92nd Birthday

March 5, 2015

Dearly Departed Dad,

It's snowing in Milwaukee, but spring signs are everywhere. People are out of parkas and wearing thin windbreakers. It's still light when I come home from a client, everyone has a cold and cough, the forsythia is starting to bud up, the black snow hugs the sidewalk. I am here in Bay View, where my house has no view of the bay but is surrounded by neighbors running, walking dogs, and carrying toddlers.

You wouldn't recognize the country: the economic mayhem, with Wall Street greed at its source, is stunning and grotesque allatonce. People can't find jobs, though Botticelli got an internship right out of college, in a metal fabricating studio in New York. We are back out on the streets protesting, in all fifty states, which is what it's going to take—people with guts standing up to outrageous tax cuts for corporate America and the wealthy. We're talking about 665 American families making 80 percent of all the income last year, with folks with just average experience making $1 million a year moving money around for clients, the wholesale rape of an economy where Health UnCare punishes the ill and skims off so many lives which could have been saved. It's unimaginable. A new disaster every hour on CNN and MSNBC. I supplement the crisis du jour with classical, reggae, and show tunes. 'Course, I remember you—there isn't a day I don't hear your wisdom:

Give 'em hell.

Give that truck wide berth.

You'll be back on top, Julia.

Take the farthest parking space to take more steps.

You couldn't read your large tomes any longer. I have them here and am working my way through the biographies. Remember, we wrote a condolence letter together to Arthur Miller after the death of Inge Morath—but first, we traipsed to the fine stationery store in Sarasota to purchase some good writing paper. We went three drafts over two days. Only at the end did you ask me whether you should say something about your health to your former customer. We added a closing paragraph about that. You were dead six weeks later, three days after your birthday. I can barely remember the sound of your voice and laughter. But I will always remember:

Tennis in Fulton Park

Visits to me in Oakland, Maine at camp for seven summers

Diorio's Restaurant on Friday nights

"Daddy Fix," as you miraculously could fix everything

Planting thousands of flowers and hundreds of small fir trees

Fighting with you for months to get my ears pierced

Your special shrimp and apple concoction

The way you missed your mother and wished she could see Botticelli "for a minute"

Winning two cars by beating you twice in tennis.

I've been very ill and that has changed my life. In my solitude and in my pain and grief, I have written every day—poetry, articles for the press, an innovative line of greeting cards, an Op-Ed lead piece in the Milwaukee Journal Sentinel, *and many Letters to the Editor, as you did. I am also working on a new Inversion Theory for a series of essays.*

Today is Shabbat, and it is your birthday. I know you are watching out for me, up in the stratosphere, where all your serves are aces, and there are no leaky faucets up where you are. Please take excellent care of Mom. Happy Birthday.

Love forever,
Jules

A Quick Email to Niibawi

I won't be home until past your bedtime, as I am going out for dinner. It's not a date, honey. It's just dinner with my accountant, who changed it to South Milwaukee, just a few minutes' drive for me. By the time he would get to Bay View from Waukesha, we might as well meet in South Milwaukee for a fish fry. (I did not mention I do not eat fried anything.)

Don't worry; this guy has his head screwed on right, it seems, after fifteen years of knowing 'Dennis the Menace,' but if he makes a pass, I will just run out to my car.

He ain't no you.
With abiding friendship and love,
Jules

CHAPTER 9

Julia Seeks Cures and Finds Success

J ulia stayed the course, of course, she did not quit trying to feel better. Wanderful kept telling her, "Your time is coming," and she heard Lady Jane say, "You just do the right thing, and don't worry about other people. But if you keep going like you're going, you'll collapse." Julia did; it was a series of interconnected and crippling "maladies," as Jane called them. They were unending in their Middle of the Night Terror, of nails in her feet pains, of a GI track hopelessly off track, Hal had reminded Julia, "You'll be back on top, baby" about ninety million times, in Janespeak, and he believed it. He knew his daughter was resilient, had some major league guts, would stumble, but not fall. *Ohmygod,* Julia thought one day, *were they correct?* Was she coming back? Was Niibawi right, the inestimable boyfriend, was he encouraging her because he loved her, or was he loving her to encourage her? She had a fine internal medicine doctor, the Renaissance doctor who called and checked up on Julia, who threw out failed remedies, who listened to Julia, and focused like a laser beam on Julia's GI off-track track: "*Let's cure this first and you won't collapse of pain and exhaustion, you will get well, Julia. Just a few months and you'll be fine.*" The Renaissance doctor explained to Julia about a recent University of California study that showed the biological link between pain and exhaustion. But men's testosterone protected them against muscle pain; women, however, suffered from these twin symptoms to a greater extent. Alas, muscle pain and fatigue left patients hard-pressed or unable to work or socialize. Walking to her mailbox or taking a shower was like exercise to Julia most days. Dr. Jim needed to learn more, read more reports. He was not willing to confine Julia to endless pain and exhaustion. Neither was she. There were still 12.5-minute appointments, and that was not counting the phone and paging interruptions.

Dear Reader, in a few weeks' time, along came Julia's new writing projects and high-level meetings at the American Greetings Corporation Worldwide Headquarters. They loved her creation, they called immediately, they invited her to Cleveland, One American Road, just forty-five minutes from Mini Mouse House on a little plane. *Ohmygod, don't crash, here's my big day, let's do it to it. Lefty put in a good word for me, I must not let him down.*

Another couple of big projects were coalescing, some of them in philanthropy, her passion since adolescence, some of them re the pending move to New York, and these were making Niibawi dizzy. He was getting all mixed up, but he hid it well, that Jolly Green Giant. He towered over Julia with his North Woods brain, and that affecting *aw, shucks* Wisconsin fake façade, just like Ben had (these guys in mirror image swept their eminent sophistication to the side). They weren't ever fooling Julia, but she watched them and smiled. *Good, it's all coming together. We ain't stopping. We are going to finish this marathon, bringing it home— yes, indeed. And we have the biggest protests in the history of Wisconsin coming up this very day in Madison, at its glorious Capitol, to protect public school teachers, the very vein of the state's claim to superior education, a la the Wisconsin Idea.*

As she flew to Cleveland, to distant fields, all primped in a turquoise pouf silk skirt and some new mauve shoes, Julia thought Jane would have had something to say about buying new shoes for the biggest day in Julia's writing career. "Let's knock it out, best of luck, and don't forget to take your time when answering their questions." Yes, Jane would have said those exact words. Julia got a contract to write for American Greetings, its global human relations recruiter having fallen for her charms over lunch. Oh my god, she did not eat all day, her stomach was tied up in knots in the ever-so-gorgeous American Greeting airy glass, almost silent yet bustling with hundreds of employee headquarters.

A contract.

Money enough for the next six months.

Security? Then, on the turn of a dime, it seemed that Julia had conquered fibro and Irritable Everything Syndrome. Lack of money was perhaps the worst affliction of Julia's.

A Poem from Julia

4:45 a.m.

The birds are back
Waking us up

In the dark
They find each other

Like pairs
Of lovers.

CHAPTER 10

More on Lady Jane

Lady Jane, a master chef *avant la lettre*, learned the tricks from recipe books, not classes, and made every meal an artful one, with birthday cakes in gallant shapes, such as bowling pins or trains, her perfectly poached or scrambled with cottage cheese eggs, and many foods that mere looking at will now, in Cancer World, just hasten your death with pathogens, cholesterol, and chemicals from the farms and processing plants of America. Betty Crocker was out for Jane, she found both new and old recipes from her grandmother-in-law and hauled all the ingredients up from their one-car garage, or stomp it upstairs, as she often did. Birthdays and holidays evolved many weeks in advance, and Jane wrote the invitations in Hunter Grammar (that old use of the word always made Jenny laugh) School perfect penmanship, two drafts sometimes, and always a pretty stamp, no flags or eagles in sight. Jane greeted the birthdays and all meals as a major production—it must be different, it must be elegant, but not too elegant, don't use the china or sterling, reserve that for Thanksgiving or a dinner party. And every bit of the kitchen must be meticulous before Jane could leave it for her books and her nightly shower, her head dappled with pink tape to hold her hairdo in place through the night.

Julia inherited the Party Theme of Life from Jane, entertaining everyone with Ben in their Shorewood "mansion," as Jane called it from the get-go. It was indeed large, and it was strikingly gorgeous and had lots of bathrooms, so you could crap in peace and quiet, but also a laundry shoot and a 1928 bathtub. Julia loved that for spending hours in bubble baths.

"It is good for me, it perks me up," Julia said. "And besides, my perfume bottles are stunning." Gotta have beauty allovertheplace, just like Hal and Jane, make my home a refuge, a quiet amid the storms of real life, a home as sanctuary, a place for the spirit, the art, and baubles of four generations surrounding her. But oh, the storms inside, Julia and Hal never discussed them. They went right under the Oriental or shag rugs, which Jane vacuumed seven days a week. Oh yes, Dear Reader, all evidence of dirt or mistakes or sadness, we must sweep it up. We are all fine, we are living in the sixties, and all of us are just fine. Lady Jane exclaimed, "Men, yech!" at least several times a week, and Julia could never quite understand this outburst from the lips of the raven, flirtatious beauty, who "married well" a Dartmouth College graduate, admitted during the Quotas for Jews Years. Hal was by her side since she was fifteen, devoted and stalwart. Why did she get so angry? Was it anger at her lot as a housewife and mother? Was it her anger at her parents' letting her brothers go to fine universities, while Jane went to Hunter College, costing just five dollars a year, alongside the swells, like Bess Myerson and Lauren, then named Betty Bacall? Was it the repressed memory of her pains of pregnancy, childbirth, and Jane's incapacitating periods? Julia wondered about this for the rest of her life.

• • •

The kindly but sort of on slow-forward doctors on Julia's case never knew incomparable parents as complex as Julia's, or at least they said that, who really knew? Maybe it was just a line to make you feel better, that you had survived all this crap—godalmighty—and could still get up in the morning. Julia believed it was Julia's fear turned into anger, fear of sex, a word Jane never uttered, giving Julia a book at age fifteen after she had already had a bunch of romps on the sly. "We learned all this in biology class last year, Mom," she said to her face, and never opened the stupid, glossy book. It was ridiculous, handing it to Julia instead of talking about it. "I know where babies come from, I know how not to get pregnant, I like making out, and I know I'm a damn good kisser, yes, indeedy."

Jane would storm around the house screaming bloody murder about a hangnail or a sock on the floor, she drove home twenty miles after breaking her ankle on a grizzly gray fall day at Bishop's Farms, she could be a holy terror, but she was deliriously witty, huggy, warm, and admired by a whole lot of men—the mailman Bill, her piano teacher, her brothers-in-law, and her brothers-in-fact. In fact, Hal told her constantly how beautiful a babe she was, and she didn't need to purchase $5,000 a year in face creams, body creams, eyelid creams, and toe creams. That was no deterrent. She just bought more and more of them in duplicates, afraid she would run short. Jane was, in the end, Julia thought, a shy person, withdrawn, but with a face that launched a thousand guys, erecting flirtatious comments, but just Jane's sweet half-smile, no real mirth coming back at the admirers.

"Julia, we've got to talk about periods."

"Ohmygod, I've known about that since sixth grade health class, Mom, and I'll be just fine. I'm not going to be moaning and going to bed for days and screaming up a storm like you. No way."

And it was true, as Julia tried to inform the myriad doctors that she hurt everywhere but had never missed an hour of gym class or any other class because of periods. Some dreaded diagnoses had changed Julia's response to pain, but these doctors had not known her well—they did not know the Fields' focus on determination and resilience. Julia thought, later in life, that Jane was really jealous of all of Julia's boyfriends and sexual exploits and long letters from Robert, the first dude with his hand up her. But making out was fun; it was much better than anything else. Sex was free—it was the sixties—and love was free, and marriage was stupid, Julia thought, a kind of prostitution, a weird arrangement of domestic un-tranquility. *My god, and endless dishes. Can't we eat like normal people, without an appetizer, four things for an entrée, and dessert?*

Nope. Jane loved to show off—her perfect knitting, her luscious meals, her whiz kid math, New Math or Olde Math, Jane did it all in her head. She was a genius, and none of this was obvious to onlookers. Every minute you turned around there was a letter at camp, a note in your lunch box, special terms of endearment, in jokes and puns, and zillions of toys, dolls, and clothes, and cheering on Julia at tennis—one ace every ten years—or the ultimate swoon when she met Ben. Hal said he'd never seen her happier since Julia was a pipsqueak—now there was a man to match Julia's skills and kindness. Julia remembered Jane coming in at night to comfort her during a childhood illness, and rubbing her back and saying, "Ah, ah bay bee" about fifty times in a row. Julia tried to get guys to lay atop her back to recreate that motherly warmth, that comforting weight, and maybe they could squish some weight off her, ever envious of Susan Stein and her bod, a size 6, or even a 4 in her wedding dress, what a sight. Jane hugged and kissed Julia a lot, she was all over her, it was a BIG HUGS and tons of kisses family, and it was in a time and a space of Parcheesi® and Monopoly®, and always Walter Cronkite at 6:30, with the family's occasional wins on radio call-in quiz games, with department stores organized by items of clothing, not by stupid, flimsy designer-ish sections. It was red Keds or white Keds, and you didn't have to mortgage your house for a wardrobe when your size changed or you needed a different style in your wardrobe. "Anyway," Julia confided in her teenager friends. "Why are we spending all this money on fancy bras if we are not gonna show off the merchandise? Let's rip it off and have sex, but oh no, we cannot discuss such things, 'it would not be ladylike,' and besides, 'we hate men.'" It was nonsense to an adolescent. Jane had inverted it, Julia thought as an adult—we love men, but they hate us. They think we're their mommies, but we are not going to be covering up *forever* for their errors. We are working women, and we can do many things well allatonce, while they may have all they can do to get to and from the office, change a few light bulbs, and use the remote.

Journal Entry from Julia

It's another horrible day of symptoms, and I spent the whole day testing to see whether my adrenals are responding to the new treatments. My new internist is responsive and scientific, extremely well read in many disciplines. He suggested a new supplement for fibro. It helped me a lot in just five days, for seven dollars a vial of arnica montana from Outpost Natural Foods. Nice. No prescriptions.

All of my medical problems were and are physical. I have told the truth, though I realize some folks can't handle the truth. I fight every day and at an exorbitant cost of energy, time, and depleted finances, for my health. He seems to understand my case, knows there are reactive symptoms to toxins in home and office environments even if others diss this.

Managing the doctors is not fun. The lawyers and bankers can even be worse some days. No one calls back! I am not calling to shoot the breeze. I moved heaven and earth for dying parents' care. It is hard not being a daughter any longer and being the advocate and the patient. I coped with Jane's relentless depressions and anxieties.

I carry on with grace and courage, most days. Fortunately, I have a fighting spirit. Fortunately, the foot pain evaporated with a special new $40 insole. The $750 one from 2008 is dead as a door nail, providing no support whatsoever.

I'd welcome a legal acknowledgment of toxic contaminants as the source of my illness. Still pursuing that.

Most days I am generally cheerful about the future: be yourself and teach your children well, or in my case, teach those around me to persevere. Alice and Wendy cannot believe I have endured all this pain while living alone. Their pains of indeterminate origin keep them up half the night, but they've got retired husbands to run their households and provide companionship. "How did you ever get through those years?" they keep asking me. "We would have taken a gun to our heads if it weren't for Frank or Al." It is my redemption, hearing that, getting their acknowledgment of my triumph, alone in the thousand nights. Folks without the skills of empathy and caring will eventually lose out. While it may be difficult and uncomfortable to revisit the past, it is also not seemly to ignore it. We are what we eat, think, and feel.

CHAPTER 11

The End of Time with Niibawi

Julia had a feeling that there was something going wrong with her time with Niibawi. He was totally distracted by his students, ever more in love with his job than with her, she had come to feel and admit to herself. But, so far, their time together hadn't changed enough to break it off...that is, until one day when he cancelled their date at the last minute. This did not sit or stand well with Julia, who had prepared dinner for hours on Thursday night for their Friday night Shabbat meal. It was things like this that drove her nuts about Niibawi, despite his ever-so-charming ways, his incessant emails and texts, and his incredible indulgence of her every whim. It was a lot to give up, but it was inevitable. May as well do it now, as she had been thinking of doing it for a year or more.

There is no easy way. Paul Simon's fifty ways to leave don't cut it. Breaking up is hell, Julia thought. She couldn't do it in writing, and she was afraid to do it in person. "Christ Almighty, get some courage," she said to herself. This is not feasible in the long run, so let's call it quits now.

No way, not with his birthday next week, she decided. No way, there are parties coming up with their friends. No way, no way, a thousand excuses. "I'm through," she blurted out accidentally on the telephone. "I can't do this anymore." Niibawi screamed. He was not expecting the Lady in Waiting not to wait any longer. Julia held to her decision and told him why she thought it was over. He got off the phone and came to visit the next day, calling in sick, but it was no use. When Julia made up her mind, nothing could change her from that decision, come hell and the bath water.

It wasn't easy in the weeks and months of solitude that followed. Julia missed Niibawi's voice, his wit, his emails, his texts, and his fabulous ways of loving her, in bed and on the couch, and their secret jokes and puns. *It's tantamount to a divorce*, she thought, but then, Prince Hal had often said her breakups were like a divorce, and now, after decades, she finally understood what her dad meant. This pretty much sucks, coming home to an empty evening of nothingness and no one to call up and eat dinner with on the telephone for an hour, even with him at the opposite end of Wisconsin. Not to mention that Julia had this Herculean need to talk, and if she weren't talked out, it was hard to sleep or to focus. She lay in her bed for nights, sleeping just an hour here and there, nothing restorative, for many weeks, turning and turning, replaying their last date. Had she done the right thing?

A Poem from Julia
"Being Home"

Being home is acceptance
Moments of peace, laced with memory
Coupled with newness

Facing radiant sunrises
With pictures of those gone forever
Like the sailing winds.

Homes shift, crash, stifle under the weight
Genetic homes sting, burn, slice to the quick

Without you,
There is no
Home.

CHAPTER 12

A Letter to Julia's Women Friends

Dearest Pals,

When we spoke recently, I did not have the time to update you in full. My complex case was consistently misdiagnosed and mistreated by the "medical establishment," which for better or worse included primarily male doctors quick to judge, who over prescribed dangerous psychotropic drugs, and were even quicker to trot out newest, unproven drugs on little more than a whim. The drug companies are the only ones to promote their own clinical trials, and experience be damned. My list of medical trial and errors runs three pages long. Trust me, I've referenced all the documents from my files. The resulting damage to my career, bank account, and friendships was deep and hard. All these downers and uppers were tried by those who wanted to silence me. I just happened to be going through MenoSTOP (ha ha). I just happened to be a vibrant, passionate East Coaster, transplanted to the Midwest. We talk faster in New York, 'tis true. We are often multi-focused, creating businesses, as I did during this time of only gigs for us senior, white women. I just happened to lose the role of being a daughter, being on call to Mom, at the same time I lost my roommate and husband in the same month. I lost these roles I needed—I need to take care of others, many others.

My noble female friends, new and old, you have provided the glue for my brain and my actions through every day and sleepless night. The misery, the many simultaneous traumas of a 75 percent decline in household income, the inability to walk to the corner, insomnia, and increased trauma, all these are now receding into the horizon.

Life will be wonderful again if I encounter some good luck. This is my view on a summery Sunday afternoon.

From bed,

Love,

Jules

Sent from my Verizon Wireless BlackBerry

A Poem from Julia's Doctor
"Bleary"

Once there was a wench so bleary
All said she thought so clearly
But they had not researched clearly
What was making her so weary.
One day a gent came upon the wench
He was a saint, right off the bench.
He was irreverent, jaunty bow ties,
Twice her brains and saw more clearly.

Take this path every day:
Life is short and very searing;

Do not fret
Do not be perverse
Whatever doctors say

Do the INVERSE.

CHAPTER 13

Music as Remedy, Refuge

Along about her sixth incurable diagnosis, aside from the two left feet, and years of phony diagnoses, and her thirtieth bottle of vitamins, micronutrients, and enzyme fix-it-uppers, at an exorbitant monthly cost of $1,000, Julia had had it. She was practically in the prime of life before this saga began in 2007. Thinking about another time and another place, Julia decided one May evening to rock out and listened to these songs, her most immediate and fulfilling remedy for all this pain, she'd long ago decided: "One More Night, Gimme One More Night," "We've Got a Groovy Kind of Love," and "Islands in the Stream." And Julia blasted the sound out over Superior Street, with her perfect sound system from Beardog—it bounced off the old wood of 1904 vintage and resonated the seventies and eighties, hearkening a different time and a heartfelt, different focus: Love. Romance. Time to dance. Dance partners. She made a mix for the red Beetle, which is to say she hired her twelve-year-old neighbor to make it in thirty minutes. "Mix 'em up. Here are my very favorite CDs."

It was copied by the neighbor as a thank you gift for the Kindly Octogenarian, tied up in a silken, red bow in a box and in a large bag from Sendik's—the delightful Milwaukee yuppie mini supermarket with thirty brands of olive oil, but barely any toilet paper or cleaning products. He knew Julia's story about the Friday flowers. He knew the story of Ben getting her roses at Sendik's for every Shabbat, and the Advancing Attorney romancing Julia, his sweetest. She swooned for the roses—hey, not luxury, they only cost $9.99 some weeks—but they were her very favorite, and he never forgot, not once, and had them delivered when he was traveling.

Dreadlocks blasted his music, twirling Julia from time to time on the nonexistent dance floor in his Chock-Full of Files house. "I can't throw anything out, I might need it," he explained, knowing it was advanced bullshit, but Julia listened patiently, as taught by her Kindly Octogenarian. *Who cares? I'm getting into his groove and he into mine, and ten thousand pieces of unfiled paper and catalogs ain't changing that, no way.*

A Poem from Julia

EASTER SUNDAY 2015

We are risen into
Life and into love
In hearts stopped or continued

In life or in love
For each other.

We are steered to service
With deep wounds
From life
From God's love.

We are together, in death or in life.
We rise, to fall or falter:
We live, we love, with
Hope to soar like the first sight of spring
On Easter morning.

Rising tulips, crocuses, and snowdrops
Also fight for their
Spaces of glory
With measure.

We are risen to meet monstacles head-on,
To provide charity and forgiveness for
Each person and flower
In hope
And in memory.

Acclaiming this day as all others
For service and mere delight of flowers
Risen to glory.

(Monstacles is my 1972 neologism, combining monsters and obstacles, in case you've been wondering.)

CHAPTER 14

Confessional to Julia's Mother

Dear Lady Jane,

Mom, you've been gone nearly eight years, and it's been a daymare of epic proportions, for those of us left bereft, for your dear neighbor, Ruth, for the old guard in Heritage Village, for the folks in Milwaukee who remember your eyes and your coy, captivating allure, but especially for Pipsqueak here, it's been horrific. It's about time I fessed up: you predicted everything correctly. I collapsed from the emerging emergencies of TOOMUCHSTRESS, annuities were the best investment, and hospitals are wretched places that make you sicker, that eerie-ogenic word I could never spell or pronounce.

It's lovely to wear some of your clothes or shoes, but it's kind of horrible, too, especially when I get a stain with my first meal at a client's at eight a.m. and have to prance around like a jerk all day and half wreck your beautiful ensemble from Saks or Nordstrom.

But the Downer Cleaners fixes everything in a flash, after you mortgage your life savings.

Mom, you never met Guilford. He was your estate attorney. This guy's got class, he took me to the fanciest restaurant in New Haven last week; he's got some big brains and a big heart. He lives in Guilford, and his name is Guilford, how quaint. There was nothing simple about the simple estate, oh well. It was only money.

As for my health, where is it? Did you take it with you? I follow the Susan Stein diet, but nothing fits. People can say that I've got curves in all the right places, but it is not my cup of scotch. Scotch?! You did a blind testing and naturally could tell the difference between Bells eight- and twelve-year old Scotch. They thought you couldn't, but you aced it. Like the New York State Regents, you got a nearly perfect grade in math—they never knew someone could get a ninety-nine. The Ojibwe boyfriend, Niibawi, was something else, oohing and ahing, quite the gentle man, and so smart and literary, the guy has brains and mirth, and even if his Yiddish is nonexistent, he's a mensch. He's about seven feet tall, or at least I saw it that way for years. But it was going nowhere; it's over.

I make all your recipes and still celebrate month-long birthdays, and, of course, Valentine's Day is the best triple holiday of the year. N and I were definitely not getting married; we both work long hours, and I have enough work around here without picking up socks or scraping double crumbs off the floor. He loved twisting me around on the dance floor and was very good at everything he does, and yet, I had to break it off. No future there.

His wardrobe would have made you plotz with mirth. Do they really only teach three colors to men in Wisconsin? Do all shoes have to be brown and laced? Isn't a guy supposed to wear black socks to *work? Oh, it's not that important, it's the way it is, but guess what? He was a great friend for years. And that was a lot more than clothes ever meant, and besides which, look at all he saves at the cleaners— enough for more jewelry...hey, a girl's gotta live. I had planned to move back to New York, put a deposit down on a house, but decided against it.*

I absolutely L O V E M I L W A U K E E!

Love,
Me
Pipsqueak

CHAPTER 15

Julia Attends a Professional Hockey Game

Okay, so Julia sits there for fifteen minutes before being able to figure out which team is Milwaukee and which is Peoria, and anyway, if they play in Peoria, why are they playing in Milwaukee? The jerseys have no team names, just the players' names, but Julia cannot tell the former coach and general manager who invited her to the game that she does not know this basic detail, of the jerseys without the names of the team— he might toss you off the balcony at the Bradley Center; he might ditch you right then and there and require you to take a taxi home to Bay View. It was difficult to figure this out, until the Milwaukee Admirals scored a goal in the first period and the crowd, sort of no crowd, exploded in cheers. It could not have been a worse setting for Julia— long legs all cramped in the seat, mind-splitting noise, lights as from the Grand Inquisitor blasting her neurons, and so many children yelling their heads off.

Julia just thought about poetry and music to calm herself. She looked at the three-million-dollar, brand-spanking-new scoreboard and counted backwards with it until the period would be over. She took the Date Man's arm going down the steep stairs the first time, but he forgot about it the second and third time, so she just concentrated really hard: *Do not fall. You can do it. Remember that your legs did not used to hurt, and you did these stairs so many times before. Ohmygod*, Julia thought, but now with FibroFuckingMyAlgia, and Irritable Everything Syndrome, she weighed much more than she used to. *Am I turning into a blimp?*—just like the Admirals blimp circling the Bradley Center, another whirling dervish to set Julia's mind at stress allovertheplace. She survived. There was water to drink. There was the man with his monographed shirt. He explained some of the plays to her. It was a raucous evening.

But Julia wondered, *Would I be happier at home reading poetry and with my music playing? When will I have time to pay my bills and rest, godalmighty? Will I ever be caught up and have the energy I used to? Do the doctors know anything or am I just their guinea pig? They aren't thinking about my case, they are watching some sort of game or going to fancy restaurants, probably, or thinking about someone else's case or getting laid.* Well, it was a night out, if brief. It was "free food," but she couldn't eat anything but the salad, and it was bland iceberg, at that. It was a lot of walking, lo unto many circumferences of the Bradley

Center, which she had watched being built when Ben and she had started their life together in 1986 in Brew City. *Ohmygod, I have not been in this building in seven years. I missed the Bucks on New Year's Day, couldn't go out two days in a row, must rest, must wear a nightgown, must putter around Mini Mouse House and cook great food for unknown guests, must work on my health, try to find it in a cupboard, in a book, on the telephone to the Medical Team of Fine Repute (unlike the Bank), must do the* Sunday Times *crossword puzzle, must rearrange everything in the tiny house so one doesn't fall down on the three socks left out or the plants going gangbusters.*

Dear Reader, Julia was a champ. She went for broke. She did anything once, but this Admirals thing—*maybe next time we sit in a box. I mean, you ran the team for thirty-two years; come on, let's have a little comfort and our own toilet. We can still watch the puck from there, right?* At least the Admirals won. We taught Peoria Riverbend a lesson: don't come to Milwaukee expecting to win. We've got the Brew City advantage, even though our crowd is filled with obese people to the max (so Julia's medical team doesn't really feel her weight is a problem). *Fine,* Julia thought, *I'm sending the doctors the bills for clothes that fit.* That's right. It was spring in Milwaukee, and Julia had a trip to New York City coming up—*a girl needs a basic black suit, fer Chrissake, and a few other trinkets to show off her Lady Jane legs, gotta keep the fellas comin' by.* As for clothes, half Julia's possessions were in a storage unit in Cudahy, four miles away, but it might as well be on Pluto, as you must hire men and a truck and, organizing that?...you may as well schedule four dates, as

249

they will cancel or forget at least once, or the truck rentals will be "unavailable," as the Handy Handyman will wait until the final second to call. And then, when you get there, no one can find what you need, fifty boxes are jammed to the ceiling, and the labels are all facing away from view.

Oh well, it's possible these doctors did care, but they were overloaded with three million pieces of paperwork from the insurance companies, whose thirty-five-dollar co-payment really wasn't worth it, everyone filling out forms and placing Forever stamps and quadrillions of emails and statements that were often false. They were probably doing the best they could with Julia's intransigent, seven-year case from hell. And they also had to fight with the lawyers, don't get 'em started, they will never look at your medical history once they start on the lawyers. These medical professionals had not gone to the Lady Jane Medical School, so what would you expect? There were no get-well wishes at the end of a visit or phone call. They knew Julia was incurable, and Julia was doing so much better than her other co-sufferers. They often never looked at the patients, but at a computer, and they probably were also sick, as was nearly everyone in Millennium World. Or their wives or girlfriends were sick, or their parents were dying, or their children were following in their stead, attending eighty-thousand-dollars-a-year medical schools, blow the roof right off Boomers ever retiring. Many Boomers had their children so late, they will be working until at least seventy-two or seventy-eight years of age. Really, what's Julia's seven-year stint of insomnia and pain? They could not define it, they could not cure it, and they started looking at their watch at 12.5 minutes into the appointment, if they did not get interrupted for two or three phone calls before then. There was never enough time to listen to Julia. She had written down all her questions the night before, but the docs, some of 'em, they just wanted to schmooze her, it seemed. Had they ever known chronic pain? They had certainly not lived through it alone, Julia realized, each of them sporting a shiny wedding band. And, most importantly, no one had robbed them of the remainder of their lives by saying, "This is all I can do. Sorry. Your neurological pains are multi-factorial and idiopathic and cannot be solved." *THANK YOU SO MUCH, MAYONNAISE CLINIC! For this, I could have stayed home. I at least had the illusion I was on the road to recovery. What?! Never recover?!*

Julia's world was shrinking around her head like a vice, the possibilities for her future life, love, and work seemed to go *poof!* in a microsecond. *They cannot mean this, there is no cure, it is all genetic, so, dammit, blow up these genes, give me my life back, and stop the torrent of money for doctors and their pills*— which seemingly to Julia, produced more ills, and blew her up to a dreaded size sixteen. Soon, she would no longer be able to window shop at the exquisitely appointed Aversa in Bayshore City Center? Shop therapy was not listed in the *Physicians' Desk Reference* book, but Gretchen and Jean and Patti and David and Jon and Mary treated her kindly, knew she was definitely not there to purchase the $2,000 dresses, and they knew that if Julia saw something she liked, even if it didn't fit yet, it would fit soon. Julia was there for the third markdowns at the end of the season or the more moderately priced items, newly available in the Second Depression.

Godalmighty. A whole wardrobe to deduct on her tax return as medical costs. Sure, why not! It was necessary; Julia could not appear in public in her bathrobe. Although, she once wore the lavender one, under her coat, to an appointment, fulfilling a double dare from Essex. Julia would do anything, Dear Reader, for a laugh, even with her multiplying illnesses and issues. Maybe not every day, but once in a while, she just had to go for broke, mess up people's minds, and tell a rip-roaring tall tale (they, by the way, did the very same thing), but they did not expect Julia, so educated, so in control, to tell a white or any other color lie. *Fukitol,* she thought. *That makes me want to do it more often, blow their minds a wee bit.* Anyway, the doctors would have seen her in a bathrobe if they still made house calls as in the 1960s, which made a tremendous amount of sense to Julia's way of thinking.

CHAPTER 16

The Prince of a Guy Passes into Beyond

here were many niceties, Dear Reader, that defined Prince Hal, and these were observed and remembered by no one except Julia. There was the momentous challenge that if she ever beat him in tennis, he would buy her a car. One Labor Day weekend in 1979, they were playing a tough set in Fulton Park, Waterbury's finest, designed by the premier American landscape architect Frederick Law Olmsted who also designed Central Park and Lake Park in Milwaukee. Abundant trees, elegant firs eighty feet tall, surrounded the courts, which were empty that Sunday, just the two of them slugging it out. The score crept up to six to five, Julia's advantage, and suddenly, there was no more small talk at the net when they changed sides, there was no more "good shot" when Julia hit them. There was now an eerie silence, empty of Hal's nice remarks thrown her way for good shots. *Finito*. It was serious business now. They arrived at the final point, and Julia had her dad 40–15. She served a winner, and Hal hit it back, but into the net.

With his huge, toothy smile, Hal met Julia at the net and said, "Congratulations. I'll buy you a car when you can afford the insurance." Well spoken, as Julia then lived in Manhattan and had no use for a car. The parking would cost as much as her three-hundred-and-eighty-dollars-a-month one-bedroom apartment, with twenty-four-hour doorman on the Upper West Side—the carotid artery of the civilized world. It was just a two-hundred-foot walk to the bus or subway, which city folk now call the train. It was a different city with people living alone, with apartments priced to one-quarter of one's earnings.

Julia beat her father at tennis, finally, after twenty years of Hal's lessons from the age of eight and many games of singles in Waterbury, in Longboat Key, and on their favored Lake Park courts in Milwaukee. When Julia moved to Milwaukee, Ben didn't believe the story. But then, he had only known Hal a short time. "My father's word is his bond," Julia said. And sure enough, sharing Ben's Passat was satisfactory for only about two weeks.

"You better get a car," he protested. And, so, she did, picked out a shiny red Celica, her first car, at age thirty-five, two weeks after moving her life's possessions to Milwaukee for a new chapter of her life. And Hal sent the check, just like Julia knew he would, once she purchased the car at Andrew Toyota, a car dealer with a heritage, also a second-generation family business, with class and customer service at all times. Julia seemed to remember everything about her life, her family, her friends, what she wore to a certain occasion, phone numbers, and birthdays. Ben nicknamed her "the walking encyclopedia." But she could never remember the circumstances under which she won a second car at a different tennis match. She tried hard, but it totally escaped her; it had blown away. Nevertheless, the second car was a minivan, teal blue, better for hauling their soccer and camping gear here and there. Hal again simply put the check in the mail, as promised. It blew Ben away.

Years later, when her father lay in terminal cancer pain, Julia found the words one day needed to ask Hal to tell her where their money was invested, how did they deal with his pension, all sorts of things that he had never explained, because, Dear Reader, Hal was gonna lick cancer. He told the doctors: "You don't know me. When I am down 5–love, I come back and win 7–5." And that was true, up to a point. The first words out of his mouth were, "I have fulfilled my obligations to the Jewish Federation and United Way." Hal was a quiet philanthropist, who also took care of many individual people in need, such as a cousin fallen on hard times, Jane's alcoholic brother, the wonderful Wanderful, and elderly neighbors in Connecticut who wouldn't drive in the snow—he'd ask them what they needed at the store if he was going. But not that day in Fulton Park. "Dad lost, fair and square, believe me," Julia said. "He did not give me one point."

On March 8, 2002, when multiple cancers ended his seventy-nine-year life, or as he phrased it six days before—

on that final Saturday when Julia was there to say goodbye forever—"Dr. Moore, I have had seventy-eight years of good luck, and a year of catastrophes." For once, Hal was not exaggerating a single Seabee bit. Yes, he wanted to begin hospice care, right there and then, without discussing it with his high school sweetheart. He died six days later.

This memory cruised Julia's brain daily, as only she had witnessed his decision. When Doctor Moore left the half-room assigned to Hal, he turned to the subject of Julia's return to Milwaukee, as her plane was delayed for three hours, due to weather.

"Baby, you are so near your goal," he said, meaning that Julia had spent two weeks in Longboat Key, caring for him and the ailing Jane, and that she had managed everything in a New York minute, making all the arrangements for their hasty departure from Longboat Key and from Sarasota Hospital whilst fulfilling her client obligations, packing up their clothes, emptying the fridge, and securing the apartment at Bayport for the next winter, one he would never see.

"Yes, I will be leaving for Bradley Airport in a few minutes," Julia said, knowing that the final goodbye to a living poppa was imminent.

"How are you getting to Bradley?" Hal asked, barely able to move his head or get the words out.

"Cousin Melody is driving me."

"Where is she, babe?"

"She's standing out in the hall."

"Tell her to come in and stand at the foot of the bed."

Melody was a fine and empathic niece, she was the kindest and most devoted one, and she stood just where Hal wanted, and they, too, had their final goodbyes.

When Julia kissed her dad, she gave him a strong bear hug, Fields family style. She smiled glowingly, with tennis matches, trips to Sarah Lawrence, Stowe, and visits to camp in Maine all a blur in her mind. She was stolid, that Julia. *Show him I can take this, the final goodbye kiss,* she thought. As she walked into the barren hall, wallpaper peeling, the air filled with Hal's roommate's screams for help, Julia burst into drenching tears that lasted all the way to Bradley and all through the Art Garfunkel concert that night at the Marcus Center. She barely heard a song.

The *Waterbury Republican American* published a front-page headline of Hal's two-page obituary the following week: "Business Leader's Death Ends Era." Before Prince Hal was gone, he had celebrated his final birthday party in bed, Jane feeding fine strawberry shortcake into his nearly closed mouth, with eyes already gone under. Their sixty-two-year romance was ending in a drug-induced silence, accepted by his two brothers and his beloved Chinney, his tennis partner and personal and corporate attorney, there to celebrate the seventy-ninth birthday of a Waterbury native, heroic and stalwart champion of his family, his family business, friends and neighbors, and his beloved Lady Jane.

He spoke of his diseases rarely, and of his immanent death only to Wanderful: "Promise me that if I don't come back from Florida, you will take care of Mrs. Fields," as they loaded the final suitcases into the car.

"Of course, you don't have to worry one thing about that, Mr. Fields," Wanderful replied. "I'll be here for her."

Death, taxes, money, or sex—these subjects were verboten to Julia's parents. They were private matters too hurtful to discuss among family. They were only whispered in a cold garage in Southbury with doom and gloom—not in Hal's lexicon, not to be shared with the fragile Jane, but only with Wanderful, who revealed them privately to Julia. He knew he was dying, but he never said one word about it to Jane or Julia, who recoiled from the subject.

It was a time and a place of mind speak, silent utterances.

And that is exactly what happened, Dear Reader.

• • •

Mattatuck Museum Auditorium

Julia's Eulogy to Hal

March 10, 2002

Dad, Harold, Mr. Fields, Monk—these are all names we have used to honor the man whose life we celebrate today. You led an exemplary life, cut short by cancers at seventy-nine years plus three days, sixty-four of them with your beloved Jane. You were a warrior until the last week of your life.

You exemplified daily all that is good and worthwhile in a human life.

Hal the optimist—he looked at a cup as three-quarters full and less than one-eighth empty.

Hal the detail man—my father recounted the experiences of any given afternoon or evening with references as far flung as engineering, mathematics, plumbing, art, The New York Times. *Invariably, he cited these references in full detail—of his parents, of the Seabees, and to his beloved Jane and to me on the proverbial Ma Bell invention of the "one-minute long-distance call." His lasted a minimum of thirty minutes.*

Hal the father—you always sang me a miserably off-key "Happy Birthday" on every birthday, even during junior year abroad in Paris. You were the father who drew Chanukah menorahs or birthday cakes on every check or card I received.

Hal the athlete—we played mixed doubles on my birthday last year, and you continued on, three sets a day, three days a week, until March first.

Hal the helper—to everyone you met, to your widowed neighbors in Heritage Village and in Bayport, and to the many people in my life in Milwaukee, including your tennis and sailing partners in Brew City.

Hal the father—you taught me to "Do it now." "To work like hell and to play just as hard," that "Life can be so beautiful," and to remember that when it is not, to use the grand metaphor of them all, "Racket back, eye on the ball, and follow through."

Hal the bridge player—you went out on a grand slam in our last game in December, even though you had to finish from a standing position, legs swollen to elephantiasis from lymph nodes.

259

Hal the traveler—seven am to the tennis courts, applying one final dose of SPF 45 on your beleaguered nose. A shell and glass collector on long beach walks, you arrived at Longboat Key on December 11, optimistic that you were "in paradise," despite chemo twice a week.

Rest in peace now, Dad, in God's final paradise.

CHAPTER 17

Years Pass as Julia Continues to Seek Solutions

October 12, 2016
Yom Kippur Morning

Dear Renaissance Doctor:

As a linguist, I am pretty good at comparing prefixes and roots of words:

So, try this on:
Hypoglycemic: yes
Hypercritical: yes
Hypertension: yes.

Hey, some of my team at least got the prefix right—how about that, nine hundred visits later, too many pills, causing hypertension and weight gain while eating the same food and exercise when I possibly could. "Oh, Julia, I am sure you can cut back on your caloric intake, and you can exercise more." You try exercising when everything hurts, and you are exhausted from just getting ready to leave the house.

Right. I followed the Susan Stein/Dr. Patricia Dolhun portions diet for the first fifty-three years of my life, and then wham bam, *started on sleep "aids" and some other doozies, gaining fifteen pounds in two years eating and exercising the same, while living in my marital home and eating all meals with others, and similar weight gains every two years thereafter. Terrific. Blimpo City. At that time, I was doing 100 daily crunches and ate only 1,200–to 1,500 calories a day for ten weeks. I seem to have lost weight only in my wrists, already small enough for my schoolgirl bracelets from the sixties. And those medicines brought on Julia-cidal depression, just like the interminable warnings state.*

My blood pressure was always low until the Pills Ills began in 2005. Your predecessor internist said that's why I must take Valsartan until the end of time. It is at least covered by the Semi-Affordable Care Act of Mr. Obama. Hey, it's something!

On this Yom Kippur morning, when though I have slept nine hours, I am dead tired, due to chronic pain and the exhaustion of being both the nurse and the patient, here is my final word on the past nine years. I have no ride to synagogue, and besides, I am already kaput at eight in the morning. Unless I stop showing up where I'm expected, no one can understand my pains unto the heavens and utter exhaustion.

In 2008, I presented to El Shrinko as a determined, if combative patient, eager to redress the permanent neurological damage caused by The Loft to Die For and to Die From's chemical exposure to perchloroethylene (also called "perc") from all the dryers vented inside for months from all the lofts and the air exchange recirculating that fetid air among thirty-five homes. I was also exposed to methylene chloride, from the polyurethane dust from the two coats layered on my great Great Room, which dust was swept into the floor vents, also recirculating methylene chloride 24/7 in the loft. M.C. affects the central nervous system. The EPA has finally proposed a rule to ban it, which its manufacturer is naturally lobbying against. Fibromyalgia is an over sensitization of the central nervous system: You taught me that. And so, on top of that, I have C. N. S. disruption, via chemicals 24/7, since I lived and worked in the same space. It only takes a couple of months to wreak havoc, as we now know. Some say the toxins would have washed out of my body long ago. That is definitely incorrect, as the nerve damage is permanent.

Going back, sciatica was diagnosed in 1972, when I lived in Paris. The next back event was spinal stenosis, first diagnosed in 2001. It has worsened with each successive move forced by financial downsizing. I have charted my well and sick times during these past nine years: packing up fifteen hundred books and sixty pieces of art will do that to a back in middle age. Plus unpacking all the stuff three times. The pinched nerves at services last night drove me out of my mind, but okay, it was Kol Nidre, so I made it through.

I lost two close friends/male clients in August 2007 and November 2007, but the latter, who consulted with me two hours a day, as his surrogate shrink—from his Highland Park driveway to his St. Luke's parking space—that loss hurt me deeply. He could not get treatment or diagnoses for months even from the hospital where he worked. Then, whiz, stomach cancer, and Dick was gone in ninety days. A great loss of a senior exec, who was new to town, so I taught him the ropes about nonprofits and the donor community.

As is often the case, where lonely marriages, his second, prevailed, he needed to vent to someone else about work. Those two contracts provided very ample income and security, without which no trial separation was possible. Then, in late October, the tender words, at eleven o'clock, after my three-day business trip to D.C. and private two-hour deep talks with Essex and the Goodly Senator (the godfather for the marriage, pleading with Ben at Elsa's to get off his duff and marry "that gorgeous lady" [130 pounds] from Manhattan). No one, including Lady Jane the prior week, dissuaded me one half an iota from a trial separation. The Fields had become Ben's new family, Jewishly, affluence-ly, and a shower of love, East Coast style and not buttoned up, as in the Midwest. We got married at thirty-five and forty for the first time. My brother-in-law, Beardog, has empathized with me. He thinks he has Lyme, is in constant shooting pains, like me, but I tested negative for Lyme.

As referenced in our appointments, during a brief vacation in November 2007, my new great room floor was polyurethaned, but only in February was it discovered that the HVAC vents were still loaded with the polyurethane dust swept up after each coat. I was already deathly sick from neurological and other damage once I spent a full month there, following mom's Shiva. *As you may remember, my mom died on her seventh day in ICU, her first hospitalization since a 1965 goiter operation. I pleaded for a private nurse, but you know hospitals, these quasi-military operations, they are sure they know best—when she goes to a private room, fine, okay, then, but here in ICU, she has plenty of help, just a call button away. Her male doctors were another group of choice Boomers who, unlike you, are dismissive of real pain, not knowing labor, childbirth, and forty years of menses. They get a hangnail or a headache, and you hear about it for days on end (joke). I was on my feet for six hours a day at the ICU and repaired all the broken things in my mother's apartment, in case a miracle happened and she came home. I continued to run my business, and cleaned out and reorganized her seven closets—yes, more physical stress, more packing and unpacking.*

Then, three herniated discs were diagnosed by the kindly Indian doctor in Savannah-la-Mar's clinic in late January 2008, when two Julias shared a room in Negril. Caribbean docs are quite expert, and that one, from India, used no machines, just twisted my legs this way and that, as I screamed bloody murder.

Jane had come back for twenty-three years, after a brain dead reading from a massive overdose at age sixty. That hospital also made the wrong call, but Hal refused to pull the plug, and she woke up five days later.

So, on this Yom Kippur, I recognize that you and others have spent inordinate time on my case. My co-author, as well, even on Saturday nights, with calls to and from Jamaica last summer. But, other than her, none of you knew me when I was well, tout simplement. *You thought of my high gear, high executive function as a diagnosis, rather than who I am. My mother-in-law, may she rest in peace, always said, "Julia, you must have an extra gene." She should only see me now in slow mo.*

You certainly did not know the genetic lineage of the genetically hyper Fields clan of Waterbury, all within four blocks, four brothers, eleven grandchildren, grandfather and grandmother off the boat, with just one suitcase and no ability to speak the language. Grandpa had a solo show of his paintings at the ACA Gallery on Madison Avenue in the 1950s, in his sixties, after building a plumbing and

265

heating supply business from scratch, beginning in 1917. And my grandmother, illiterate, held the family together, with the wisdom birthed in immigrant survivors of ninety-hour workweeks in sweatshops in Lower Manhattan.

"You are very resilient," my father said ninety million times. "But, hey, Dad, how about having someone here to help me out?" I am operating on an eighth of a tank, as I keep telling you, since you asked to take over my case. Off all the benzos. I sleep great every night, but my energy is fizzling after two hours puttering around. Of course, I now have hyper-angst about going through another period of low-earned income, my fifth time since November 2008. These are directly correlated with severe depression/hospitalizations that I now realize were from male doctors locking me up, shutting me down, hospitalizations that cured or solved practically nothing and created exorbitant bills. Obamacare covers only so much.

And by the way, we all know that male depression is very differently played out. The hospitals had 90 percent females, but the men who are driving us "crazee"? They are drinking, on drugs, yelling at us maybe, running around with women or men. No one is sending them for behavioral health treatment, much to the country's detriment.

So, again on this Yom Kippur morning, I forgive the harsh on my bod medicines you and others prescribed to me: some were EXTREMELY helpful in calming autonomic neurological damage from horrible, creeping spinal stenosis and rheumatoid arthritis, from Bertha Stern—would not inheriting her heirloom jewelry have been enough? Why did I need to inherit this, too, dammit? Some meds worked for better sleep, briefly. They all made me F A T and, with plantar fasciitis and three Morton's neuromas diagnosed in January

2008, the extra weight was killing my feet, naturellement. *With those meds, there goes your sex drive, 'course there are no available men in Milrideee in the first place, but a girl's got to dream, doesn't she?*

In my solitude, I worked hard on finding new writing voices.

I have learned to L O V E *my solitude, playing my* mélange *of music—reggae, rock, and classical, as I work.*

I have learned the power of prayer in the hard times, a true comfort.

I have adopted the power of gratitude for what I still have—the resilience, the fortitude to get to the bottom of my health issues, and to be at the new top of my game, if in a diminished state.

I have seen the enduring power of my parents' and my grandparents watching over me, through many hasty treatments and advertent (there should be a complement to "inadvertent") diagnoses. You may recall that I had a traumatic recovery from tonsillectomy at age five, two weeks alone in the hospital. I got braces way too young (at age eight, Jane insisted, therefore, exposure to mercury toxins at a tender age). The foul Waterbury air and water: Bury the Water! A stabbing at twenty-two in broad daylight before Central Park was dangerous in the morning. It was within spitting distance of Sixty-Eighth and Fifth; you know the rest….

Together, we used the victorious patch medicine for depression, Emsam—despite the surgeon's and the anesthesiologist's heinous crimes against me during the last ECT—she did have one good idea. I now have the mental acuity I admired in my Ben from our 1986 first date, in which he proposed BEFORE the appetizer, beating Jerko #6 in the City (who proposed after one long weekend of dates, also, that one, a blind date). Now, amazingly, I can sit sooooooooo long that I get very stiff because I am so focused. IT IS A MIRACLE. Me? Sit still for hours?!

I cannot sit in a play, movie, or concert—went to three last weekend—without falling asleep…. I cannot do it, but I can read or write for hours on end, a blessing.

Acceptance of chronic pain has taken me years, but I still fight the pain signals every day.

Acceptance of these DISUNITED UNITED STATES? I fight it every day with my community-building, writing for clients.

Spinal stenosis to Beat the Band and the Hands, all numb, no small motor facility, I drop everything, broke a stunning apple jade bracelet of Jane's yesterday, one bought at Gump's in San Francisco in an inimitable Hal-we-must-commemorate-trips gifts. I do NOT CARE anymore what we name these: What the hell are S O L U- T I O N S?! Give me some protocols. Geez, Louise.

Vasomotor Rhinitis, thank you family quackity quack doctor.

Ankylosed teeth: two horrific oral surgeries at fifteen; more mercury, braces reprise.

There are Julia-cidal Depressions. They come up like a hurricane. As you well know, the brain is the most important organ, but if you have therapy in MKE, you must not talk about it. That is very early twentieth century, don't you agree? I am not afraid of dying, 'tis true: I am afraid of living! My dear, there is no Healthcare Worth Its Pills in the "affordable" uncaring society.

With American sloth and rudeness (some of your nurses, who need a good woodshed talk—we are old enough to be their mothers or grandmothers); they should not act snippety because they hate their jobs. *We are there because we are S I C K. We do not want to be in your offices, sorry, Charlie.*

You wisely recommended I create a five-year plan. Here it is:

1) Develop more clients.

2) Will weigh 120–130 on my forthcoming sixty-fifth, look and think like forty-fifth birthday—THERE IS NO STOPPING ME WHEN I DECIDE SOMETHING. BEN IS THE VERY SAME, but women? Ohmygod, if we do it all, career, marriage, social engagements, then we are Manic Mondays. How goofy. Boomer women, we all did it all, we overdid it, no one can do it all.

3) Will go to India, spending $$$ on that instead of on a party.

4) Try to take four vacations a year; should satisfy my need for a calmer, more pro-active, more sophisticated mindset than gun-slinging America—and hey, the docs did not ever suggest that I should take a vacation from 2011–2016. Oy vey. Not once.

5) Finish my two book projects. Get them published.

6) Self-publish by fall 2017—at least the novel; maybe write a second edition of the women's health book with Pat, who claims there is a mystery re women's weight, as many of her patients do exactly what she says and do not shed an ounce.

So, dear Renaissance Doctor: How do you take a healthy fifty-five-year-old and destroy her health? *Please, slow down and read this twice:*

You take away her ENTIRE local support system

You do this in 60 days

You knock off Lady Jane about five years too early

You create monstacles, knocking her down, here and there, Banks of Ill Repute or the Non-System of Health Uncare.

Renaissance Doctor, I cannot explain to you the trauma of the second parent to die. Horrific. Be careful. Do not work yourself to death as I did.

You have all the supports of a successful marriage, children in town, and especially daughters, and a zillion other things. A big reputation (deserved), and no creepy people breathing down your neck.

This, my dear Dr. Renaissance, is my very last letter. If you want to know the test results from my mammogram cum lymph test Thursday or the EMG the week after or whatever goddamned other thing will happen next, you have my phone numbers.

It was a total pleasure being your patient.

Blessings and gratitude for all your hard work from June 2011– September 2016,

Julia

POEM FROM JULIA
"These Graces"

These graces
These noble spirits
And tenacity
Taught since childhood

To never stop trying to figure out
Where it all began
And to restore sanity, some glimmers of it.

Outside these windows

270

Providing community to common folk
Seeking work, and mere blocks away—
The need for cash for food!

II

We all want for more mothering
So we marry them, reproducing
Lost   unperceived   warrior
Childhood struggles.

It is very deep to learn to listen and argue and
fight and still love our mates.

III

Millennium World:
Male fumbling and incessant turmoil
Goes underground   undetected.
It leaks out in other ways,
Unlike women's rage.

Little counseling, shrinking, or therapies of any sort—
Gotta keep up their pristine
Images at all costs

Even if it costs the marriage or
Children's missed dinnertime tales
While at work.

IV

The second parent to die is
An entirely different death
Than the death of the first.

Some restart child's play
Run the show and the table,
In an inversion of roles.

V

It is the Boomer Men
Deprived of deprivation:

Suddenly
In male MenoSTOP (it is o v e r, not paused)
They wimp out.

Tired, and with reason,
They cave.

In temper tantrums
Of epic proportions

Beyond law

Beyond caring.

CHAPTER 18

Things Reconsidered in Julia's Psychoanalysis

There were two date rapes, one in early 1972, another a month later. There was no concept of date rape, especially in the hippie and post-sixties world of the 1970s at Sarah Lawrence, Villanova, maybe also at Yale. It was a world of allatonceness. It was the twenty-first century version of hookups, but it caused pain, it left women with illusions of relationships, of initiation to friendships or sex, of living, studying or traveling together.

And the date rapes left lasting scars on Julia. These scars were deep-seated. They popped up only in 2016 when, during her profound psychoanalysis with the Kindly Octogenarian who truly listened, was there for her, no monkey business. This dude in his splendid collection of colorful silk bow ties, tied anew each morning, and suits, as doctors ought to be, in Julia's view—was there for her.

Doctors were not supposed to dress casually for serious business. *Was it perhaps, now, their view that lifesaving work was just business casual?*

The Kindly Octogenarian had a different vantage point.

For two entire sessions, he just listened.

"Aren't you going to say something?" Julia asked at the end of the second session.

"I am going to listen a bit more," was music to her ears; it was the best thing a doctor had said in a decade, rather than rash conclusions, drawing parallels that were askew, did not pertain to her case, were not the sources of her pain. *A man who listens?* It was Julia's heart's desire, a trait so infrequently found in Millennium World, where the telephone had taken a last-row seat to instant and overlapping texts, emails, and deletions, unread so-called communications.

When the K.O. finally spoke, his scarce words rocked Julia's case to completion. "You are living in solitary." "Your mother did the best job she could do, but no mother can do it all." And the clinker, "You have terrible anxiety, and that is an exhausting way to live."

It was enough for years' more work, but their time together grew short. Kindly had announced his retirement in May, and there would come an end to these tranquil resolutions of trauma and anxiety and, inevitably, the last appointment. Their work included years of Julia teaching Kindly some Jewish humor, so often misunderstood in Smallwaukee, its ironies mistaken for rudeness or brashness, as Julia had learned as a transplanted New Yorker.

Julia delved into these profound diagnoses and mined them in her work and in her weekly studies to train as a lay psychoanalyst, yet another new potential career in the gig economy. She traipsed through her life to see where the traumas originated and shared the events with Kindly.

"Open marriage" and "free sex" sounded arcane in Millennium World, but they were actual and created deep wounds in Julia. She knew about hushed voices in the living room while she was ill with rheumatic fever at age ten, discovering that the Doctor Who Makes Us Sick was spending hours talking to Lady Jane, not making his next house call. She now knew what caused a rupture with her mother for fifty years, until the about-face apology in Longboat Key, an apology that opened their vistas to intimacy, trust, and five glorious years of talking late into the night at their West 52nd Street hotel in New York, at beaches in Montauk, after concerts at Tanglewood, and hours spent in the Lenox, Massachusetts storied knitting shop. A mother's love abridged, now explored, took hold of Julia during those last years as they rediscovered each other in clarity born of communication across the phone lines and in reams of ordinary letters and cards.

Julia discovered her unconscious anxiety with Kindly's pointing her in the right direction and with the Renaissance doctor slowly removing the benzodiazepines that had brought on horrific insomnia—with not a dream or REM sleep for many years. Their paradoxical effects on

Julia had left her sleeping just an hour here and there, no real sleep, and the lack of sleep made her anxious to her core, unable to work, write, or read. The benzo withdrawal was difficult, but it ended in a few months, and with it came restorative sleep. As throughout her case of a decade, medicines that did not work were seldom deleted by her medical team until Julia pushed the issue forward.

"Why am I taking all these medicines?" she implored over and over again. "They are not working! They are having the opposite effect on me."

Through her own research, Julia found one medicine she had never taken for fibromyalgia—and Kindly deemed it a trusted, old medicine with few side effects. *Bingo!* Gabapentin worked to relieve her fierce fibromyalgia pains, like knives sticking into her legs, back, arms, and hands. But the sleep of nine hours was no longer enough. Julia fell asleep in every movie and play for years, with her Botticelli daughter and gifted son Joshua jabbing her to wake up. It took six months to obtain an appointment at Stanford Medical Center where the chair of the Chronic Fatigue Syndrome/Myalgic Encephalomyelitis Clinic had prepared for their appointment by studying the requisite Stanford "personal summary" essay and all her charts sent from Milwaukee. Julia had spent three weeks on the essay, cramming her answers into four single-spaced pages. Dr. Breditto gave her a ten-point quiz about CFS/ME, and Julia checked off nine of the ten indicators. She even squeezed in an extra ten minutes of consultation to ask all her questions, though the nurse pronounced at sixty minutes that their appointment was over. It was time for his next patient.

Miraculously, Julia's blood pressure was at its lowest in a decade at Stanford: it showed that she was relieved, had arrived at the planetary experts for Immune Diseases, as a costly last resort, to Stanford, where bro-in-law Beardog's life was miraculously saved for four more years. Breditto continued mining Julia's case with telephone calls, follow-up tests at Stanford and in Milwaukee—there was severe spinal stenosis in seven discs and nerve damage incomparable in his lone career. He prescribed new medicines for inflammation, and they worked. The pains vanished.

Months earlier, Kindly had put his head down and thought for thirty seconds. Julia thought he might have dozed off, as at eighty, he had every right to be tired, still working six days a week, while returning all pages and calls promptly, from all of his phones, even in semi-retirement, as he continued Julia's case. And he did this all without the benefit of a secretary, with the original small, white, medical appointment cards. It was non-electronic medicine in all respects. Kindly had studied under the eminent neurologist and psychoanalyst of Vienna, a four concentration camps' survivor.

"I studied for a year at the feet of Viktor Frankel. We learned about waiting for circumstances to change and how patients could learn patience, which gives way to hope."

Alas, Dear Reader, patience was not in Julia's genetic makeup. Hal and Lady Jane never rested, except on their annual, beloved Caribbean off-season jaunt to Antigua or skiing weekends in Vermont or at Catamount, that blessed snow-kissed mountain with tri-state accessibility from Connecticut, New York, and Massachusetts. They never expected her to rest, either. Life was a relentless push toward achievement, helping the less fortunate in Waterbury or wherever they were. Life was about stretching one's boundaries, getting all As, studying the piano, learning Hebrew, Sunday school for three very long hours, volunteering with the youth groups, planting hundreds of trees in Waterbury and in Torrington, marching against the Vietnam War as a family, attending Memorial Day and Veterans Day parades, true parades with early arrivals and flimsy fold-up chairs.

Rest? There was none of that in Julia's childhood or in the "dry years." Much of her reading was for classes, as Julia always took a course and taught one or two writing classes a year. Reading had now become her favorite pastime in the Decade of Disease. She explained that it was very difficult to save money in the dry years by borrowing books from a library, as Julia needed to note passages that were important, had to underline or highlight them, cataloging them as they related to her work.

With Jane and Ben gone in the same season, Julia had lost her nurturing roles in life. As her diseases ramped up, these two pillars were no longer present to take care of her—to provide the daily reflection of her day, to encourage her how to vault over the twin economic disasters, insurance, and medical care in one of the nation's most costly states, how to overcome the excruciating pain and how to survive the unslept years.

After receiving three hundred books from Jane's estate, Julia had slowly delved into them, reading many, giving some as presents. One of her three rabbis received, ever so graciously, one of Julia's grandfather's books written in Yiddish. Some received Hal's Dartmouth books that she knew she would never open like *Tess of the D'Urbervilles*, hated it in high school, was never reading it again. These books were primarily history, biography, and politics, with a few novels, but those were seven- or eight-hundred-page novels, the kind that Hal read in retirement years.

"I don't know how I ever had time to work," Julia's dad said often, as he took over doing the groceries for their neighbor, Ruth (who would outlive them both, dying the week after her one-hundredth birthday). Hal's four hundred daffodils went on seemingly forever, as did the dawn redwood, planted by Hal's brother Jerry for Jenny as a seedling, quickly reaching forty feet in the Southbury hills, the rolling landscape of Connecticut hills that Julia forever missed in the pancake flat terrain of Milwaukee.

Finally, the subject was not roses; it was about the peonies. Since they had not yet cracked through the surface in Bay View, Julia could not dig up and transplant them in her new home, an ever smaller third-post-marital, rental apartment on Milwaukee's Lower East Side with wraparound evergreen trees, nicknamed her Country House in the City.

In 2016, America was more and more a place of nothing being on the straight, of bankers and property developers evil and greedy, of promises broken allovertheplace in many businesses and homes in THESE DISUNITED STATES. It was all day long, the phone trees of anguish, calls picked up in the Philippines by people whose English was implausible, whose every word was indistinguishable, whose slowness harkened back to Lady Jane's oral history: "My life began with turtles."

She had spent summers during the war in New Jersey, picking strawberries and having her sole other youthful flirt, a football player who went off to war when the summer ended. She graduated from college, during which she had a job selling gloves at B. Altman's, wherein a crew of observers drove across the George Washington Bridge from Paterson to check out this beauty, this New York maven, this sterling example of a woman, witty, charming, and with hazel eyes to rock anyone's socks or stockings.

Hal and Jane were indeed married on Valentine's Day in 1946, adjacent to Central Park, and Lady Jane told everyone she would give birth on Valentine's Day, and so years later she did. Some had also called her crazy, these predictive powers producing anxiety to the max in others, and yet often, precisely the predicted outcome. Dear Reader, it was not psychic, it was intuitive, it was an algorithm of Jane discerning desires, facts, and observations, sifted through in lightning speed, in Fields

Time, rapid fire, without a prisoner taken, with the speed of light, with the light of the nations, with honor aforethought, it was all of these things, and Julia had inherited it, and with that, the sobriquets of malicious people that she was screwed up, cuckoo to the max, not really sick whatsoever.

"Please don't diagnose me," Julia insisted. "There is no test for that, and you are not a psychiatrist. The stress you are causing makes my FibroFreakingMyAlgia, Chronic Fatigue Syndrome/Myalgic Encephalomyelitis, and PTSD worse. Those are my doctors' diagnoses."

Shortly after the eleventh Valentine's Day anniversary with his one and only, Hal would receive a call from Arthur Miller, setting up a time for fiancée Marilyn Monroe and him to drive to Torrington Supply Company, Inc. in Waterbury to choose plumbing fixtures and appliances for their new weekend home. The family business was nicknamed "Torrington Soup" by Cousin Paul. The young actress would know both worldwide fame and penetrating sorrows, despite her many doctors' and her own desire to rid her soul of childhood goblins entrenched in her mind. Marilyn did not live even until her forties—though her image and frequent, new biographies, seemly and unseemly, multiplied in peoples' minds and on bookshelves for decades.

As Julia reexamined the times past, she recalled them all in minute detail for K.O., the one who, with his simple, infrequent sentences, knocked her case to completion.

It was, Julia thought, a very good session, she as Shrinkette, and it was going to be all right, this ending commentary. They would no doubt run into each other at a couple of funerals or Milwaukee Symphony concerts in the next decade in Smallwaukee. These memories, these actions and discussions in REAL TIME, these small steps, the emails sent, read, or tossed, these things were all-important, they brought balance to Julia's life, in a time when life was cruel to life.

Whether in a land of RESPECT, Dear Reader, in Jamaica, that church-going nation, wholly starved in a scarce economy—or in America, these fifty states torn asunder, with life for many stretched beyond the break point, its families gripped with fears, anxieties, and new twenty-first-century illnesses, the parallels and differences were breathtaking to Julia. Crime with guns was rampant in just a few neighborhoods in Kingston, which Julia had visited many times and saw its main street filled with world-class brands of shiny storefronts. Like Milwaukee, with center city crime on the rise, as well as Nordstrom and many fine boutiques, like Aversa, in its newly remodeled sterling store in Bayshore Town Center,

It had also become a nation with healthcare reform passed, in present time, taking a senator of courage, charm, and determination, whatever it took, to bring it to a vote, to closure, to provide some relief to all the Julias lacking health insurance and lacking the ability, therefore, to return to work or to meet the demands of their current jobs. Ill common folk or billionaires could afford healthcare, those who merely sought the best healthcare for themselves and their families, an ordinary occurrence in all the other Western industrialized nations.

Hey, it was something, it was a start. The nation had turned the corner and more jobs were coming online, offline, and the nation would be all right, Julia predicted, with her fervent and hourly prayers said for occurrences of empathy, of words meaning what they said, of no more walls between people, of opening up the whole country.

It was a time beyond time, with instantaneous communication posing as real communication, with fake sources repeating gossip as fact, with dreams for tomorrow eclipsed by the present need for tens of millions of Americans to survive on practically nothing. At least the red herrings in her case were gone. They would vanish like smoke, their falseness blown to smithereens, like the bridges and roads of Okinawa, where Julia's father had built desalinization plants, roads, and bridges, ones driven over by her mover, a man with a deep soulfulness, who quickly found her a pillow and a blanket among the dozens of moving boxes. Julia paid him and was ready to collapse on her assembled but unmade bed.

Julia's spirits were strengthened, not broken. Her health was evanescent, tamed at times, rent apart at others, quite unpredictably to herself and to others. Energy sometimes flowed through her like a sieve, left her strong of mind and body at other times.

Her mind was mindful of all these things, and their long years of work of unraveling her past was coming to an end, Dear Reader. It was, in deed and in fact, the very best and the very worst of all times imaginable on God's very good earth. Lady Jane's possessions, the silken scarves, the special love seat, the sterling flatware: all these possessions reached their next resting place at Julia's new home and writing studio, the small ranch-like two-bedroom apartment on Water Street, on the hilariously named "Lower East Side," with not a decent bagel within miles.

The Kindly Octogenarian looked long and hard at Julia. They arrived at the waning minutes of their last session, and it was his call, she felt, how to tie up the loose ends.

"You have turned my diagnosis into a cure, Julia."

"Really? What do you mean?" she asked.

"You have turned 'living in solitary' into joy, into your life's work as a writer, into healing old wounds and finding joy in ordinary things. You have told me your life story, and I wish you all the best."

They shook hands. As Julia walked to the car, the early, fleeting snows of November fell for the first time that season, a season of resonance. Kindly and she had delved into decades of myriad, intractable joys and pains. They had worked to piece them together, tale by tale. While together, in synchrony, the patient and doctor came to a place of healing and meaning.

Living in solitary was the diagnosis, and it spelled a distant goal. It was not a prison sentence. It was a reflection of Julia as Kindly had heard and responded to her spoken and unspoken words, all of them remembered and retold in reverent time, a time of healing.

PART III

A DEADLY VIRUS STALKS THESE UNITED STATES IN PASSOVER SEASON

CHAPTER 1

A Marilyn Poster, Recovered by Dreadlocks

A las, Dear Reader, Julia lived on Social Security and retirement funds, now depleted by eighty percent, due to the skyrocketing cost of aides, complementary medicine not covered by insurance, and prescriptions. She expected a high measure of promptness and hard work. Some helpers, like Dreadlocks and Lisa, appreciated that. Others ripped her off, plain and simple.

Dreadlocks was a stalwart, had stood by Julia's side since 2010, the day she moved in next door to him. He drove her to dozens of medical appointments, as only he could drive, slowly and carefully in a time of everyone rushing everywhere. *Where in hell are we? Will we ever get there?* Julia often wondered, as they perused local streets unknown to her, even after decades of life in Milwaukee.

"I drive like an old man, I know," he said with a twinkle in his iridescent, blue eyes.

One day, he brought her a surprise, quite unlike Dreadlocks, so surely predictable in actions and habits.

"What?! You found my poster of Marilyn Monroe?" Julia shrieked. "Where was it?"

"It was in my storage locker up in Oostburg. I cleaned the dump out last weekend and thought you would like it back."

"I gave it to you?! I don't think so, Dreadlocks."

"Well, you did, as you thought that you wouldn't have enough space on Water Street for it. Here are a couple of other pictures that were hidden way in the back of the dump." He handed her a poster of Jerusalem, tinged with gold leaf, and a small painting by a friend.

Julia reached up and gave him a bear hug. "Thanks so much. I do have places for them, or I will just take down a few pictures."

Seeing Marilyn's face and flirtatious pose brought back memories of meeting her in 1957 in the eighteenth-century Connecticut farmhouse that Prince Hal had specked for new plumbing and heating supplies. The World's Most Famous Actress was Hal's often told tale, as it also became Julia's. Now, the poster would greet her every morning. It, like Lady Jane's clothing, china, silver, and jewelry, was part of Julia's home, successive ones, as the mighty press of medical and economic disaster ground on to her renting smaller and smaller apartments. Many pieces were sold to pay for astronomical medical costs, at pennies on the dollar.

In the end, Dreadlocks was her truest friend in Milwaukee, a giant of heart and mind, a keeper, that Dreadlocks. He spent the winters up in Oostburg, a hamlet of Sheboygan, reading, playing music, and fixing up that house, as he had through his profession revamped many hundreds of houses throughout metro Milwaukee and his home in Bay View, top to bottom. Like his mind, Dreadlocks' work was meticulous. Julia could rely on myriad trips to Home Depot together for electrical and nick knack supplies. He never charged her more than the stores did, nor for any of his time or gas spent shopping. In her customary way, Julia provided gourmet meals for their regular three-hour conversations. She occasionally fell in love with Dreadlocks, and then, the feelings passed. He was much younger and apparently, a lifelong bachelor, no children. Julia's search was for an ever-present companion, which he could never become at age fifty-three, no, never.

CHAPTER 2

Unraveling Julia's Medical Case

Julia felt something was missing in her medical case. Was there, perhaps, a link connecting these horrifying and repetitive diagnoses? If not all, maybe there were connections among some of the key ones? She arrived one day at the Kindly Octogenarian's office with a single sheet of paper in tow for her final appointment for the second time around. He had retired from his administrative work but had kept her on without any fees. Quite unique, this doctor of doctors.

On the paper, Julia displayed her primary two physical illnesses and the main two psychological ones.

"Is there a connection between anxiety/depression and PTSD on the one hand, and fibromyalgia and myalgic encephalomyelitis, cruelly labeled chronic fatigue syndrome, on the other?"

"Yes, Julia, they are all four diseases of the central nervous system."

"I see. I am not surprised that they are related, as my memory, so keen about things from even sixty years ago, plays into both fibromyalgia—remembered pain—and all the traumas feeding into PTSD. Traumas survive, I think, in an ever-expanding echo chamber of memory and pain, as I battle these illnesses while 'living in solitary,' to quote your phrase," she responded, a quiver in her voice and tears in her eyes. Julia was startled and pleased by the doctor's ongoing, supportive encouragement of her thirteen-year-long quest to make sense of her case. How do you take a perfectly fit fifty-five-year-old and destroy her health? This remained the overriding question since Julia first began to question her diagnoses in 2008.

"Quite right," Kindly said. "You are certainly very afflicted in both nervous systems   the central and the peripheral nervous systems. It is a seamless web of unusual severity." Kindly paused and considered his next comment. "And you have exquisite sensitivity to emotions and to pain. Yet, Julia, you soldier on, pain or no pain, new medical diagnoses or not. It is quite astonishing."

Compliments were rare in psychoanalysis, and Julia did not quite know how to respond, so she let the comment hang in the air for a while.

"You have played an enormous role in my healing, Doctor. Reaching into her ever-present tote, Julia added, "This is a small token of my appreciation." She presented the doctor of doctors a bottle of *Veuve Clicquot* Champagne and a new book about Freud's life. "Enjoy these in your retirement, and please know I will miss our work very much." A tear welled up in one eye.

"Why, my goodness, Julia how very thoughtful of you. This is my favorite brand of champagne, and, meds be damned, I think I will break it open tonight."

She walked to the car slowly, overcome with feelings of the final separation from this extraordinary doctor, a pro in his field and many others, the healer of her mind, body, and spirit, a rabbi of sorts, a confessor, a mentor, and yes, like a friend, but a special sort of friendship.

There was no replacing this dignified approach to medicine; none, not ever. Julia was as certain of it as she was of the fact that the four core diagnoses were embedded in her life until her last days.

CHAPTER 3

Concluding Views of the Thirteen-Year Saga: Julia
Strikes Out on Her Own

D ear Reader, this tale was coming to an end, a tale of Time across Memory and Memory across Time. It was impossible to categorize all of Julia's journeys to and away from health, but there seemed to be a deeper meaning to her story. I will be very straight with you: it was a difficult thing to end our conversations and our requisite revisiting of scenes that were and are vital to this story. In the end, Julia found connections through my tale, reconstructed from our deciphering of many experiences, emotions, plots, and twists of fate—all of these spread across a societal scene of turbulence, falsehoods, and inescapable good works by many common folk, ordinary citizens in the Nation. These connections are vital to the story and to Julia's wish that her suffering would not be in vain—that it would enlighten for others, doctors and patients, the medical fallacies and correct diagnoses pieced together during more than 2.7 million dollars of direct and indirect medical costs.

It was commonplace by 2020 to realize that the American health system was a nightmare. However, solutions and attempts to right the decades of wrongs were played out against the ferocious and mysterious COVID-19, which killed more than 240,000 Americans by the end of October 2020, one-quarter of the global deaths, from just 4.3 percent of the world's population. To say Julia was not surprised is true, but it was more than that: lax attention to nutrition, exercise, alcohol, and fresh air was for sixty years direly embedded in the American psyche, along with the architecture of windows that did not open in office buildings, hospitals, and hotels.

The Kindly Octogenarian and Julia corresponded from time to time about her condition and about his own health challenges. She would forever miss psychoanalysis, with its regular conversations about her body, mind, and spirit; she desperately sought to replace their frequent forays into thinkers and writers from the ancient Greeks to contemporary analysts. Julia read as many of the thinkers as she could, interspersed with the *Milwaukee Journal Sentinel, The Business Journal, The Small Business Times, Time, The Nation,* and *The New York Times* and continued plunging into Prince Hal's biographies and history books. She followed a nutrition plan for her illnesses: all organic, no chemical additives, and the requisite number of ounces of water detailed in her friend Susan Stein's book, *These Are Not Your Husband's (Partner's/Boyfriend's) Portions*, a

2005 precursor to increased attention paid by behemoth eateries and small taverns to the calories and sizes of their standard fare. Her grocery bill was astonishing, but necessary. And the complementary, proven doctors' medicines and compounds were never covered by health insurance. Replacing the avalanche of wrongly prescribed psychotropics were a few prescriptions for her heart and diabetes, whose advance warning signals had been woefully under attended to by Julia's physicians. The psychotropics—namely, Seroquel, Resperdal, Rexulti, Effexor, and Abilify—had created insulin intolerance, and diabetes grew to be her major health hurdle. As Julia remarked, "At least they got the prefix correct. I was *hypo*glycemic, not *hyper*active or *hypo*manic. But the doctors, being mainly male, could not square my level of energy with an ill businesswoman. In men, the qualities of tenacity and high levels of activity, despite illnesses, are lauded and promoted in every job or gig I've ever held." One doctor, a late arrival on her case, had put it very accurately to Julia's way of thinking: "We don't need to deal with all of our humanity with medicine."

· · ·

This is a story to hold near and to revisit, Dear Reader. It is one woman's fight for what she needed and deserved in a Time with myriad lies, corruption, and children deprived of their childhood innocence, with instant television and social media that spread lies and deceit taking the place of newspapers and opinion pieces. It was a Time outside of Time. It was the precursor to the pandemic—virulent, rampant, stealthily singeing its way across the world, brought to new levels of isolation and despair. It was like living in the future, a world to be reclaimed and spared the specter of nuclear arms in countries large and small, biological warfare, and the havoc of climate change.

This is the story of one Julia Fields, brought low by myriad, interlocking illnesses, a swift and unexpected divorce, the abrupt death of her mother, and rampant toxins in a new home—her health brought back to stability by keen, brilliant physicians plus a hefty dose of the sage advice of Prince Hal and Lady Jane: "Julia, you are resilient, you will be back on top. You can accomplish whatever you set your mind to do." Like all wise parents, they showed the world as one to be explored, with risks. And such did Julia prepare her beloved children, Jenny and Joshua, whose generation stood tall and vocal to the tasks ahead, from the halls of Congress to the streets of cities, torn asunder with crime, homelessness, and hunger in a land of bounty, majestic mountains, and oceans and lakes in abundance.

THE END

————Sneak Peek————

The Millennium World Playbook
By Julia Fields

Introduction

We now live in a world that is often topsy-turvy, moving along too quickly for most of us and focused on the outward life of visible, tangible resources—be they wealth, physical prowess, or business success.

- o We feel the world is moving too fast; yet, we benefit from a myriad of time-saving features and gadgets…and still stress over not having enough time.
- o We feel at the mercy of ever larger bureaucracies in medical care, telecommunications, corporations, retail stores, and conglomerates, and we feel this in both our personal and work lives, reducing self-worth, inflating the sense of our helplessness.

How can we take charge?

Inversion Theory is a concept I developed based on my Millennium World experiences that can be readily applied to many of life's difficulties in the twenty-first century.

Inversion Theory focuses on solutions for streamlining lives in Millennium World in the areas of friendship, work, medical care, and romance. Something for everyone!

In Millennium World, there is a multitude of ways to communicate: text, email, cell phones, social media, and a few of us still have a hard line. In any case, all forms of communication allow us to screen messages and calls at our pleasure or whim.

Caller ID—invented in the late eighties, but a part of every smart and not-so-smart phone nowadays—is perhaps the worst invention in history: How can we be sure that missing this call is not a lost opportunity to receive information, for connectivity in real time, or to assist someone in need? Some companies forbid employees from screening their calls, wisely recognizing the value of exemplary customer service (but this is no longer the norm). The "norm" has become an over-saturation with facts, half-truths, distortions, and increasing numbers of errors of fact; even *The New York Times* falls victim to inaccuracies, with an ever longer list of daily corrections. Attention Deficit Hyperactivity Disorder is now literally and figuratively a national epidemic, with preventable errors—due to multiple platforms of communication coming in and going out— creating fear, rage, confusion, gridlock, divorce, tragedies of all sorts, even and including death. Knowing who is calling in and not responding can lead us to a pattern of perpetual avoidance, making the likelihood of misunderstandings ever greater.

We are *under connecting* in an *overly connected* world.

We're substituting pixels for empathy, for holding hands, for walks together, for sharing a meal or a birthday toast (clinking *actual* not *virtual* glasses). We now email or text, almost to the exclusion of telephone discussions. We write replies without the benefit of hearing each other's inflections—vocal inflections and visual clues can provide us with more direct understanding. Did you know the tone of an email is misinterpreted up to 80 percent of the time? On a good day, there's a 50/50 shot your recipient will interpret it correctly. (Check out the 2006 article "The Secret Cause of Flame Wars" on www.wired.com.)

Yet, paradoxically, as a solitary woman with a variety of incurable diagnoses, I have come to find pixels and texts a necessary lifeline to connectivity with distant friends to better understand my symptoms and diagnoses, to order groceries I can no longer lift, and to limit my exposure to germs in public spaces. But then, growing up in the Sixties as a female, I took typing class; I can type at 120 words per minute and was trained in copy editing. Those who are still hunting and pecking lose out to generations who grew up with mandatory typing lasses or began using computers in kindergarten. Those who prefer an e e cummings style of writing—Millennials and beyond—without capital letters and punctuation, can easily be misunderstood. "Spell check" often provides the wrong word, as it does not correct for grammar, and "auto correct" is similarly misnamed. Those without proofreading skills can, in a word or a sentence, negatively impact a friendship or professional relationship all in the name of saving time or avoiding speech.

The second layer of miscommunication arises from "electronically" being a frequent form of one-way communication, as we can block or delete information without reading it. And we don't ever know what our recipient has read, making our subject lines a more crucial way to communicate, possibly the only guarantee that part of the message will be visible to the recipient.

Entrepreneurs and people in sales positions have more reason to respond: Their entire reputation and income depend on meticulous attention to detail. But aren't we all selling something? We are offering each other a picture of ourselves in our words and appearances but also in our electronic "hygiene."

This begs the questions of the use of time. We all have the same twenty-four hours and make choices, conscious and unconscious, about how we use each hour and minute. A wise supervisor, then the leading bookseller in New York City, taught me in my first job to "do it now" and that "most tasks take a long time to *start,* not to complete." A piano professor offered this wisdom: "Learn to get something done in fifteen minutes," even if it was just perfecting one measure or phrase of a piece of music. These 1970s lessons have proven invaluable to me in business and in life in Millennium World in particular.

Some days, starting with the last thing on the list is best. After weeks of procrastination, *invert* the order of tasks: turn your list upside down. Tackle the most difficult item first.

When a problem arises, with seemingly no resolution, I have learned that inverting the way I approach it often yields resolution. In showing ourselves to the world, we cannot decide *a priori* who is important to call or write back as none of us knows the potential of answering a call or responding to a message without two-way communication.

Through inverting the problem, we can, then, choose to follow new standards. Remember that we benefit from many time-saving conveniences. It is *how* we use our instant communication that matters.

Ours is a *use-of-time* not a *lack-of-time* problem.

Inversion Theory Solutions:

1. Under promise and over deliver in all you undertake, whether for paid work or as a volunteer, parent, or friend.

2. Proofread EVERYTHING at least once, usually twice. Imagine every text or email as a publicly printed view of you to the world.

3. RESPOND! Non-responsiveness creates gridlock for others. It's also rude and sends a message you may regret. You will seek assistance from those in your orbit in the future, so, please, respond to them now.

4. All too often we use words that are vague, such as, "Let's get together soon." Instead, take the

initiative and suggest specific dates, times, and places, so the recipient of your invite can turn to a calendar, check it, and respond.

5. Let at least one car into traffic on your daily path: Those five seconds cost you nothing and put a smile on someone else's face. And, I bet they'll think to pay it forward.

A Case in Point:

I recently wanted to schedule a citywide conference. It took four weeks to get answers via email from the potential venues about whether they were available, when a phone call and a fifteen-second calendar check could have provided a simple "yes" or "no."

Habits die hard, as they are familiar and cozy. But do they help us in the Millennium World of allatonceness? Is it better to *invert* our attitudes or disposition? Is it better to focus on the other person, be s/he a client, boss, friend, or neighbor? Or to focus on what is happening at the other end of the stethoscope over what is happening on our smartphones or in the waiting room?

Yes, the horse is out of the barn with technology but *invert* your stance and manage it, rather than be managed by technological "advances" that may leave you chronically stressed and behind the curve.

CHAPTER 1

Surviving Instant Interdependence in Millennium World

Global interdependence is now in our hands, in smartphones in third world villages and in first world commercial centers—we have it, and it is ours to use to our advantage. The exponential rise in availability and speed of communications has made us all feel connected as airplanes, buses, and trains offer satellite connectivity for phones and computers, remote vacation villages offer wireless communications in rain forests, parents and children are able to text at will, and employees are rarely disconnected from their work in any given twenty-four-hour period. Even in poor communities and in remote villages, a cell phone is a prerequisite for many. Even grade-school children have come to have their own phones since the dawning of the twenty-first century.

This connectivity implies, but does not necessarily mean, that we are fully aware of our interdependence. We text but often do not complete our thoughts. "I saw your email" is not the same as "I read what you wrote."

We have always had ways to live interdependently; this is nothing new. We rely on people stopping at traffic lights; we rely on an emergency room to be open (though in crime-ridden cities in America some are often full and closed); we rely on the grocer to have basic necessities in stock. We rely on friends, colleagues, or family members to put on a necklace with a trying clasp; to lift a heavy load; to dig out our car from a snowbank; and to lend an ear to help solve problems at the office and in our personal lives.

What we do with our presumptive, multi-layered, technologically advanced, communicative world is what matters. Do we use it to further mutual needs? To promote a sense of community? Of caring? Of empathy? Of kindness? Or, do we hide behind "being busy," "being overloaded," "being too tired," "being in a meeting," "being unavailable to take your call," or the welter of other excuses.

Here are some simple ways to live interdependently, to use time to your advantage, to avoid hurt feelings. These are helpful ways to cope with the ever-increasing amounts of information pixeling its way to you on computers, phone, iPads, and through traditional means: memos, snail mail, and, yes, through radio and television:

1) Take regular five-minute breaks from the computer and the clock and write to a friend, child, lover, or parent. It's a reminder of the importance of these

relationships and reboots your concentration for the next task at hand.

2) Resist the impulse to email and get up and walk over to your colleague's workstation. For those increasing numbers of people working from home, stand up and move while calling a client on the phone; it's physically and psychically stimulating. Grab a break from the workstation and M O V E.

3) Decrease the proportion of "bad news" to good news. All information elicits a brain response and listening to or reading each breaking news disaster has an effect. Set aside a regular window for daily events/news rather than allowing it to filter in at will with notices on your phone and computer.

4) Slow down by reading tangible newspapers, magazines, and books. Taking the time to turn pages, clipping articles to send to friends—this all works a different part of the brain than when working via computer. Use it or lose it!

5) Save yourself time and stress by scheduling "response time" into each day.

Interdependence. It's here. It's now. Use it to your advantage and to the advantage of those around you.

Invert your relationship with technology. You need to manage technology or it will manage you!

CHAPTER 2

"Millennium Mourning"
Outline for an Essay of Julia's

1) There has been a trivialization of grief. In regard to views of the hereafter, a Moslem will see seventy virgins; Christianity sees scary purgatory, hell, and heaven. Jews see immortality of the soul.

2) What is the connection between survivors and the deceased? Can we influence the fate of souls?

3) There is a burial/cremation/wake. Judaism has rituals of seven days of s*hiva,* a month of mourning, then commanded practices for a year (no music, etc.).

4) Judaism has stringent expectations with urgency after a death. It is considered disrespectful if there is not an immediate burial, due to the decomposition of the body. Autopsy flies in the face of this.

5) If one is the sole survivor and has no faith, can the heir dispose of the body in any way chosen? Often, there

is a management problem, deciding about how and where to dispose of the body or the ashes.

6) People a bit distant from the family want to forget a death quickly, e.g., those without any bodies from the three thousand deaths on 9/11, with many MIAs, President Bush hurried the national mourning. Grief is a deep psychological issue: How can we live through the grief?

7) Orthodox Judaism has special issues for seven immediate relative categories: mother/father, son/daughter, husband/wife, and siblings. The mourner is to sit on a lower chair than the guests. Mourners are not to wear leather shoes as on Yom Kippur.

8) Mourners are to fill life with other things as there is no other way to deal with all of life's pains.

9) How do people get to the point of surviving and carrying on? One way is by reciting the stories told by the deceased, by viewing pictures of excruciating pain and inhumanity, or with memories of great life events; however, these can also bring great pain. We are commanded to turn to life, invest in life, and to build families.

10) Viktor Frankel wrote of finding transcendent things to survive for, as though being miserable would fix something: No, it will not bring back the dead.

In Judaism, during the first week after the burial, mourners have no obligations in showing up for work and completing daily responsibilities. During the second week, there is still no work. After the death of a parent, there is no attendance at weddings or concerts for a year.

11) What are the changes in mourning? Faith has turned into style and become very self-indulgent and self-serving. Many of these customs hearken to the strong connections among members of the family, but for many technical reasons, with families spread out globally and the lack of trust among families, there is not full compliance. Those living alone are often left to fend for themselves. There is an old joke about a father who has died; the busy son has no time for s*hiva*. Shall he hire someone to pay a *shiva* call to his mother in another city?

What are our questions re medication to dampen grief? Recently, the pendulum is swinging back to therapy, e.g., Daniel Karlett, see the recent *New York Times* article, and also Daniel Yalom, Stanford, a leader in group therapy. Viktor Frankel believed that one can deal with almost any challenge if one has a reason to live, despite the deadening effects of experiencing life in four World War II concentration camps. Nazis deprived people of all except of the right to choose which ways they could interact, think, and feel in order to remain human beings.

Bibliography

Abbasi, Aisha. *The Rupture of Serenity*. London: Karnac Books, 2014.

Andersen, Kurt. *Fantasyland*. New York: Random House, 2017.

Arendt, Hannah. *The Human Condition*. Chicago: The University of Chicago Press, 1958.

Bellah, Robert N.; Madsen, Richard; Sullivan, William M.; Swidler, Ann; and Tipton, Steven M. *Habits of the Heart*. New York: Harper & Row, Publishers, 1985.

Beckett, Samuel. *Endgame*. New York: Grove Press, Inc.,1958.

Beckett, Samuel. *Krapp's Last Tape*. New York: Grove Press, Inc.,1957.

Beckett, Samuel. *Waiting for Godot*. New York: Grove Press, Inc.,1954.

Bettelheim, Bruno. *Freud and Man's Soul*. New York: Vintage Books, 1982.

The Bible. Authorized King James Version, Oxford UP, 1998.

Boll, Heinrich. *Wo warst du, Adam?* Germany: Friedrich Middelhauve, 1949.

Brownmiller, Susan. *Against Our Will: Men, Women and Rape*. New York: Simon and Schuster, 1975.

Cahalan, Susannah. *Brain on Fire: My Month of Madness*. New York: Simon & Schuster Paperbacks, 2012.

Carroll, Jock. *Falling for Marilyn*. Toronto: Stoddart Publishing Co. Ltd., 1996.

Chelser, Phyllis. *Women & Madness*. Garden City: Doubleday & Company, Inc., 1972.

Clinton, Hillary Rodham. *What Happened*. New York: Simon & Schuster, 2017.

The Collected Poems of Muriel Rukeyser. New York: McGraw-Hill Book Company, 1978.

De Beauvoir, Simone. *The Prime of Life*. New York: Lancer Books, Inc., 1960.

Desmond, Matthew. *Evicted*. New York: Penguin Random House LLC, 2016.

Duncan, Paul, ed. *Monroe*. Hong Kong: Taschen.

Epictetus. *The Art of Living: The Classical Manual on Virtue, Happiness, and Effectiveness*. New York: HarperCollins Publishers, Inc., 1994.

Faludi, Susan. *Blacklash: The Undeclared War Against American Women*. New York: Doubleday, 1991.

Ferrucci, Piero. *The Power of Kindness*. New York: Jeremy P. Tarcher/Penguin, 2006.

Ford Foundation. *Women in the World*. New York: The Ford Foundation, 1980.

Frankl, Viktor E., *Man's Search for Meaning: An Introduction to Logotherapy*. New York: Simon & Schuster, 1984.

Frankel, Viktor E. *The Will to Meaning*. New York: Penguin Books (USA) LLC, 1969.

Freeman, Ru. *Extraordinary Rendition: (American) Writers on Palestine*. New York: OR Books, 2015.

Freud, Sigmund. *Dora: An Analysis of a Case of Hysteria*. New York: Collier Books, 1969.

Freud, Sigmund. *On Creativity and the Unconscious*. New York: Harper & Row, 1958.

Freud, Sigmund. *The Origins of Psychoanalysis*. New York: Basic Books, Inc., 1977.

Freud, Sigmund. *The Psychopathology of Everyday Life*. New York: W. W. Norton Company, 1965.

Friday, Nancy. *My Mother My Self: The Daughter's Search for Identity*. New York: Dell Publishing Co., Inc., 1977.

Friedan, Betty. *The Feminine Mystique*. New York: Dell Publishing Co., Inc., 1983.

Friedman, Thomas. *The Lexus and the Olive Tree*. New York: Farrar, Strauss and Girouz, 1999.

Fugard, Athol. *The Road to Mecca*. New York: Samuel French, Inc., 1985.

German English Bilingual English Dictionary. New York: Penguin Random House, 2009.

Hardy, Thomas. *Tess of the d'Urbervilles*. New York: Harper Brothers Publishers, 1897.

Hertz, J.H., ed. *Pentateuch & Haftorahs,* Second Edition. London: Soncino Press, 1960.

Horney, Karen. *The Adolescent Diaries of Karen Horney*. New York: Basic Books, 1980.

Isaacson, Walter. *Einstein: His Life and Universe*. New York; Simon & Schuster, 2007.

Knight, Chris. *Decoding Chomsky: Science and Revolutionary Politics*. New Haven: Yale University Press, 2016.

Kristeva, Julia. *Black Sun*. New York: Columbia University Press, 1989.

Kristeva, Julia. *Desire in Language: Semiotic Approach to Literature and Art*. New York: Columbia University Press, 1980.

Kristeva, Julia. *Hatred and Forgiveness*. New York: Columbia University Press, 2010.

Kristeva, Julia. *The Incredible Need to Believe*. New York: Columbia University Press, 2009

Kristeva, Julia. *Intimate Revolt*. New York: Columbia University Press, 2002.

Kristeva, Julia. *L'avenir d'une révolte*. Paris: Calmann-Lévy, 1998.

Kristeva, Julia. *New Maladies of the Soul*. New York: Columbia University Press, 1995.

Lacan, Jacques. *Écritis I*. Paris: Éditions du Seuil, 1966.

Lacan, Jacques. *My Teaching*. London: Verso, 2008.

Laplanche, Jean. *Life and Death in Psychoanalysis*. Baltimore: Johns Hopkins University Press, 1976.

Lawrence, D. H. *Fantasia of the Unconscious and Psychoanalysis and the Unconscious*. New York: Penguin Books, 1921.

Lehrer, Jonah. *Proust Was a Neuroscientist*. Boston: First Mariner Books, 2008.

Lerner, Gerda. *The Female Experience: An American Documentary*. Indianapolis: Bobbs-Merrill Educational Publishing, 1977.

Lewis, Michael. *The Undoing Project*. New York: W. W. Norton & Company, 2017.

Miller, Arthur. *The Crucible*. Boston: A Bantam Book, 1952.

Miller, Arthur. *Death of a Salesman*. New York:The Viking Press, 1949.

Miller, Arthur. *Homely Girl, A Life*. New York: Penguin Books, 1966.

Neff, PhD, Kristin. *Self-Compassion: Stop Beating Yourself Up and Leave Insecurity Behind*. New York: HarperCollins Publishers, Inc., 2011.

Niebuhr, Reinhold. *Moral Man and Immoral Society*. New York: Charles Scribner's Sons, 1952.

Nieves, Myrna, ed. *Breaking Ground: Anthology of Puerto Rican Women Writers in New York 1980-2012*. New York: Editorial Campana, 2012.

Ornish, M.D., Dean. *Love & Survival: 8 Pathways to Intimacy & Health*. New York: HarperCollins Publishers, Inc.,1996.

Quinnett, Paul G. *Suicide: The Forever Decision*. New York: Crossroad, 2008.

Redfield Jamison, Kay. *Exuberance: The Passion for Life*. New York: Random House, Inc., 2004.

Rickman, M.D., John, ed. *A General Selection from the Works of Sigmund Freud*. New York: Doubleday Anchor Books, 1937.

Sacks, Oliver. *Gratitude*. New York: Alfred A. Knopf, 2015.

Schecter, Ellen. *Fierce Joy*. New York: Greenpoint Press, 2012.

Siegel, M.D., Bernie S. *Love, Medicine & Miracles*. New York: Harper & Row Publishers, 1986.

Stoler Miller, Barbara. *The Hermit and the Love-Thief*. New York: Columbia University Press, 1978.

Stoler Miller, Barbara. *Love Song of the Dark Lord: Jayadeva's Gitagovinda*. New York: Columbia University Press, 1977.

St. Germain, Mark. *Freud's Last Session*. New York: Dramatists Play Service, Inc., 2010.

Strunk, Jr., WIlliam; and White, E. B. *The Elements of Style*. New Jersey: Pearson Education, Inc., 2000.

Tarr-Whelan, Linda. *Women Lead the Way: Your Guide to Stepping Up to Leadership and Changing the World*. San Francisco: Berrett-Koehler Publishers, Inc., 2009.

Tauber, Alfred L. *Freud the Reluctant Philosopher*. Princeton: Princeton University Press, 2010.

Todorov, Tzvetan. *Hope and Memory: Lessons from the Twentieth Century*. Princeton: Princeton University Press, 2003.

Turner, Jack. *Teewinot: A Year in the Teton Range*. New York: St. Martin's Press, 2000.

Vernon, Mark. *The Meaning of Friendship*. New York: Palgrave MacMillan, 2010.

Viljoen, Edward. *The Power of Meditation: An Ancient Technique to Accept Your Inner Power*. New York: Jeremy P. Tarcher/Penguin.

Von Dorn, Mark; and Lapolla, Garibaldi M., ed. *The World's Best Poems*. Cleveland: The World Publishing Company, 1929.

Weiss, Peter. *Marat/Sade*. New York: Pocket Books, 1966.

Newspapers and Periodicals:

Daily Kos, online
FOX News, online
Harvard Business Review
Milwaukee Business Journal
Milwaukee Journal Sentinel
The Nation
The New York Times
The New Yorker
Time

A VALENTINE
TO AMERICA

Ten percent of royalties from *Valentine* will go to Feeding America Eastern Wisconsin.

https://www.feedingamericawi.org

Made in the USA
Columbia, SC
03 March 2021

33823842R00205